Dirty Blonde and Half-Cuban

Dirty Blonde and Half-Cuban

a novel

Lisa Wixon

rayo   *An Imprint of* HarperCollins*Publishers*

HarperCollins books may be purchased for educational, business, or
sales promotional use. For information, please write:
Special Markets Department, HarperCollins Publishers Inc.,
10 East 53rd Street, New York, NY 10022.

FIRST EDITION

Designed by Chris Welch

Printed on acid-free paper

Library of Congress Cataloging-in-Publication Data
Wixon, Lisa.
Dirty blonde and half-Cuban : a novel / Lisa Wixon.—1st ed.
p.   cm.
ISBN 0-06-072174-X
1. Young women—Fiction.   2. Fathers and daughters—Fiction.
3. Americans—Cuba—Fiction.   4. Havana (Cuba)—Fiction.
5. Birthfathers—Fiction.   6. Prostitutes—Fiction.   I. Title.
PS3623.I96D57   2005
813'.6—dc22   2004063407

05   06   07   08   09   DIX/RRD   10   9   8   7   6   5   4   3   2   1

for Joey

In the dim light of early morning I saw the shores of Cuba rise and define themselves . . .

Here was a place where real things were going on. Here was a scene of vital action. Here was a place where anything might happen. Here was a place where something would certainly happen.

Here I might leave my bones.

—*Sir Winston Churchill*

One

1

I felt his hand on my bare shoulder, and it was all over.

In the oppressive August afternoon, the heat from another's touch had the chilling effect of ice on a radiator. I'd been sitting alone, in a café in Havana near the former Hilton hotel—the one ransacked by Communists and renamed Habana Libre.

Free Havana.

The stacks of papers on my table were askew, some stained by the *café con leche* I chain-drink to keep my spirits up. He came at me from behind. I looked up into a tanned face and silky blue eyes framed by deep lines. Late fifties, I guessed, and not unattractive. He asked to sit. I shrugged casually. He asked if I spoke English. I nodded. Then he asked for advice—best bars, best beaches. My advice warranted a rum over ice, or so he measured, and he offered to buy me one.

I sighed. The papers were in a fantastic mess in front of me—evidence of my bootless investigation—and, today, had not been revealing the clues I'd hoped for. I piled them neatly. What the hell. A rum would be nice.

He smiles. I pretend, despite the mounting evidence to the contrary, that I'm a First World girl in a First World city, being offered a friendly drink by an attractive man. That at the end of this exchange, we will trade business cards and a flirtatious smile, and in a few days I'll find a message on my cell phone and, who knows, there might be dinner and maybe a movie or a stroll and, you know, a date.

But I am not in the United States, my home, and he assumes he's not sparring with an equal, a woman of his socioeconomic rank; give or take a few rungs in either direction.

He rolls an ice cube on his tongue, momentarily losing himself to the pleasure of coolness amid the humid soup that is summertime Havana. Another drink, then another. He talks only of himself in determined pontification, and asks no questions of me. It's how he signals he's expecting to pick up the tab. This one, and the next.

I ask where he's from. "America," he says with a mixture of pride and complicity, as do all Yankees who sneak into Cuba.

"It's *norteamericano,*" I say, playfully scolding. "We Cubans are offended that you claim the entire continent for yourselves." He's not listening. Greedily, he takes in the size of my chest, the green jade of my eyes, the curve of one thigh crossed over the other.

"So," he says, leaning across the table. "I'm on the eleventh floor of the Habana Libre." He looks at me expectantly, while holding the check in his hand. "What'll it be?"

I CAN'T BLAME him necessarily for the blunder. The café's bathroom mirror is not kind in its judgment; cracked and faded, it reflects my freak-show appearance. These clothes, bought new in Washington, D.C., three months ago, are frayed from wear and harsh soap and sun. I carry my things in a plastic sack—the Cuban girl's purse—as my leather one had been stolen months before. My body, once a healthy size eight, has shrunk to a gaunt size four. Hipbones jut out for the first time in my life. I am easily bruised. A Cuban diet does these things.

I am an American, in the sense that my passport says so, in that my university degrees and professional stints and taxes paid cement my belonging to her.

But I am Cuban. My first breath was Havana air, and my father—as I recently discovered—circulates the blood of Cuba in his veins. I am a Cuban-American. Like marbles in a tub, I noisily roll the moniker around in my head: Cuban-American. The hyphen is the fulcrum, the teeter-totter that swings up and down. Some days I'm more heavily Cuban. On others, I weigh in more American.

But today, this day, as the man's condom-covered cock slid between my thighs and his chest spread my breasts, as he heaved over me, pushing and pulling and pushing hard still, and as I ran my nails hard down his spine, a painful reaction to the pleasure I didn't expect to feel, as his face crinkled and he collapsed and rolled over and dressed and threw American scratch at my knees, and as I gathered the bills from the floor and tucked them into my bra—isn't that what prostitutes do?—and as I took the elevator eleven floors to the lobby and walked past the smirking guards, and as I passed through the doors into the cruel sun of the afternoon, I realized that the teeter-totter had landed with a thud.

At that moment, I was only Cuban.

2

The lever on the 1970s Russian pay phone was stuck. Jiggle. Jiggle. Twenty centavos more did the trick.

"Camila!" I said, finally getting through the hospital switchboard. "I slept with someone."

"Finally, Alysia!" she said with her tinkling laugh.

"It's not like that. I—" Looking around, I lowered my voice. "I got paid."

She laughed harder. "You're a Cuban girl now," said my best friend here, a respected Havana heart surgeon nearly a decade my senior. "Tell me."

Talking faster than a wet parrot, I relayed the details of the afternoon into her sympathetic ear. Camila's morality is shared by the majority of Cubans: sleeping with foreign men and getting paid—usually in the form of clothes and perfume and money for family emergencies (for one always comes up when a love-struck foreigner is around)—isn't actual prostitution.

There is a word, in fact, for women seeking out a rich boyfriend, either for marriage or regular remittances, and that word is *jinetera*. Spanish for jockey. Jockeying boys and girls are the hopeful light of their supportive families. To jockey is to dream of a successful future, to dream in a country that feels so free of hope, of promising careers, of stable relationships. It's also the only way for many to make dollars in a country where lawyers earn $18 a month and a meal in a decent restaurant costs twice as much.

"What did he pay?"

I had no idea, so I rooted around in my bra for the money. "Two hundred," I said, a bit surprised.

"*Dios mío.* You're going to put us all to shame," Camila said, laughing again. "You *rubias*"—blondes—"are always worth more . . . When do you see him again?"

"Never," I stammered. "I'm never going to do this again!"

"Right," she said knowingly. "Next time, *mi vida,* don't ask for money so fast."

"I didn't," I said, feeling I'd let her down. "I refused to see him again, so he made some snide comment about how if I wanted to be a good capitalist, I'd better learn to set a price up front."

Camila sighed. "You weren't being a bad capitalist, you were being a bad *cubana.* These men here aren't looking for a one-night stand, they want a Cuban girlfriend while on holiday." Then, wistfully, her voice trailing off, she said: "If he gave you two hundred dollars for an hour, imagine a whole week . . ."

Camila is thirty-three and one of the sexiest women in a country of sexy women. Her hair is cropped short to showcase a graceful neck and a dancer's erect body. The $32 monthly surgeon's salary doesn't pay for much, so Camila's acquired a handful of foreign boyfriends who deposit money into her account each month. When they arrive in town a few times a year, she dutifully attends to them.

"I'm not going to be anyone's girlfriend," I said. "I've got more important things to do."

"Any news on your father?"

"I'm off to check," I said, and hang up. The raging sun was starting to set, and the line across the street for peso ice cream stretched down the block. *La Rampa,* as the street is known, was packed with boys who cuff their jeans like James Dean. Boys looking for men who love boys. Men with money to spend.

Shivering in the heat, I made my way home.

3

The first I'd heard of José Antonio was in the hospital. My mother was battling an indefensible foe, one that attacked the very molecular structure of her cells.

We watched her waste away in the cancer ward at a Georgetown clinic. She'd just landed in her fifties. A mere month before, a vibrancy hummed inside her small body, as if there wasn't enough physical space to contain her spirit. Now even her breath hinted at the internal decay. Her long blonde hair had lost its luster, and her eyes their incessant gleam. Her appearance frightened me, but I tried not to show it.

No one told me she was going to die, or thought to prepare me. Whomever I asked just patted my head and told me everything would be all right. Afterward, it took me a long time to trust an adult again.

One afternoon, my mother's nails dug into my skin, and she pulled me close.

"José Antonio," she cried softly, touching my face. "Find him for me." My mother's eyelids only shut halfway, stuck on dry membranes—one of the desiccant effects of the morphine that dripped into her veins. "He's in Havana, with his family," she whispered. "They're expecting you."

Havana. I was born there in 1978, as an American, the first and only child of my diplomat parents serving abroad. My father and my mother returned to the U.S. in 1980, my one-year-old hand in theirs, just before the Port of Mariel unleashed a torrent of hopeful rafters bound for Floridian shores.

When I was growing up, my mother never spoke about Cuba, and I barely registered the country as my homeland. Diplomats' children born abroad think of themselves as having been delivered on U.S. territory, on a little island of America within the foreign country. That I could have ties in Cuba, with Cubans—that someone was waiting for me—was information that couldn't register in my young brain.

"You have to find them, my little monkey," my mother said.

Little monkey. Hearing my pet name made me grin. My first-grade teacher at the foreigners' school in Dakar gave me my childhood nickname, from the *Curious George* books my mother had shipped from back home during our tour of duty in Africa.

In the mornings, the teacher would read the books aloud in class, and in the afternoons, my mother would translate the stories into French to an audience of Senegalese children who'd gather near our house. Children who giggled as loud as me over the misadventures of the baby primate.

From the hospital bed, I carefully counted each time my mother called me her little monkey. I'd listen to every sentence, every pain-fueled rambling, in hopes of hearing the magic phrase. I invented a game: that on the tenth time she said my pet name, she would be healed, and we'd all go home together.

She never made it that far.

In the throes of her battle she appealed to friends long vanished, to her parents recently deceased. To ghosts. But José Antonio was the one who most agitated the peace of her unconscious mind. I'd never heard of him and, at first, believed him to be a manufacture of the morphine and the pain.

The look in Aunt June's eyes told me differently.

Aunt June flipped through the guest book that lay bedside on the hospital table. "See all these visitors here come to say good-bye?" she asked, exaggerating her Mississippi accent whenever it became necessary to change the subject. "Your momma was always so popular. Glad you two had the foresight to bring her back instead of letting her rot in one of your Third World hellholes."

"They have excellent medical care in South America," retorted my father, who walked in with the doctor. "But my wife preferred to return to the States."

His eyebrows slightly rose at seeing my aunt. My father was tall and lithe in one of his beautiful suits, carefully threaded by the fingers of the underprivileged.

"A girl your age should be in one place, not tramping around the world," June said to me, but loud enough for my father to hear.

"Nice to see you too, June," he retorted.

Born and raised in Natchez, Mississippi, Aunt June and my mother were the final offspring of the Montgomery family, an upstanding kind of folk with a proud past. Long before the sisters were born, cotton mills shut down and the family's land became worthless. But when my aunt and mother were teenagers, oil was discovered in the thick, burbling underbelly of the forgotten dirt, and the once-worthless crop fields became gold mines.

Aunt June was the spitfire eldest, and she'd multiplied her small fortune in the horse-breeding trade. She was a proper Southern belle in lipstick and diamonds, but with the cowboy boots and men's tailored suit that certainly drove her mother bonkers.

"Hello, John Briggs," said the doctor, shaking my father's hand. "Bad news. It's metastasized to the lungs," I heard the doctor say quietly to my father.

My father showed no reaction at the news, but his eyes rested on my face, and in them was a sorrow I'd never seen before. My instinct was to jump up and embrace him, but I knew a hug, or any physical affection, would fluster him.

My father quickly became engrossed in hushed conversation with the specialist. I leaned over to my aunt and repeated the question.

"Who is José Antonio? She keeps calling for him."

Aunt June studied my father's profile and then looked at me. Her eyes were indecisive.

"You're too young to lose your mother," she said. "Thirteen is too damned young."

4

My mother died six weeks to the day after she'd first fainted in Montevideo, a few kilometers from the home we'd been assigned at our new post in South America. My father was in his twentieth year with the U.S. Foreign Service, the State Department, and whatever overlapping federal bureaus employed his intelligence.

His peripatetic lifestyle—a new foreign assignment every few years—was the thing that most enthralled my mother about him during their courtship two decades before. Each new country, she claimed, she loved more than the last.

My mother told me of an African religion that held that each person was born the child of a specific god, and took on the god's characteristics through life. I'm certain hers was a gypsy god, one that infected her blood with the love of the open road, the unknown, the shock that comes with the discovery of a new, earthly beauty.

Her enthusiasms steered the journeys we undertook in the poor countries that were more home to me than my own America. We shared close-knit bonds with other foreign-service families—and it was how I met my best friend, Susie, herself a diplomat's daughter. Together with our mothers, we explored the sand dunes and deserts, oceans and rivers, and the cultures and customs that make up a foreign nation.

It was a dream childhood.

Although my father worked harder and longer than the other fathers, the few moments I spent with him each night were the highlight of my young life.

My father would come to my room before bedtime, straight from a grueling day at the embassy. Our ritual rarely wavered: he'd drape his suit jacket over a chair, unloosen a red tie, and swing his long legs off the side of my bed. Then I'd be told to pick a title from the stack of books on my nightstand. I would pretend to consider the choices, and he would feign shock when I chose a shopworn copy of *Curious George*. I loved the way my father read those stories, even more than my mother's recitations, because I always imagined he was the Man in the Yellow Hat, the stringbean scientist who claimed the monkey from his habitat and oversaw his perennial mischief. It was this way I always thought of my father, benevolent if distant, kind if reserved. A protector.

But while my mother withered away in the clinic, I began to sense a shift in my father. His voice became more stern, his gait more rigid, and when I caught him looking at me, his eyes betrayed a bewilderment and fear. What lay dying on the bed was not just my mother's life, but my father's connection to his own.

A few nights before she took her last breath, I awoke next to my mother, the two of us chilly under the antiseptic sheets of the hospital bed. The perfume of jasmine and lilac, her favorite flowers, overwhelmed the air. Aunt June's head hung off the chair next to the bed, her gentle snore keeping a calm rhythm.

"Darling," my mother said in a turbulent whisper. "You have to find your father for me, you have to promise you will."

"He's down the hall, probably," I said, climbing out of bed to fetch him, careful not to entangle the tubes and wires that plunged into her skin.

"No," she said, gently pulling me back toward her. "Your real father."

Your real father. I told myself the morphine was talking, and not her, but tears of panic welled up in my eyes.

"José Antonio," she whispered. "That's his name."

"No, Mom." I felt sheer terror. "You're sick, I don't understand—"

"Promise me you'll find him," she said, reaching for me. She was speaking now with too much certainty, too much like her former self.

"I think you need more medicine," I said.

"I've taken enough."

I looked over at Aunt June, who'd quietly awakened. "*Dad* is my dad," I said stubbornly.

"I'm sorry."

"He is," I insisted, while my peripheral vision folded in on me. "I don't understand."

"You will when you find him. You'll understand then. Please, promise Mommy."

She used her French-manicured thumb to wipe away my tears. I would've promised her anything. Would've said anything—if only she climbed out of that hospital-issue gown and back into my life, to resume her role as the woman who loved and protected me. To be my mother again.

"Promise."

At that, I watched as the door to the hallway closed, and my father, who'd been listening in the darkness, left me alone with the smell of jasmine and lilacs and death.

5

The Vietnamese believe that when a person dies while young their spirits roam—silently and imperceptibly—through the kingdom of their old lives. That they carry out unspoken conversations with those among the living.

Although my mother was dead, I held more conversations with her than with my father. Upon her death, he returned to South America and placed me at a boarding school near his parents' home in Connecticut so they could look after me. Part of me believed my father was simply grieving and would one day send for me, and we'd live together again.

Whenever I'd silently tell my mother how sad I was, and how much I missed my father, she responded the same way:

"Be forgiving with him. He does his best."

My father and I never spoke of that last night in the hospital, or of my mother's deathbed longing for José Antonio. Though he was an intrepid traveler, the only territory through which my father never ventured was the emotional terrain that my mother had navigated with ease. He had lost more than his wife, and I more than my mother. We'd lost our interpreter.

But that didn't stop my father from employing a substitute.

"We need to speak," said his mother, the Briggs family matriarch.

My grandmother wore Nancy Reagan suits and a blonde helmet of hair, each strand bleached and blown and sprayed into submission. She pulled me into her study the summer after my mother died, during a party on the Fourth of July.

"We're very sorry your mother has passed," she said, her breath humid with vodka. "But we think it's best you spend as much time as possible with your grandfather and me, while your father is away and focusing on his career."

The notion of spending more time with my grandparents tied my interior in knots. My mother must have understood this. When alive, she refused to ever leave me alone with them.

Knuckles tapped on the other side of the door, but my grandmother continued. "I understand your mother said some strange things to you about her time at one of your father's posts." At this, she waved her hand nervously. "Cuba, or some such place." The knock came again, and this time she opened the door.

"Dr. Wagner," said my grandmother, introducing me to a lumbering man, his inebriated eyes rimmed in red. "This is Alysia. Our granddaughter." Then she turned to me. "Dr. Wagner has agreed to take a few moments from the party to speak with you about hallucinations."

For a moment, I was terrified, believing she somehow knew of the conversations my mother and I shared. Or perhaps she could feel my mother's presence the way I did, and in that very room. But the doctor was there to dispel a much more mysterious notion.

"Hallucinations," said the doctor, "are quite common in cancer patients." With downcast eyes, Dr. Wagner blundered his way through a speech about the effects of pain on the minds of those near death.

"So you see," said my grandmother impatiently, "you must ignore whatever she said to you. It was a figment"—she waved her hand again—"of her vivid imagination."

"Absolutely," said Dr. Wagner, taking another drink and refusing to look me in the eye.

My grandmother leaned into me and patted my knee in what felt like a slap. "You're my son's daughter. You're a member of the Briggs family. If you ever say or think otherwise, you will have a very, very difficult life."

She said this with a smile, but nothing about it was friendly.

6

This is what my father provided: Classes in ballet and French. Medical and dental. College tuition and math tutors—of which there were many. An apartment at the Watergate. Books and pencils. The clothes and accoutrements he deemed necessary to broadcast his family's stalwart political status.

What I provided my father was the promise to attend his alma mater and study hard for good grades. That I'd complete graduate school and eventually go into the foreign service, following in his footsteps.

Our arrangement was made indirectly, with subtle gestures and inferences, and I never found the courage to test those boundaries with my disobedience. I believed if I just worked hard enough and did precisely what he expected, then one day I could have a relationship with the man who raised me.

Every test, every term paper, every scribbling of notes had been done in the hopes that I could please my father. During the last of my senior finals, I collapsed from a pain gnawing at my right side. Within hours, I was hospitalized with appendicitis, and as they prepped me for the knife to remove the inflamed appendage, I could think only of my mother. She'd died in a clinic just blocks away.

"It doesn't look good," said my father over the phone. "I'm on business in New York. I'll try to make it tomorrow or the next day."

I told myself it was my father's fear of hospitals—a phobia developed in the wake of my mother's painful death—that kept him from seeing me. But truthfully, I barely recognized my father as the same man who read me Curious George stories all those years ago. Or who seemed so alive in the presence of my mother. As the years wore on since her death, he became more like his own Connecticut family and less the man who chose, against his parents' judgment, a gregarious and effusive Southern woman as his wife.

That night in the hospital, a searing pain jarred me from unconsciousness. Aunt June was snoring, her head hanging from the chair, looking very much the way she did those many nights we held vigil at my mother's bedside. I started to cry, wanting my mother and father.

"Hey now, honey," she said, fumbling in the semidarkness. "I'm here, it's all right. The surgery went splendid."

"Where's Dad?"

"He . . . He says he'll try and make it, darlin'." She gave me a hug as tears flooded my eyes. For the next week, knowing my father was only a short plane ride away, I watched hopefully each time the door swung open, praying he'd walk through any moment.

But he never did.

My mother, though, was rarely far away. As I wrestled with the healing and pain, I'd feel a touch on my forehead, a caress on my cheek, and as my body got stronger, the olfactory senses picked up notes long forgotten in the thicket of my memory—the jasmine and the lilac, the sick and the antiseptic—and then I heard it again, her voice whispering in my ear.

They're expecting you.

José Antonio.

Your real father.

AUNT JUNE SAUNTERED in after breakfast. "Monkey bait," she said, tossing a banana on my tray. "Phlegm cutter." Orange juice in a Styrofoam cup.

"Why haven't we ever spoken about Havana?" I blurted out.

Aunt June looked at me a long while and went right for her purse. She opened a Chanel compact, inspected her morning face, and made a big production of creaming her hospital coffee.

"Been a-waiting and a-waiting," she said finally. "For you to say something."

"How do I know she was telling the truth?" I asked excitedly, pulling myself up. "You were there, she was talking crazy. Was is just a hallucination? Is there any proof?"

"Proof? Look at yourself lately?"

Instinctively, I touched my face and felt the contours of my lips and nose. Aunt June pushed her compact in front of me.

"You look about as much like John as Buddha does Christ," she said, laughing. "You got all the proof you need right here." She looked at me as if in disbelief, and lurched to her feet. "You mean you and John never talked about it all these years?"

"Never." My aunt paced in her pajamas, the red silk between her thighs rustling in the quiet room. She was furious with my father; I could tell by the way her fist clenched into an alabaster ball.

"That man's cold as an old ice box," she said.

"Tell me," I said, motioning for her to sit on my bed, "what you know. Please."

"John," said my aunt, exhaling a long sigh and handing me my orange juice, "wasn't able to have children. Your mother told me."

"Well, she managed to get pregnant."

"Precisely," she said softly. "And John knew that you weren't his. But he couldn't admit to his family, or to himself, or to your mother, that the marriage had broken down. That's why his name's on your birth certificate."

"For appearances."

"For appearances. That's all that counts with that fool family of his in Connecticut."

"My grandparents, they don't buy it for a second," I said, the pieces starting to fall into place. "I can tell, the way they look at me." Then it dawned on me: the undercurrent in my relationship with the Briggs family had always been precisely about my paternity. Their accusatory demeanor had little to do with the imperfection of my performance as one of their grandchildren, as I'd always assumed. It had everything to do with their son accepting me as his own, when clearly—to everyone but me, it seemed—I was biologically not.

"You're lucky they don't buy it," she said, throwing her head back and laughing the way my mother would. "I mean, do you really want to be accepted by *them*?"

Looking out the window, I realized she was right. Slowly, I raised my Styrofoam cup to meet hers in a toast. In the clarity, I felt a burden released, and also an empathy gained. If I, as a grandchild, had been tormented by the expectations of the Briggs family, how much more had my own father suffered under them and their demands? And what of my mother, did she, too, endure his torn loyalties?

"Why didn't she leave my father?" I asked my aunt. "If she was so in love with the Cuban?"

"Perhaps because our parents dug it into our heads to do the right thing. And whatever was pleasurable was *definitely* not the right thing."

"You got over it," I said, laughing.

"One does," replied June, with a secretive smile. "Given enough time."

"Well, I guess I'll never know," I said wistfully. "About José Antonio."

"Nonsense," said June. "You can go down there to Cuba and look him up, see what he has to say. I'm sure he'd love to see you."

I shook my head vehemently. I was overwhelmed by the idea of searching for my mother's former lover in a country I was not even allowed to travel in. "It's illegal to go to Cuba. If I'm going to be a diplomat like I promised Dad, there's no way I can risk getting caught."

Aunt June shrugged and looked out the window at the cherry blossoms that make springtime in Washington a sensory treat.

"It's *illegal*, Auntie," I said, exasperated. "And Dad will *kill* me if I go looking for José Antonio. Oh my God, what am I saying, it's too ridiculous."

"We all make our own path in love and in life," said Aunt June. "All I know is our daddy, your grandpa, was the greatest man who ever lived. Imagine my life without my father, without your grampa? Nothing would've been the same."

Remembering my grandfather, I smiled. I studied Aunt June, suspecting there was much she wasn't telling me.

"Do you *know* this José Antonio?" I was leaning so far forward I was nearly falling off the bed.

"No, no, I don't know him. What I do know is how your momma talked about him. She said he was good-looking and strong and quick." Then she lowered her voice. "He was the great love of her life."

"Did he know about me? Or did he think Dad was my . . . *dad*?"

"I don't know."

The whole concept was difficult to wrap my mind around. If José Antonio was indeed my real father, it would've been tricky for him to find me, and, as I learned in school, Cubans are rarely allowed to leave their country. On the other hand, he may not want anything to do with me. And the risk of hurting my one living parent was too much.

"Forget it," I said. "I've got graduate school in London this fall, and then a job to worry about. I don't have time for this." But as I lay in the hospital bed, I couldn't help but remember what I'd promised my mother when she lay in hers. Promised I'd find José Antonio.

"Too bad," said Aunt June coolly. "Because I was thinking dancin' and rum and a few weeks in Havana would make a real nice graduation present."

"Oh, no," I replied, shaking a finger. But I knew I couldn't refuse my aunt. "What about Dad?"

"If John finds out, you blame it all on your old Aunt June." She cackled wickedly. "Your *chaperone*, Aunt June. 'Cause I'm going too. So, whaddya say?"

7

*O*ur plane lands just before daybreak.

Inside the airport, officials wear fatigues as if at war. Women officers, lovely and tanned and quick with a smile from behind bulletproof glass, sport micromini skirts in army green. Officers wear military jackets with a thread count so low we see skin through cloth.

"First time to Cuba?" asks the customs agent.

"Absa-too-da-loo-tely," says June. I nod and hand him my double-thick passport filled with stamps. He checks a computer screen.

"Want to give me another answer?" he asks, his eyes narrowing.

Aunt June shoots me a look of support, and I answer him. "Ah, yes. I was born here. It's my first time back."

"Welcome home, *m'ija.*"

While we are waiting for our luggage, the habit of childhood travel prompts me to study a map of Cuba. I trace an index finger along the page in my guidebook. I like looking at maps, and I can't help thinking it's the same perspective my mother shares, one from above, looking down on it all. Cuba, with its archipelagos and satellite islands, mountain ranges and rivers, claims the biggest landmass in the Antilles. Sharing its latitude are Haiti and the Yucatán; on longitude is the United States. The tapered fingers of the Florida Keys stretch longingly toward Cuba, but fall a mere ninety-two miles short of the Caribbean capital.

Culturally, the guidebook tells me, the isolated Cuba—by accident and by design—is a social version of Darwin's Galápagos, where creatures form and evolve in unusual and beautiful ways, quarantined by endless miles of water.

Within that isolation is the hopeful dream of finding my father.

We've chosen a sweltering morning to arrive in Havana. As we taxi into the capital, I tell Aunt June how I'm reminded of being nine years old, and riding with my parents for the first time through the streets of Beijing. The red Mandarin symbols looming over every shingle captured my imagination. China, to me, seemed not like a new country, but a different planet entirely.

As in China, Cuba's scenery also proves otherworldly. Billboards that in any other land would advertise Shell Gas or Nike blare revolutionary slogans with doe-eyed guerillas waging a war against the goliath Uncle Sam. These fervor-pitch banners give Havana the overall effect of not being a modern city at all, but a Berkeley dorm room circa 1969.

"Never could figure out your momma's passion for travel," says Aunt June, trying to appear relaxed in her maiden voyage abroad. I stare at Aunt June's profile under a broad straw hat and smile, grateful for the remaining family I have left.

As we ride in the back of a poky Lada—the ubiquitous Russian sedan one slight letter off from sharing the Spanish word for tin can—a new dawn breaks, and a glowing sun kisses the enigmatic city with its light.

Seductive as a striptease, Havana begins to reveal herself. We stare out the window at the startling loveliness of the city: something Arabic 1500s here, something Spanish 1600s there, something American 1950s here. Nothing aesthetically contrived, centuries accidentally blended. Organic and unexpected beauty.

Once-opulent houses of worship and opera and theater stand shivery and peeling. Havana, a European-style capital long forgotten, is magnificent and gray. A baroness at the end of her long life, numbed by a destitution not foreseen.

Aunt June gasps at the beauty and the destruction.

"Goodness," she exclaims. "It looks like a war movie!"

TRUTH IS, THE first trip to Cuba turned up *nada*.

Though I found the hospital where I was born, and confirmed John's name on my birth certificate, little headway was made. I could barely get my bearings. *Charanga* played everywhere. Roosters crowed at all hours,

and vintage American cars cruised along battered roads. Precious paint-
ings were housed in buildings of restored Art Nouveau. In the distance, a
deep sapphire sea was fronted by turquoise waters floating over coral and
limestone.

Royal palm trees hovered as tall as skyscrapers. Cocktail lounges and
discos blared with tango and flamenco, rumba and *cha-cha-chá*. Cubans
were loud, friendly, and always seemed to be dancing.

What came over me, slowly and imperceptibly, as I drank in the spectacle, was a burning desire to find José Antonio. At first, I'd just wanted to
see the island where I was born, but soon the possibilities of finding him
and his family captured my imagination. In the context of all this beauty,
in this culture of Cuba, this *cubanidad*, I realized that I'd be inheriting
much more than a Spanish last name. I'd be gaining a heritage. And so it
was this way that my mother's wish finally became mine, and the promise
I'd made to her to find José Antonio became the promise to myself, to discover this secret link into my past.

When I told this to my aunt, she seemed more than pleased.

"All I can say is I'm glad to know where my poppa was from. Mississippi. Fun to spell, easy to navigate, signs in English. Not like *this* god-
forsaken place," she said, shaking her head.

Aunt June spent our month at the hotel, a former American Mafia
haunt, enjoying the citric pleasure of Hemingway daiquiris delivered
poolside. She rarely left the grounds, but over the days warmed to the easy
rhythm. By the time we left, she claimed Havana to be the most beautiful
city she'd ever seen.

"Don't know if your momma loved the man or the island," said Aunt
June. "Can't say I ever would've left."

After our time expired, we did leave, though neither of us voiced our
disappointment in not tracking José Antonio. At the airport terminal
with Aunt June, I realized what the trip had truly been about. It had been
about her spending time with me, her only niece, and encouraging me in
whatever way possible to seek my own happiness, knowing I'd been dealt
a strange deck of familial cards.

I'm certain my aunt understood that in this archeological dig, we were
just brushing at the surface. She also must have known that I never
would've had the courage to take this first step alone.

At the airport, I threw my arms around her in thanks. "I'm going to miss you," I said, not knowing it was the last time I'd ever see her.

In Cancún, she flew to Mississippi via Houston, and I to Hartford through New York. After an uncomfortable July spent in the company of my grandparents in Connecticut, I snuck back into Cuba for a few weeks in August, this time brave enough to go alone.

THE MAP OF Havana was $7 in the tourist shop, and a *cafécito*—a thimble shot of dark, sweet coffee—helped me study its possibilities.

Although maps are central to my personal history, to understanding my family and their life as diplomatic tramps, the map of Havana tells me only one thing.

How very lost I am.

"What's your hurry to get home, anyway?" Victor Alvarez interrupts my thoughts. He's a meticulous government man in his late sixties, and the first fruitful contact I've made in Cuba.

"The best way to do this difficult search," he continues, "is to move here. Become a temporary resident."

"Isn't that impossible? I'm an American. I'm not even supposed to be here for a weekend."

"*Mira*, it's easy, actually. Just sign up for a student visa." Victor fiddles with buttons on a suit that could've been the same one he wore when the revolutionaries first burned through town in 1959. "You can stay a year. You can't leave during that year, but you can stay."

"Just like Hotel California."

Victor looks at me quizzically. "You need to be here to find what you're looking for, and even if you're here full-time it will take months just to find the address of your parents' home. But you're not going to progress *como así*. No one trusts a tourist."

"I can't stay a year," I say. "I can barely stay a few weeks. Can't I just phone you?"

Victor emitts one of his long laughs that implies he's dealing with a clueless outsider, an *extranjera*. "The people who can help you, and you'll have to meet many before you find them, won't trust you unless they can look you in the eye."

The frustratingly slow progress I've made thus far confirms for me that Victor is telling the truth. "Student visa buys me a year?"

"*Sí, mi amor.* A whole year."

Still, I shake my head. As much as I love Cuba, I feel in my heart I may never, ever find my needle in that haystack. I love the idea of owning Cuban blood, but living in Havana, with its chronic shortages and blackouts and suspicions of long-term guests, is not something I could prepare for. Victor is wrong, my search could take more than a year. It could take my whole life.

On the plane to London, where I was about to begin graduate school, I resigned myself to knowing that I'd tried. I'd made an effort to track José Antonio, but found myself understanding even less than when I began. A State Department family's life is a closely guarded secret in enemy territory, and I had no idea where to begin.

Finding José Antonio—if, indeed, he even existed—would take much more than a preprinted map of that immense, sun-soaked city. It would take a seer. A higher power. A conversation with the dead.

If my mother truly wanted me to find José Antonio, surely she'd provide a divination. I floated that wish, silently, onto the cumulus clouds the 747 glided through on the way to London.

If you're listening, I prayed, then send a sign.

8

Four months later, and a few weeks before Christmas break, in the middle of exams and a winter so extreme twelve people died of frostbite, I received a call from my father, who, in an anxious voice, asked about my studies. As a conversational afterthought, he relayed the news that my Aunt June had been diagnosed with the same killer that had downed my mother.

I dashed to the airport, but no plane could get me there fast enough. Aunt June died while I was en route. My father, who'd known about her cancer for nearly two weeks, insisted she not call for me, so as not to "break the concentration" of my studies. At first, I felt betrayed. And then, later, I just felt lost.

At June's ranch in Mississippi, after the horses were auctioned off and the house sold to new owners, I found myself alone, going through her effects. I remember being grateful then to my aunt for having done the same with my mother's things when she died ten years before.

It was at the end of the longest week of packing and tossing and sorting that I opened the moldy cardboard box that changed my life.

Inside were notebooks. As I flipped through, slowly at first and then faster, I recognized the handwriting inside. These were my mother's words. I remembered then she had written in journals nearly every evening, a cup of green tea in her hand.

The journals' years went backward from 1992, the year my mother died, to 1981, the year after they left Cuba. I searched frenetically. There had to be another box with the earlier years—there *had* to be. I grabbed at the nearby pile, sneezed from the dust and mildew, and peeled through tape with my bare hands and teeth. I went through five boxes, then six. The room tipped. I was possessed. Why were these in Mississippi with my aunt, and not in Washington at home with my father? Had Aunt June forgotten about these journals? Or had she intended for me to read them someday? It occurred to me, sadly, that I'd never know.

It was in the seventh box that I discovered my prize: my mother's journals from the Cuba years, 1977 to 1981. I scanned through them until I saw José Antonio's initials: J.A.

J.A. and I took Alysia to the beach this afternoon.
J.A. and his family played with her all day.
J.A. is frustrated when we leave for home.

That José Antonio knew of my existence changed something in me. He loved me. Or so said my mother's diaries, all of which I read nonstop in a week at my aunt's home. If José Antonio wasn't allowed to leave Cuba and find me, then it became my responsibility to look for him, and with the help of my mother's diaries, the impossible suddenly felt within reach.

Without telling my father, I canceled the last semester of graduate school, caught a flight to Washington, and applied for a license to travel to Cuba long-term to find José Antonio. While awaiting an answer, I reread the diaries and then scoured our Watergate apartment for the missing crucial clues: José Antonio's last name, his address, or the address of our assigned home in Havana all those years ago.

But my mother, unlike her sister, saved few things, believing clutter to be the bane of a traveler. I considered returning to my aunt's Mississippi ranch to look more closely through the piles of June's papers, with the hopes of finding at least an old letter with the return address in Havana. But U.S. diplomats in most countries use the military's mail system, and any envelopes to my aunt from Havana would contain a return address with only a box number now long expired.

My mother's diaries brought much clarity to the story of José Antonio and the narrative of our lives in Cuba. But she made cryptic the technicalities of my biological father's whereabouts, and the only mention of him was in the use of his initials, J.A. I imagined her doing so out of fear that my father would discover the terms of the affair. I would never know for sure. I couldn't help but think that if she hadn't said José Antonio's name in the hospital, or if she had never confided in Aunt June, even the mystery of his first name would have died with her.

While this was sinking in, I received word that the U.S. government had denied my request to visit Cuba. Determined to go anyway, via the illicit route Aunt June and I traveled, I phoned my best friend, Susie, and a few of my closest friends. Over dinner in Georgetown, I explained that I'd be going to Cuba for a year to fulfill a promise to my mother and find my biological father. The faces of skepticism that greeted me were quickly supplanted—once the shock wore off—with encouragement. But my friends, many of them on the foreign-service track as well, did not hide their chagrin at the fact that visiting me while I was in Cuba was illegal and, if they were caught, it would be detrimental to their careers. We agreed to keep in touch through e-mail, as phone service in and out of the Communist land was sketchy at best. The thought of not hearing each other's voices for a whole year made nearly all of us cry. My friends made me promise to tell them if I needed any help, and I swore I would.

Susie stayed the weekend, and together we pored over my mother's diaries, each taking turns in reading them aloud, and taking meticulous notes on legal pads. Susie's methodical mind was invaluable in mapping out a strategy to connect the spaghetti-thin links I had to José Antonio's whereabouts.

"All you have to do is find where you lived in Havana, and then ask the people who worked for your mother about José Antonio. They're probably still gossiping about the affair down there," said Susie, her eyes sparkling. "Boy, I wish I could go too."

We spoke about John, and how I felt betrayed by him, and how I could never forgive him that I never had a chance to say good-bye to my aunt. But I also felt loyalty. Genetic father or not, hadn't my father fed and housed and educated me? How could I tell him I was going to look for José Antonio? In looking for the family that might have been, would I lose the only family I had left?

The weekend was spent considering the answers. Susie and I chattered in the shorthand and clipped phrases only best friends can understand, and she rehearsed with me the conversation I was shortly to have with my father, in announcing my intentions to look for José Antonio. I cried when she dropped me off at the airport. We promised to e-mail nearly every day. I think she made me swear if I didn't, I could never smoke a Chesterfield again.

In my suitcase, I had the $25,000 my aunt had left me, more than I'd ever had in my life. It would barely last me a year in Havana, a city as expensive as any world capital, but I was determined.

I flew to Cancún, and in the airport lounge, awaiting a connecting flight to Havana and safely distanced from the U.S., I phoned the father who raised me to tell him I was looking for the father who did not. As the operator placed my call to his cell phone, I took a deep breath.

It was the first time in my life I knew exactly what to do.

9

The office of student affairs for the University of Havana lies in the heart of Vedado, on palm-lined streets of the formerly wealthy class who prospered under the tyrannical reign of Fulgencio Batista. The *mulato* leader exiled himself—to great cheers and jubilation from his subjects—on the first day of 1959. Many in the neighborhood fled as well, to planes that landed in Miami and Newark and Madrid.

Sporting an olive military jacket over pink Lycra hot pants, the woman who authorized my yearlong visa—from July to July—looked at me sternly as I signed my residency agreement. I couldn't, she lectured, leave Cuba for a year without written permission. In asking for an exception, I must request permission, in writing, one year in advance. When I questioned the nonsensical nature of that rule, I was answered with a shrug and an *"Eso es Cuba."*

I pay tuition for classes I'll never attend, and sign my new *carnet*, a British-racing-green booklet with metallic embossing. I am semiofficially a *cubana*. For a year.

The room I rent is in Miramar, in a Spanish colonial home with Arabic tiling on the ceiling, and crossbeams of burnished wood. The family, three generations of esteemed doctors and medical professors, happily take me in. My $400 monthly contribution will supplement their combined $62 monthly salary the government doles out in worthless pesos.

The celebratory bottle of rum I shared with them over a *criollo* meal of black beans, rice, pork, and fried *plátanos* was my first as a Cuban. With my bags and notes, I settled into the tourist room, the home's nicest, feeling guilty that the others share cramped spaces along the western end of the house.

By the light of an oil lamp, I studied the map of Havana. Streets A through Z ran parallel. Numbered ones crossed them in between, like gloved fingers entwined in another's hand. Obispo for pedestrians cut from the wharf to Central Park. There, Calle Neptuno picked up and ran from boisterous, slummy Centro to middle-class Vedado. The waterfront curved around the barrios and swooped north through the glimmering suburb of Miramar.

The miracle of a map is that it shows how disparate neighborhoods come together; it delineates where and when they connect, eventually—at first divergent and then harmonious, like a composition by Beethoven. There is hope in a map. The exact space where latitude meets longitude is the promise it keeps.

I blew out the light and tucked in for a sleep that wouldn't come.

In the morning, I took my thousands of dollars and taped piles of money to the bottom of the room's furnishings. I should have known every Cuban is acutely aware that a *norteamericano* may only use cash. That the American embargo prohibits wire transfers, advances, credit cards, and checks of every kind. A *norteamericana,* in Cuba for one whole year, would have to bring *a lot* of cash.

I was thinking this as I taxied home from my first meeting with Victor.

By the time I arrived at my *casa,* the money was gone.

No one was home. Later, the family blamed the neighbors.

The policemen just shrugged.

I had $500 to my name.

I cried for a week. I cried because the only person who could bail me out was the last person I wanted to speak with.

John.

10

This is what I remember doing. I remember changing my round-trip ticket to leave Havana the next day. I remember the man at airport customs, when I explained what'd happened, and how he said no, I couldn't leave for Mexico; sadly, as if he wished to help. Next came the office of student affairs, then the Cuban office of foreign affairs, and finally, without care as to my punishment for being there illegally, the U.S. Interests Section, the building where my father reported to work every day more than twenty years before.

"You're in a pickle," said the woman behind the counter at the Interests Section, when I explained my situation. That's all she could say, that I was in a pickle.

When I did finally phone my father in Washington, I had just enough money to cover the call.

I explained my plight. No, I couldn't access cash. No, I couldn't leave the country. No, there were no jobs for foreigners. I told him this, but heard nothing. I was sure the line had gone dead.

Finally, he spoke. "You called me two weeks ago and said you wanted to find your 'real father' in Cuba," he said slowly. "You want to be a Cuban? Well, now you're going to get just that. You get to spend the next year seeing exactly what your life would have been like had I not . . ." His voice trailed off.

"But I promised Mom I'd look for him—you remember, don't you? That night in the hospital?"

But he was not listening. "I gave you a life most children, Cuban or not, would kill for. This is how I'm repaid?"

"I'm not here because I'm ungrateful," I said, appealing. "Wouldn't you be curious about your family, if you were in my shoes?"

"No, I wouldn't," he said sharply. "I wouldn't at all. I'd be damned grateful I could pass for a Briggs and I'd leave it at that."

I barely heard his words, or the full force of his Connecticut snobbery behind them. Instead, sensing his finality, I pleaded. "I'll pay you back," I said. "Every cent. I just need to make it through the next twelve months."

A protracted silence.

Then, swallowing all my pride, I asked this: "Could you make a few calls, use your connections and see if I can get a visa out?"

His voice faltered, and he cleared his throat. "I've already lost one woman to Cuba. Do you think I want to lose another?" Then a sigh. "Is José Antonio going to take everyone precious from me?"

"Dad, please come and get me," I said. "My friends can't come here, you know this. They can't get a license. You can. They can't send money without violating the embargo and jeopardizing their foreign-service careers. Dad, *you* are the only one who can help me."

"How can you call me 'Dad' and then go look for José Antonio? No. You want to go look for him—you go look for him. You've gotten yourself into this situation—"

"You can't leave me here!" I was shouting then, sheer panic in my voice, and it ricocheted across the marbled lobby of the hotel. "If you leave me here . . . If you leave me, Dad—"

He interrupted. "I did everything I could to raise you like my own. I said this to your mother, and I'll say it to you: It's me or it's him. You're on your own."

"Don't—"

But he cut the phone line.

With the few dollars left on the calling card, I numbly began to dial Susie. Then I stopped myself. Of course Susie would come for me. She would wire me money and in doing so she would cast aside the risk to her own career ambitions. My other friends would do the same. For a moment, I wavered. But my father was right. I'd opened the wounds of my family's history. I'd gotten myself into this mess, and it was my job to clean it up. Even if I had to do so alone.

As the receiver clicked heavy under my fingers, and as I glanced wildly about the hotel lobby, I realized that at that very moment I'd been abandoned. I was the biblical Abednego, and Cuba was the furnace Nebuchadnezzar had thrown me into.

But the more I looked around, at young, beautiful women on the arms of the tourists—ones temporarily privileged by the economic disparity of an impoverished land—I knew I wasn't the only one left to fend for herself.

Just as it was for my brethren, the people of Cuba with whom I'd now share a life, the morality of my upbringing would begin to crumble around me, first in small, dusty pieces, and then, as the storm worsened, in bigger, heavier chunks. It was the day I agreed to debase myself. The day I began to exchange what was dear for eating, sleeping, and finding the one thing I desperately wanted.

My real family.

I looked around as I walked to Miramar to collect my things. Scenery I'd once found sad now brought encouragement. Well-dressed men on rickety Chinese bicycles. Tattered laundry hanging from the balconies of mansions of former opulence. A dignified old woman, whose jewelry no longer held its stones, hawking black-market cheese.

If these were my people, and I no longer doubted they were, they'd have to teach me exactly how to survive.

And survive I would.

Two

11

’m shivering in the nude. The nurse hands me a ratty gown and ushers me into a room that looks like a Byzantine torture chamber. Cracked plaster and rusty metal contraptions hang off the walls.

"We don't have beautiful facilities," says the doctor behind the clipboard, reading my mind. "But guests from all over the world visit us. Our staff is the best in the hemisphere."

She's striking, early thirties, with an air of easy sophistication and skin the color of caramel flan. A nurse introduces the woman as Dr. Fernandez de Valle, head of cardiology at the Instituto de Cardiovascular. I'd soon know her as Camila.

An icy stethoscope slides over my chest and back. I breathe deeply. Camila dismisses the nurse, unfolds her glasses, and reclines in her chair.

"You're Cuban."

"How can you tell?"

She arches a brow. "You've had a panic attack," she pronounces. "Your chart says you're only twenty-three. Now, what on earth does a lovely young *rubia* have to be nervous about on holiday? The boys and their *piropos*?" She smiles. "They *are* overwhelming, all that whistling and carrying on in the streets."

I study my feet. I'd never had a panic attack before, but I was certain I was going to die. The palpitations started just as the family of doctors— my landlords in the home where my money had been stolen—proclaimed frostily that I had to leave by the weekend, as it was nearly July, and tourism was on the upswing. As it sunk in that I was homeless and broke,

I couldn't catch my breath. First, my heart beat quickly, and then more rapidly still, until it felt as if it would burst from my chest.

"Well, *muñeca*?"

The adrenaline makes me feel confessional, and the whole story spills from my mouth. I tell her about my mother and stepfather, the robbery, and my search for José Antonio. She listens carefully. When I'm done, she jumps from her seat.

"*Ay, candela!* How could you live with those *ladrones*?" Thieves. "They took *los mangos bajitos*! All your money was gone?"

"All of it . . . I'd only left the house for a few hours."

"The family robbed you. No question." She thinks for a moment. "You need to get out of that house *prontito*. A woman I know owes me a favor. Pack your things." She scribbles on paper. "Meet me here around seven tonight. You'll be having dinner with my family."

I grab for my pile of clothes. "Thank you," I say meekly.

"*No pasa nada*," she says. "Some of us Cubans are lucky enough to have a bit of Arabic blood in our veins. And that means we're obliged to help travelers. Besides, it's been a long while since we've had a *norteamericana* in the flesh. This will be fun."

THAT NIGHT, ON the patio of Camila's family home, neighbors and friends and cousins gather to hear for themselves the story of a *norteamericana* looking for her Cuban father. In a country where time and *chisme*—gossip—are the only items in copious supply, I quickly give up any notions of privacy.

I'm the new neighborhood *telenovela*.

The soap opera everyone will follow.

Camila negotiates a tiny room for me in the Vedado home of the woman who owes her a favor. A few days later, I meet my new landlady. Our arrangement is black-market and illegal. I'm warned to keep in the shadows, away from the police.

12

Red paper lanterns swirl in a tropical gust. A tiny block of Chinatown, with its raucous cafés and curio shops, forms an oasis of bobbing lights in a darkened city. Under the scarlet glow, preteens in silky China-doll dresses giggle seductively at aging tourists.

Like them, I'm waiting for my black-market job to begin, and I check the time on my watch. Ten-thirty.

Consulting my map, I walk a few blocks along Calle Zanja to a deserted square, near the former Shanghai Theatre—a rollicking stripper's cabaret and dirty-movie house made infamous in a 1950s Havana known for its gambling palaces and whorehouses and peepshows.

When drugs, money, and thugs ruled the streets.

On these same streets now, violent crime is rare, and women walk alone without apprehension. Still, in the dark, as I wait at the appointed corner, my radar is in overdrive.

The black 1951 Studebaker Champion screeches to a halt, and both doors swing open. I jump a little, but breathe easier when the driver introduces himself as Mario. I squeeze between two *cubanos* on the burgundy bench-seat, its springs underneath long retired, and we take off. After each successful pass through an intersection, Mario pounds the roof twice in lucky exclamation. A man next to me launches into a heated argument about an umpire's call in a World Series game—one played thirty years ago.

As we drive through Centro, I stare out the windows, fascinated. Front doors are flung open. Old mansions have been quartered into apartments, and their inhabitants bunch inside, or spill onto streets. Music tumbles from every balcony. The flickering of fluorescents illuminate interiors and the lives inside: old men hover over chessboards, women scrape at pans, and young children toss jacks with grandmothers.

Mario drives out of the poorer Centro, and we arrive in a ritzy section of Miramar. The bullet-nosed beast slides into a driveway. Mario walks me past a large banyan tree that obscures the main entrance and hides the mansion's bustling interior.

A woman named Blanca greets us and ushers me past the warm lights, antiques, and roomfuls of foreigners dining at small tables. Blanca clarifies that it's a *paladar*—a private restaurant—and hers is run illegally.

"We don't make enough money to pay the monthly tax," she explains. "So we just take our chances."

"If you get caught?"

She laughs and nervously waves off my question. We take a side door and climb a sumptuous, curving staircase so old that countless footsteps have worn arcs in the marble. Blanca sits me down in a small room and instructs me to wait. Several people, she says, will come in with a list and cash, and deliver their requests. She smiles at me funny.

"It's on Camila's word that we trust you," she says. "Good luck."

Pedrín is the first to enter. His lashes are long and curled at the tip, but his body is masculine and strong. His skin feels like leather as I brush his cheek with a kiss. Pedrín sits down, awkward in the small chair, and looks me over.

"You're Cuban, *verdad*?"

"*Creo que sí,*" I say. I guess.

He laughs. "*Mira,* you'd know if you're Cuban."

"How?"

"You'd be intelligent and inventive and you'd die for your country. Or—" he leans in with the punch line—"you'd die trying to leave it."

Smiling, I ask: "What'll it be?"

"A microwave." He pulls out a paper from his wallet and reads from it. "Sheets, two sets. Rice cooker. Some Advil. Multivitamins. Cough syrup for children."

I write this down. He pulls out some twenties from his wallet.

"Your markup is twenty percent?" he asks.

I feel embarrassed. "I wish I could say it was zero."

My advantage, one worth a twenty percent commission, is that I'm carrying a foreign passport. With that, I can walk into the *diplomercado*—diplomats' market—and buy items off-limits to locals. Oftentimes, the same items are available to Cubans in dollar stores, but Blanca tells me there's been a shortage for weeks now and the *habaneros*—Havana residents—are getting desperate.

"Don't worry," says Pedrin. "The *habaneros* who work at the *diplo* charge a hundred percent markup, if they can sneak the stuff out. This"—he gestures at my list—"is a deal."

"Can I ask . . ." The question is too personal. I hesitate.

"*Dale,*" he encourages.

"How do you get dollars? I thought everyone was paid in pesos."

"My wife has a *yuma.*"

"A what-a?"

"A *yuma.* A foreign boyfriend. The *yuma* sends money pretty regularly, and we need it; we have two kids, plus my wife's mother."

"You don't mind the boyfriend?"

He says nothing, and looks down at the desk. "He's *gordo, viejo, y feo.*" Fat, old, and ugly. "Why should I mind?"

Pedrin stands up, a bit too fast, and hurls U.S. dollars on my desk.

"*Vaya con dios.*"

La yuma, I'd later learn, was originally slang for the United States, and *una yuma* identified a *norteamericano.* The word was derived from old western films where the township of Yuma, Arizona, played a character, such as *The Wild Bunch* or *3:10 to Yuma.* Today, *yuma* means any foreigner, from any country. And it's especially used to indicate a naïve tourist who assists—unwittingly or not—a Cuban in his daily quest for dollars.

AT THE END of the night, Blanca says that what I've heard is not unusual. She explains that Cubans are paid only in pesos, but that most necessities can only be bought in dollars, at dollar stores open to Cubans.

In the dual economy, the pesos are nearly worthless.

"So if everyone is paid in pesos," I ask Blanca, "but most things are sold in dollars, how are people supposed to get dollars?"

"Each day we wake up, *mi amor,* to answer just that question."

Later in the evening, Camila tells me that remittances sent from abroad are the island's biggest source of income.

"More than money from tourism?" I ask. "Or cigars?"

She nods, and pulls the night's dinner from the 1940s rust-bucket fridge. "It's not just the families who've left for Miami. Cubans marry foreigners and then move to Europe or Canada and send money home." Camila arranges black beans and salted tomatoes on a plate and then, quietly, says, "And if you're Cuban with a *yuma* boyfriend or girlfriend, they send money here as well."

"If you don't have anyone to send money?"

"There's free education, free health care, and those with houses don't pay rent. There's also a *libreta,* which gives us enough food to get us through the first few days in the month. The rest," she says, patting her stomach, "we have to *inventar* in some other way."

As she heats my dinner in a microwave, I chew on my lower lip. Camila doesn't have any family abroad. Her job as head of the prestigious Instituto brings in the peso equivalent of $32 a month. Though four times the average $8 Cuban salary, it's hardly enough for basics.

Yet the signs of dollars are everywhere in her home. A color TV, a stereo, beautiful clothes.

I don't dare ask where it comes from.

13

The first time I noticed Walrus was my eleventh trip to the *diplo-mercado*. First, I saw him in the aisles, tugging at his mustache, and then later, watching Mario and me load goods in the back of the Studebaker.

By that trip, I'd made enough money for a month's rent, and Camila and I had celebrated the night before with a bottle of rum we shared on the seawall, the Malecón. In a city where no one has enough space, the long, concrete couch on the bay has become Havana's living room.

"I think this whole *diplo* business," I said cheerily as a parade of transvestites wobbled by on pavement slick with sea spray, "is the answer to my prayers."

Turns out I'd been imploring the wrong gods.

On my twelfth trip, the July sun is overhead, and the ocean carries no breeze. At a corner near the exit of the *diplo-mercado,* Mario obsessively wipes the Studebaker's wraparound rear window. I struggle with boxes and bags, squinting through flashes of sun on metal. I call for Mario. He heads toward me. From a distance comes a strange whistle. A signal. I look around, scanning for the source, but see none.

Mario, without looking, stuffs his buffer in a pocket, cranks the engine, and roars off, the muffler dragging behind like cans on a wedding car.

I turn to see Walrus standing next to me. "The only thing slick about that," says Walrus, pointing at Mario's car, "are the tires."

Pasty white with shocks of thick brown hair and a large, unwieldy body, Walrus studies me. Knotted rope loops through his pants, and sweat mars his white shirt. Quickly, I hail a cab.

I'm pushing the last bag into the taxi's trunk when his wrist lands on my neck.

"Staff says you've been in the *diplo-mercado* every day this week. Using a U.S. passport. That true?"

"Who's asking?" I shake off his hold and slide into the cab.

He points at the trunk. "Are you setting up house here, *princesa*? 'Cause if so you've got enough for a castle."

I refuse to answer. The Walrus smiles, motions for the cabbie to wait, and lights a Popular cigarette—unfiltered Cuban tobacco that lets out a brume of smoke. Walrus leans into the car and sneers. I can smell his lips.

"Careful here, *princesa*."

BLANCA DOESN'T ANSWER the door or return any calls. The Studebaker is nowhere in sight, so I stash the purchases at Camila's house. A few nights later, Mario cautiously turns up, and we make the deliveries.

"It's just freaking rice cookers," I say. "You'd think I was dealing opium."

"You must have a Chinaman walking behind you," says Mario.

"A Chinaman walking behind me?"

"It's a saying. Means bad luck. The fat cop is *singando*"—fucking—"with you. Happens to all of us, sooner or later."

"How lucky. What kind of cop is assigned to the Advil aisle, anyway?"

Mario taps two fingers to his shoulder blade, to indicate the dual stripes of a military uniform.

"G-2. Security police," he says somberly. "What you *don't* want are those *chotos* walking behind you." We glide through a crowded intersection, and Mario bangs on the rooftop in thanks. Dangling from his rearview mirror are a rosary of beads and bones and shells to ward off bad spirits. In the back window, he hangs blank CDs, because he swears it deflects the other evil—police radar.

"Why would the G-2 follow me?" I ask. "Because I'm the child of a Yankee diplomat?"

"*Mira,* if you're going to live in Cuba and you're a *norteamericano,* you've got to accept you're going to be watched. Almost all long-term foreigners are watched. *No importa.* The G-2 were trained by the Russians, but now—now they've got nothing better to do than follow around pretty, young girls," he says with a laugh. Then, with a roll of his eyes, says: "Or anyone who's a risk to the *'triunfo de la revolución.'* "

The Studebaker stalls at a light. At a corner café, an elegant, dark-skinned woman in a nurse's outfit waits for a tourist family to finish eating before snatching the chicken bones from their plates and hurrying away with her prize.

El triunfo de la revolución.

The triumph of the revolution.

When I first arrived in Cuba as an adult, I was overcome with the beauty of its people, with the quick smiles and kindness, the motivation and the overt intelligence. After I spent my childhood traveling through impoverished territories, the education and health and optimism of Cubans impressed me. I'm still impressed. But what I didn't expect was to feel that each day I saw a rawer, more truthful kind of Cuba. And I hoped that this onion, unpeeling in gossamer layers before my eyes, would not reveal itself to be rotten at the core.

14

Nick Wethersby is a high-class private investigator and European mystery man who now makes his living snooping on a rich foreigner's Cuban love interest. Word on the street is that he's hiding out in the Pearl of the Antilles because U.S. authorities have a warrant on his head. In this last, dark corner of the earth, chances are he'll escape detection.

In a camel's-hair shirt and linen pants, Nick sports the prematurely wrinkled face of someone who's spent too much time on other people's yachts. In Cuba, he plies his trade on the black market and lives with his Cuban wife in Guanabo, a beach town outside Havana.

"When foreign lovers are the biggest source of income for lucky Cubans, anyone who interferes with that relationship is in danger," Nick says, pulling up a chair for me on his patio overlooking the waves. "I can't lie to you, yours is a risky task." He drops a hand on my knee.

Nick's wife, a *mulata* forty-one years his junior, makes a production of adjusting a lemony O-ring halter around her plentiful breasts, securing Nick's line of sight and shooting me a look of warning. Her lifestyle, that of the wife of a coveted foreigner, is among the most luxurious in Cuba.

"My associate will be dressed as a tourist and take photos of you and the *chulo* at a disco, in flagrante," Nick says.

I nod slowly, listening, and staring at his oiled nails. Nick's reputation as the smartest investigator on the island led me to ask him for help finding my father, and he's certain he can find—using only the clues in my mother's diaries—the home where my mother lived in the 1970s as well as her lover's last name and address. Nick is in possession of one of the most valued assets in Cuba: connections. Using his, I may cut my search by months. And Nick, upon hearing my story, agreed to take my case. But it wasn't money he wanted in exchange. It was my services.

Nick continues: "Typical *chulo*'s woman is European or Canadian. She's in her forties, fifties, sometimes sixties. She's bossy and pale and can't move her hips. But she's convinced this young, usually *mulato*, Cuban male finds her incredibly attractive. She uses her money to control him, to keep his interest, and these macho Latinos don't like it much. In every instance I'm aware of, they have Cuban girlfriends on the side and are keeping their options open with other foreign women. Our job is to catch the *chulos* screwing around."

"Fidelity testing?" I smirk. "Great line of work, Nick."

Nick flashes the heel of his hand. "In this case, our client back in Norway has an investment to make. Wedding and expenses are going to set her back twenty-five, thirty grand. That's prior to his migrating. She wants to see what kind of man he's going to be now, *before* her hard-earned slips down the sewer. That's where you come in."

"If I fail?" I ask. "I'm pretty bossy and I can't move my hips, either." Truth is I could barely make eye contact with an attractive boy, much less trifle with a love-savvy *cubano*.

Nick's wife touches my arm and interrupts my thoughts. "It's a no-brainer. You're young, attractive, *and* foreign. That makes you a triple threat. If the *chulo* has a cheating tendency, you're the kind of prize he won't pass up."

The kind of prize *no* man could pass up slides through Nick's back door, her lips curled into a perfect pout. She doesn't look at anyone but Nick, and holds her hand palm-up, theatrically tossing her long black hair. Nick hastily pulls her inside.

"Modesta," says Nick's wife, whispering in my ear. "The meanest *bruja* in Havana." But I don't manage to inquire further, because Nick bursts through the patio, his calm demeanor shaken. He and his wife exchange knowing glances.

Then, as if remembering me, Nick asks: "So? You taking this job?"

The ocean today is still like a lake, and fathers are playing with their children at the shore.

It's a Tuesday afternoon. It's a Tuesday afternoon and families are laughing and carousing and swimming. I envy the great fortune of a whole generation of children who will one day recall their parents with the clarity that comes only from the spending of time together. An arrangement entirely possible in a place where time does not mean money.

"I won't sleep with him."

"You don't have to," says Nick's wife. "A photogenic kiss with some oomph will be *perfecto*. The pictures should say 'We're off to bed.'"

I think about my mother's diaries, and how I reread them each night, and imagine with her every word a Havana two decades before. She wrote that José Antonio took me to the beach and taught me to swim on those long-ago Tuesday afternoons when my mother would bring me to him, so that a father could know his child.

"How 'bout it?" asks Nick.

"I won't sleep with him," I repeat.

"There'll be a car waiting for you outside the disco," says Nick's wife, impatiently. "Just tell the *chulo* you've changed your mind. Jump in, and we'll take you out of the situation." She looks at my expectantly. "*'Ta bien?*"

Her willingness to deceive one of her own disturbs me. She reminds me of many people who are newly rich and suddenly loathe the poor and ambitious.

"Cubans are nothing if not great actors," says Nick's wife, as if reading my thoughts. "Convincing *yumas* they're desperately in love."

The complex artistry of conniving vulnerable foreigners into games of love began a decade before. Cuba's economic lean times were realized in the early 1990s, when Soviet subsidies were cut and food disappeared. The resulting "special period" of barren stores and raging fear provided the biggest economic and social upheaval in thirty years. Cuba had gone from supplying sugar to supplying tourism, and the convergence of a new poverty with an influx of foreigners gave rise to the endemic hustling and prostitution.

Jinetera, the Spanish word for a female jockey, means much more than a *señorita* equestrian. It's a fitting metaphor for what many educated and beautiful Cuban women do after hours to feed their families as well as their dreams.

Jineteras, and their male counterparts, the tourist-swindling *jineteros,* have become local heroes. Jockeys, cowboys, riders of the beast are heralded by their families as saviors.

With an American embargo punishing all who do business with Cuba, there are no promising signs of prosperity. Humiliations—damning and daily, inflicted by foreigners and police—are not discussed, just swallowed back with a swill of rum or the ubiquitous "relaxation pills" doled out at clinics like aspirin.

I wonder how many years this ridiculous system can continue. Its degradations. Its pride-for-dollars economy.

Tonight, I'm going to perpetuate the humiliation and squeeze into my shortest dress to seduce a young man. If I'm successful, he and his family will lose a lifeline of dollars.

"We're just protecting his girlfriend's assets," offers Nick, as if sensing my discomfort.

I think about this woman, this Norwegian, imagining her cruel manipulations, and also her tender insecurities. I picture her unsexiness, made all the more awkward by the inherent splendor of Cuban women, all of whom are beautiful precisely because they believe it to be so. There's a great providence in living sheltered from commercialism. For in living protected from the notion of a singular beauty, from a narrow prescription of attractiveness, loveliness may bloom on any stem.

"You in or not?" asks Nick. "We don't have much time."

I nod reluctantly. As an American, I'm unaccustomed to ambiguities. I'm waiting for the moral victor to emerge and for the bad guy to show his face. But I don't know with whom I sympathize more—the Cuban or the foreigner.

Myself a mix between the two, I find consolation only in that I'm doing this to find my father.

That I have no choice.

HE'S MY AGE, with olive eyes and skin as warm and brown and sleek as a river of chocolate. I'm whispering in his ear. I pull him under the kaleidoscope of the disco ball, and throw my hair back. I'm not Alysia tonight. I'm someone else. I'm a girl in a London club in a Miu Miu dress;

I'm in Ibiza, and it's warm and the air is wearing me like a coat and there's nothing about me that's a fraud. Music surges through my body, igniting every nerve, and his mouth is the sweet cream of a *tres leches*. At the end of this dream, when my lips leave his, and I slyly suggest we take it on the road, to my place, baby, and the flashbulbs pop like a jigger in the foreground, I'm happy, I'm in ecstasy, I'm young and alive and he's all mine tonight.

I climb into the car, feeling shattered. I watch his confused face through the rear window, one glued on with duct tape. He's young, I tell myself. He'll find another *yuma*.

I take a swill of the driver's bathtub rum, in case he doesn't.

The car stops short of my home, and I stumble through potholes on my way to the concrete couch, the Malecón. It's near dawn. The transvestites are asleep, and I sit nearby, watching the sun pull from the clouds, and letting the humid sea—tumultuous today—wash over me completely.

15

Nick strolls the lobby of the five-star Parque Central hotel with the gait of a VIP on a royal tour. In hushed tones and the gravitas normally reserved for national diplomacy, he gives the bad news to clients—more than a few of whom go ahead with the wedding anyway.

Nick signals for me to wait at the hotel's rooftop pool in the sky. There, under the brutality of an August sun, I settle into a green chaise and get to work. My mother's journal of her life in 1970s Havana is spread before me. Like any journal, it's sometimes insightful and occasionally scintillating and often dull. It's painful to read of the details of her mundane life as the wife of a diplomat, or of John's inability to show affection, to relax, or to be spontaneous and loving.

I feel shameful, prying into her innermost thoughts, but it's the price I pay in searching for clues of my father. I console myself with the notion that most journal keepers harbor, on some level, the desire to be read.

But if my mother ever considered that her daughter would one day be reading her words and tracking her steps, she surely would have included clearer information. On each read, I'm hoping the letters in every word have rearranged themselves and formed an address—one where she lived, or my biological father lived, or both.

I'm tugging at my bikini top when the stranger sits next to me and orders a Cuba libre.

"American Coke and Cuban rum," he muses in a British accent. "Volatile combination, don't you agree? Likely to combust in one's stomach."

I flip onto my back.

"Richard," he says, offering his hand. "Of London. Are you here long?"

"Alysia," I say. "Of Cuba and America—"

"Sorry," he laughs. "Don't need to order a Cuba libre. One right here."

Instantly I like him, and offer my hand in return. "I'm staying on a year. Student visa."

"Your Spanish is good, I presume."

"Don't understand half the slang, but I manage."

His drink arrives, and he orders one for me. "There's the matter of a Cuban girlfriend," he says. "We're not getting on, and the translator I've hired, he's a real wanker. Would you mind terribly?" Grateful for any work, I agree and make the arrangements to meet the lovebirds for dinner.

Richard leaves as Nick shows up, scratching his burnsides.

"Good news," says my employer, settling into a chaise and pulling out a map. His magnifying glass glides over Miramar, the streets colored in brilliant yellows and reds and blues. He punches in coordinates on his hand-held (and illegal) GPS, then scrawls a large box on the map. Somewhere within his crude boundaries sits the home John shared with my mother twenty years before, and possible clues to José Antonio's address. The parameters, wide and general as they are, make me happier than I've been in days.

Nick picks up a new stack of papers and promises to read through notes culled from my mother's diaries. Her throwaway phrases—"a two-minute walk to the beach" or "the figure-eight pool next door"—have crystallized into geographic gems.

"Tomorrow, I'll have your mother's address locked up," he boasts. "But I'm expecting you to take care of tonight's *chulo*."

"The last *chulo* didn't fall for me."

"Like you tried."

"I tried!" I say defensively.

"In flip-flops and a baggy shirt, you did," he scolds. Not to mention the greasy ponytail, I say to myself.

"Do I have a choice?"

"*This* one's tough; a lifeguard I've been after for nearly a year. Name's Rafael. He's got more *yumas* than coconuts."

"Where and when," I say with a sigh.

"Club Las Vegas, midnight." Nick pulls down his sunglasses. "Upfront and honest," he says. "You don't get him, our little arrangement is over."

16

I'm determined to bag my *chulo* tonight.

I'm twirling in Camila's nude, sheer Marc Jacobs dress I nicknamed the *bomba*—because every time she wears it men drop dead.

The neighbors are buzzing about the night's task. Everyone seems to know a different Rafael with "more *yumas* than coconuts" and I'm saturated with seduction tips like a virgin bride on her wedding night.

In Camila's teeming front room, the neighbors look me over. Opinions bellow simultaneously: The dress is too baggy. It's too long. It's rotten against my complexion.

"Only one way to test," says Camila, pushing me out her front door. I walk hesitantly along the busy sidewalk, looking back at the group of people gathering to watch.

"*Oye!* Loosen your hips!" shouts one of the neighbors.

"*Por favor!* Slow down!" shouts another.

"And *movimiento sexy!*"

Several men pass without looking at all. In a country where street flirtation has been elevated to an art form, I'm downright mortified by the lack of attention. I loosen my body. My toes start to point and I sway my buttocks.

With Camila's giggling neighbors behind me, I remember my mother writing that the streets of Havana unlocked in her a sensuality she believed long dead. Suddenly, I feel my mother's presence—the way she always appears, a slight depression on my forearm, a shift in the wind—and my body surges. It's a granting of permission to release the *cubana* inside. I take a deep breath, throw my shoulders back, and smile a bit more confidently.

A creaky old man with a cane hobbles by. "I'd pay a dollar for a bit of that!" he shouts.

Considering the economy, I take it as a compliment.

17

$\mathcal{N}$atchez, Mississippi, at one time, claimed more millionaires than any other town outside New York City. Despite its comforts, my mother's low threshold for boredom, coupled with her heightened sense of adventure, had her aching to leave long before the end of her high school days.

She believed that growing up on the banks of the Mississippi, for a girl like her, was an inexorable torture, for the river itself traveled freely by and into the wilder parts of the world.

Parts she dreamed of seeing.

It was 1957 when she first saw the boys from Latin America. They'd arrived at the station carrying trunks plastered with exotic port stickers, and wearing linen suits and felt hats. The young students were whisked off to Jefferson College, a nearby private military school newly fashionable with privileged families in Bogotá and Mexico City and Tegucigalpa.

It was only then that Natchez appealed to her imagination.

She remembered clearly a Saturday afternoon when she was sixteen. She and her girlfriends—in starched petticoats and silk scarves—met at Mr. Paul's pharmacy on Main Street for their customary cherry colas. There, at the long Formica bar, on the weekend before a big dance, the town girls gathered on one end, and the town boys at the other, all awaiting a surge of courage.

When the Latinos first sauntered through the pharmacy doors that Saturday afternoon, clad in gray-and-blue military finery, my mother held her breath. Unlike the Southern boys in their trepidation, the Latinos waltzed right up to her and the other girls and invited them to the dance.

Their cheekiness sparked a years-long feud between the locals and their foreign counterparts.

My mother remembers hearing Spanish spoken for the first time that afternoon, and could never forget the way it sounded like a baroque symphony, the way it made her blush.

The first boy from Havana arrived a year later, in the autumn of 1957, followed by several others, all sent in anticipation of a bloody revolution brewing in their homeland.

Alejandro, she remembers, was shipped to Mississippi precisely because his family feared he would join the rebels in the mountains.

Alejandro taught her many things. He taught her about José Martí, a bard whose verses were written in blood. About the dignities of social equality, and a people's pride in governing themselves. He spoke of atrocities in his city, of a Havana where death and penury held court. Where outsiders reigned, and natives served.

Alejandro took her to a ballroom dance. Then he took her outside, on the dewy grass under a magnolia tree, and taught her to move like a Cuban, to dance *timba,* to feel the clave rhythm of a music only he could hear.

Alejandro possessed a sense of entitlement that frightened her.

Alejandro believed in a *tierra libre.*

Alejandro left for the Cuban mountains in 1958 and never returned. On the first day of 1959, my mother awoke to a New Year's headline. Revolutionaries had made a triumphant march through Havana.

My mother read the news and dreamed. She dreamed of a hillside held by romantic and erudite rebels. Of the dead poet who foretold a reckoning. She dreamed of an island so green and lush it called men from the sea.

She dreamed.

18

The jockey has an outfit. A whip. Riding boots. Jodhpurs, the breeches with reinforced patches at the knee and thigh, where the rider's legs grip the beast.

"You know this dress is like eight hundred bucks," I tell Camila as she rolls my hair around empty beer cans and secures the cans atop my head with three-gauge wire, *a lo cubano*. I fiddle with the label. "Marc Jacobs."

She pulls my hair up so tight, my eyes slant like a cat's.

"Ouch!" And then, blithely, I say: "Anyway, whoever gave this to you was *super* nice."

"Alysia, my favorite Yankee. Before you go out *singando* with the lifeguard, you and I need to have a little chat."

I smile to myself. I want to hear it directly from her.

I wiggle into Camila's Marc Jacobs dress for the second time that day, and, without anesthesia, surrender myself to hair and makeup as administered by a surgeon's hand, and listen as she speaks.

About a *jinetera* who, in her teens and early twenties, entertained foreign dignitaries at the behest of her government. And who, as a reward for her success and beauty and brilliance, and upon finishing medical school, was granted the prestigious position as head of the renowned heart institute. And with it, continued access to foreign men.

Camila talks about a *jinetera* who receives regular remittances from sometimes handsome—but always wealthy—suitors abroad. About the countless marriage proposals she's turned down to stay in her country, with her family. To continue *la lucha*. The struggle.

Camila graduated top of her class. She speaks five languages. Dignitaries from Mexico and South America and the Middle East subject their hearts to her expertise—in medical matters and those of love.

The *jinetera* tells me about her counterparts in ancient Greece, the hetairai, who were talented in the sexual and conversational arts. The hetairai studied dance and theater and gallivanted with powerful men while their wives toiled in domesticity, bearing children and keeping house.

The hetairai, Camila says, were not confused with simple prostitutes, and never placed a day rate on their affections. Her ancient counterparts accepted gifts of jewelry and property from lovers and companions. The hetairai were prosperous and esteemed and wore beautiful things. Bracelets and anklets, necklaces and thigh bands. Transparent, clingy gowns.

I play with the fringe on Camila's sheer dress.

The modern-day courtesans in Cuba, and most particularly in Havana, speak foreign tongues and hold respected degrees. In a society that praises a woman's sexual talents and beauty, and makes no judgment on the trading of those for money, the Cuban courtesan—the *jinetera*—lures the most discriminating men in the world.

With precise fingers, Camila drapes gold chains around my neck and ankle and belly.

"Prostitutes accept pay for one night," she says with a dismissive wave. "*Jineteras* use their education and skills to weave fantasies of love." Our eyes meet in the reflection of the mirror. "Never forget that distinction."

I would never forget that distinction.

Camila unwinds my sun-streaked hair and flutters her nimble fingers through my beer-can curls. She tells me of the etymology of the Cuban *jinetera*. That in Arabia, the *jinete* was a cavalry of pint-sized horsemen with bows and marksmen's pulls. And that Cuba's modern-day *jinete* is a brigade of provocatively suited lancers with the aim of Eros.

She stands me in front of her mirror, and I barely recognize my eyes in thick liner or my body in heavy gold. Approving of her own work, Camila kisses my cheeks, and tells me the night is mine, and sends me off into it.

19

Mario has exchanged his wife-beater for a prodigious safari shirt and white socks tucked into sandals. I tell him he's gone overboard in the costume department, but he just grins and spit-wipes the lens on his touristy camera. I adjust, for the hundredth time, my décolletage.

"*Coño,* you look fine, now just move," says Mario, swatting my rear. "Don't fuck it up this time."

The two of us separate into the flow of Las Vegas, a former cabaret near long-shuttered American mafia casinos, and now a sleazy after-hours joint. The walls in Las Vegas are plastered with maroon drapes, suggesting a faux glamour of the club's namesake. An elderly gent in a shabby tuxedo oversees the lone pool table, its green felt patched with duct tape.

Girls of the night parade past, frenetically touching their nostrils and smoothing their skirts. Las Vegas at four A.M. is the discount aisle in a supermarket that slashes prices on perishable goods. And shopping for deals are men from Italy, Canada, Argentina, and Spain.

Mario signals for me to follow him around the corner and into the disco. A trio of sexy *mulata* singers work the mikes in tight, tattered sequins and wigs.

Daytime Cuba may live in the province of the 1950s, but nighttime Havana belongs squarely in the 1970s. Men in wide lapels and women in halter dresses and corkscrew heels practice not the four-four lockstep of disco, but the three-two clave of salsa. Musky cocaine flake—an uncut delicacy, as in Cuba fillers are more expensive than the drug—fuels the vibe, one bereft of worldliness and full of an innocence only an island experiment can preserve.

Loose confederations of young Cuban hustlers—ranging in shades from *blanco* to *negro,* faces and bodies culled from the best of human genetics—mark their territorial corners, backs to the wall, eyeing one another for the external signs of *jineterismo* success.

Rafael the lifeguard *chulo* holds court in a favored corner and is flanked by leggy brunettes. He's tall and broad, with a square jaw and a tousle of clove-colored hair and eyes. His smooth, *dulce de leche* skin stretches over naturally carved, abundant muscles. Sitting next to him, I notice, is Modesta, the scary, dark-haired woman from Nick's patio. Her wrist hangs off his shoulder. I turn around and walk out.

"I can't do this," I say to Mario as he follows me back to the bar. "That guy is so *guapo*"—hot—"I can't do this." My hands are flapping by my face. "Plus he's sitting with like freakin' supermodels."

Mario grabs my arm. "*Cōno,* Alysia, you're just as pretty. Now get your *bollo* out on the dance floor and make eye contact."

"I can't dance."

"You can't dance?"

"Right."

"*Pero, coño,* you're Cuban!"

"Half, technically," I offer weakly.

He grabs my waist with both hands. "You're Cuban from this part down, as of *right now.*"

Knowing I'm about to make a buffoon of myself, I take a deep breath and attempt to visualize my reward—a sacred address on a piece of paper, the house where my family once lived. But I can't get Rafael's face out of my line of vision. I think about my mother, and the way she described first meeting José Antonio, the way her bones turned to water. My knees, too, are liquefying as I cross the darkened dance floor. But I avert the humiliation of dance because I bash directly into a waiter. The two of us come crashing down.

"Marc Jacobs dress! Marc Jacobs dress!" I shout as I roll away from a tray of collapsing Cuba libres. Several hands reach down to help me, and I choose the nearest one. I'm yanked to my feet and find myself staring into his face.

El chulo.

He's breathtaking. I can't help but stare at his full lips and take in the subtle scent of mint and aftershave. Rafael's massive hands nearly cover my whole back, and he pulls me away from the puddle of liquid forming at our feet, and into a corner of the dance floor. His grip is firm.

"Think you can pull off *una estafa*?" A scam. "Trying to rob me of my income?" He is seething.

I'm baffled. "How'd you know?"

"Camila. She's watching my back," he says.

"Camila?"

"She knows Las Vegas is mine on Tuesdays." Confused, I stare while he continues. "She told me to help you get your photo, that it's important. Something about your father."

"What about your *yuma*?" I whisper.

"*Puta* doesn't deserve me. Besides, she was *mala hoja*." Bad in bed.

I look away as the realization hits me: "Camila doesn't think I'm sexy enough to seduce you!"

"You're a bit clumsy," he says with a shrug. "Besides, when I'm off duty, I prefer *cubanas*." I look over at his table and see the hatred in Modesta's glare.

I turn back to Rafael. "I *am* Cuban," I say indignantly.

"Right."

"Am so," I protest. "Half."

"Not the half I like."

My face burns. "Like you're a great catch. How much does your *yuma* pay?"

He rolls his eyes. "*Ay*, now who's the *puta*?"

Neither of us says anything for a long while. The dance floor around us is thick with fancy footwork. I fold my arms.

"*Mira* . . ." he says, fumbling.

"I'm not used to . . ." My voice trails off. "Everyone I meet thinks this is no big deal, but I'm having a hard time . . ."

"You think too much."

Mario's flash goes off nearby. "Forget this," I say, turning away.

But Rafael pulls me back toward him. "*Vamos.* Let's get your photo. I promised Camila."

Our bodies move closer and he gently traces my lips with his fingers. His face softens, and it's so lovely I can barely stand.

"You're sure you don't mind?" I whisper. "About the photo?"

"If you're going to be a Cuban," he says, whispering in my ear now, "you have to know we think nothing's more important than *la familia*."

Rafael's hands lock in mine, and I close my eyes, accepting his mouth, his warm kiss, a perfect kiss, one generous and demure in equal measure. I'm wondering how something so magnetic could be an act, an improvisation for the camera that will flash any moment, and as I fall into the frisson, my own bulb goes off, a new illumination, and I back away, pushing against Rafael's tremendous chest, and turning on my heel.

My sympathies, I realize, are no longer confused.

My father is Cuban and my mother loved him, and here—in this treacherous place, this innocent place, this Babylon—I stand proudly on *mi patria*, with my Cuba.

With my Cubans.

Ignoring Mario's bewildered expression, and knowing I've lost, for now, the chance to find the Havana home where my mother lived long ago, I walk out with my head held high. Finally fitting into the spirit of this dress, I leave Las Vegas.

20

My landlady is asleep on the couch, wearing polyester underwear in functional beige. A Cuban *novella* blares on the radio. A woman is sobbing because her husband won't stop *singando* her best friend.

But my landlady doesn't stir. She's a biomedical engineer so depressed by the lack of employment that she's sleeping her mid-thirties away. I tiptoe past into the high-ceilinged, Spanish-tiled rooms I rent illicitly. The web of neighborhood-watch types she has to bribe to keep quiet is too complex for me to unearth.

I bathe away the sex on my legs and stomach. I convince myself that my accidental *jineterismo* earlier this afternoon, in the Habana Libre hotel, with the handsome American who approached me in the café, was an isolated mishap. A sordid miscommunication I can wash away under the flaccid shower. I've only been in Cuba two months, though it feels like dozens, and I've a niggling feeling I'm becoming someone I don't know. In my confusion, I try to think of a pleasant face, and it is Rafael's that springs to mind, despite the fact that I haven't seen him in the week since we met.

But it's the *norteamericano* hovering over my naked body who remains in my head. I dress, and stuff his bills back in my bra.

Camila's wrong, I vow, massaging my temples. This won't happen again.

In the living room, I read my messages and dial. "Victor?" I ask into the receiver.

"*Oye*. I'll swing by tonight."

I rush to the Internet café, needing a lifeline to reality. I answer Susie's e-mails. Because I tell her nothing about my money being stolen, or about my first sexual experience in Cuba, I feel like I'm lying to my best friend. Instead, I fill my briefing with the hopes that today may yield the address of the home where my family lived in Havana.

Later, at our appointed time, I wait by the side door for my Cuban spy. As a government worker, Victor has access to classified records. He looks at me carefully.

"You look different tonight," he says. "Anything wrong?"

I shake my head, and we crouch on the creaky wooden staircase. Victor pulls out his notes and modulates his vocal cords down to a whisper.

"Your family lived here in Havana under President Carter, and your father—"

"Stepfather," I interrupt.

"Your stepfather was employed at the U.S. Interests Section." Victor adjusts his glasses. I stare at a slick chunk of hair that has slid rebelliously over his forehead. Victor's hesitation tells me he doesn't want to say what he's found.

"Your father—"

"Stepfather—"

"Right. He was born in Connecticut, worked in the diplomatic corps. Your mother, she was also American."

"From Mississippi," I say impatiently.

"Like all Americans, they were under routine surveillance while living here. The notes I found indicate your mother had repeat encounters with one Cuban male in particular. They appear to have been romantic."

I nod impatiently.

"I have dates, and a description of the man you believe to be your father. It's all in there. Including the address of your family's home here in Havana." Victor hands me the papers. I take them gleefully.

"Did they follow him?" I ask. "Was there an address, a place where they were secretive?" I was hoping for José Antonio's home address.

Victor swats away the errant hair. "I can find out," he says. I interrupt him with an enthusiastic nod. "That, of course, will take some time."

It always takes time. It took two trips to Cuba to find Victor, to find someone with both access and willingness to disclose information. In the eight weeks since I've moved to Cuba, he is the only person I believe to have legitimate connections. Using the same bills from the afternoon encounter, I pay Victor his bribe and kiss his cheek. It's the first concrete confirmation of my mother's account, and I'm both encouraged and daunted by the news.

Encouraged because I believe in my heart that I may find José Antonio. But daunted as it becomes clear what I must do to fuel the search, and to afford to scrape by for the next ten months. That what I thought was a mistake—this afternoon's fling with a tourist in his hotel, my first ever with a stranger—was now obviously the only way I could make $200 appear in the tuck of my bra.

At ten P.M., Camila rings the doorbell as I'm touching up the dark on my lashes. We're bound for Macumba, a trendy club packed with the richest tourist men. I look at myself in the mirror, a strange confidence reflecting back at me. I've made up my mind. With my money stolen and with no legitimate way to make a living, I've reluctantly joined the ranks of the Cuban demimonde. Educated. Professional. Hopeful. And part-time hookers.

I'm American, but I'm also Cuban. And to live on my island home, the place I was born, the land where my family surely resides, I've little choice.

So I jockey. I ride the beast. I control the beast.

The beast is the tourist man.

Three

21

My mother ventured as far as her family permitted, to Nashville, Tennessee, where she studied history and Spanish at Vanderbilt. On the 1959 campus, women still garnered curious stares.

John's gaze lingered the longest. She remembered him a dashing senior from Georgetown breezing through the Southern states with his debate team. He was tall and elegant and pursued her with a relentlessness she couldn't defy.

John spoke of a purposeful career in foreign service, and in following in his father's political footsteps. He promised her a life of travel, of stimulating discussion and intrigue, of nights spent staying up late and pondering the wonder of whatever culture they were experiencing. John promised they would be happy. That they'd have a large family and raise their children to be aware of the wider world.

My mother believed he was the answer to her prayers.

John believed my mother's insouciance, enfolded in a genteel graciousness, was her real beauty—more so than the gleam of her cactus-green eyes and piles of long, blonde curls.

My mother promised to be faithful.

John promised to never leave her.

They married in 1962, just before the Cuban missile crisis played out on the world stage; when youngsters dove under desktops in nuclear drills, and the planet anxiously watched defiant Soviet tankers carry warheads to Cuban shores.

My mother didn't sleep during those fretful days, thinking of the Cuban friends she'd made in Natchez. She pictured their proud faces and wondered how a people so intrinsically linked to hers could be engaged in the scariest conflict the world had ever seen.

When John told her about his disdain for Cuba, and his desire to exact change in the Communist land, my mother kept quiet, knowing he could never understand. She thought of the poet José Martí, and the Cubans' innate desire for self-determination.

John swore to one day serve in the diplomatic corps in Havana, so he could execute his ideals. My mother remembered touching his hand and telling him Havana was her dream as well.

Fifteen years and five continents later—their marital promises all but broken—a plane carrying the first U.S. diplomatic corps in Havana in nearly twenty years touched down at José Martí International.

A perfumed gust flooded the tarmac. My mother never felt anything more liberating on her skin, and knew those winds hinted at much more than the scent of mariposa.

22

At the dollar shoe-store in the Habana Libre I'm standing like a stork in front of the foot mirror, wobbling on a new pair of four-inch heels and looking every bit the Cuban equestrian.

My young companion, Dayanara, is pacing.

"Calm down," I scold as I pull out my new dress and smooth it over my frame, shoes and heels a perfect match. Skin spills out of every stitch, but I still cover more than your average *cubana* behind a mop and broom.

"*Mira!* We have to hurry," whines Dayanara. "I have to practice."

I motion for the cashier to box the shoes. She glares at us. For we're Cuban girls and we have dollars to spend, and unless we have family in Miami, that likely means one thing: we're engaged in the oldest profession.

Dayanara—Daya—is a *guajira*, a country girl who moved to big-city Havana to strike gold. It's barely noon, yet she wears a minidress and leopard-skin heels that lace up midthigh. Coppery glitter shimmers on each centimeter of her skin.

I'd met her over dinner with her fifty-seven-year-old British boyfriend, Richard, who offered to pay me to translate their conversations of love. I'll never forget first laying eyes on her, and how I realized my breezy gig would entail much more than translating. I would also be enabling Humbert's *latina* fantasy. I slugged three rums neat before I had the courage to ask the age of his Lolita—fifteen—and by the fourth rum, and upon her beaming mother's arrival, I realized I was the only one who had taken any pause.

In the two months I've now known Richard, and on her mother's insistence, I've begrudgingly agreed to oversee the transformation of his girlfriend from intractable *guajira* into urbane moll.

Today, I hurry Daya past my landlady, who's gossiping with the neighbors, and I ignore her furious gaze. I'd promised to keep a low profile. This teen is anything but.

Daya lifts the flap off the DHL box that has arrived at my house, a gift from Richard. For the third time that day, out comes the box of Tampax. She pulls one from the delicate wrapping and follows me around the house, holding it like a tube of arsenic. Richard has sent them in advance, along with clothes, makeup, and strict instructions that I'm to oversee their tasteful assembly.

"Teach me, please," she says, stomping her feet. I can tell she's scared—tampons are virtually unheard of in Cuba, and aren't sold anywhere but at tourist hotels. "My period arrived today and"—she gestures at the box—"*he* arrives tomorrow."

I sigh. Once she uses the tampons, the messy alternatives Cuban women employ will seem intolerable. But, because they're about $2 a tube, regular Tampax usage is a luxury, the way Harry Winston baubles are back home.

Daya falls listlessly onto my bed and watches every move as I adjust my dress in the mirror.

"Do your schoolwork," I say, plopping down her books. "I'll return in two hours."

My landlady is back in her underwear, sipping *aguardiente*—firewater—and fanning herself in the heat. She acknowledges my wave with a blank stare.

More than anything, I want to find my father, to meet the Cuban family I've never known. Each day I get closer still, and Camila tells me to be patient, that in Cuba, time means little and information is slow to turn up. Knowing I'm in for the long haul, I take a deep breath and head over to the hotel.

I try to ignore Walrus, who is leaning against his Lada, smoking a *puro.*

Wobbling on high heels, I trip in the street and skin my knee. Walrus smirks.

A graceful jockey I am not.

·   ·   ·

DOUGHY AND SOFT, Terence is an amateur sculptor of hard bodies. He's in love with Communism, and is convinced Cuba is a place where it's practiced. Normally, I'd debate the merits of Marx, and the misapplication of his theories in my homeland, but my job is to be sweet and pretty.

I'm standing in Terence's hotel room naked. A Polaroid hangs from his neck, and a tape measure slides between his thumbs. He jots down the circumference of my thighs, the width of my hips, and, as I roll my eyes, the minutiae of my genitalia. He promises to send a photo of the life-size work he's basing on my body.

It will be without a head.

Terence is my first official boyfriend, and the only foreigner I've been able to procure since the incident at the Havana Libre with the American a month before. Terence and I have been "dating" for a week. The Canadian barely lets me out of his sight.

"That man needs a sheet of Bounce," I tell Camila, but the island's lack of laundry luxuries makes the joke fall flat.

A plane will take Terence home in a few hours, and Camila instructs me to get some good-bye cash. Thus far, I've been given $480 for reasons of my own invention—"cab fare," "medicine," and an "ill grandmother."

I'm one of the lucky ones: I'm a *rubia*, a blonde. As a Cuban girl's skin darkens, her worth on the foreign-man market decreases. But I insist on condoms—most Cuban girls don't care—so my price plummets.

In actual time with Terence, I've earned about $2.85 an hour. Or, conversely, if you add up my sexual tricks (seven blow jobs; eleven tries at intercourse; two hand jobs; and public sex in the Jacuzzi on the rooftop of the Parque Central), it comes to about $22.85 per act.

A biochemist makes $13 per month.

Roach poison is $6 a bottle.

Band-Aids are not sold.

Blood drips from my skinned knee. Terence lies on his back. I'm on top. We're fucking. His flesh feels like wet bread; our body fluids form a sticky paste. Though the room is eerily silent, I move as though dancing to salsa, in slow, rhythmic circles. One-two-three, pause. One-two-three. It could take me ages to perfect the hip movements of the Cuban dance. The feet are easy.

I look between his legs. I've straddled him, and like a good jockey am riding the beast, clenching myself, just as Camila taught me. ("It's like when you hold pee," she instructed. "Same muscle. Do ten reps fast, then ten reps slow. Twice a day.")

Terence clutches my waist. He's small and prone to premature shriveling. I make him comfortable. Tell him he's a real man, my kind of man, baby, and when he's inside it fills me up like a tank. His eyes shine and he wants to believe, needs to believe, and so he believes. I move faster. He gropes now for my breasts. Gets a fistful, then slaps them, from the side, like the racket on a ball, slow at first, then frantic, screaming that he's about to come, and he slaps harder and my tits sting red and I'm clenching and he's pushing his hips up, inside me, faster and faster still, a frenzy of slaps and jerks, his head thrashing, and then his head burrows under a pillow, and when he comes, it's weeping and gnashing, a holy noise, an expulsion of guilt and shame and pleasure.

I roll off, holding the condom firmly to his stub so that it doesn't slip inside me. I lay next to him, unfulfilled, panting slightly under the ceiling fan that chugs above, grinding through rusty gears.

Terence keeps the pillow tightly over his face and turns on his side, in a fetal position. He cries and shakes off efforts at consolation. I shrug. I'm not a shrink. I wait, listening to his sobs, until my own thoughts drown the noise.

But I'm tortured. I refuse the force that wants to reason with me, with what I'm doing. I don't want to stop. I want to find my real family, the family that is here, somewhere in Cuba, and considering the love and affection Cubans shower on their children, I won't risk not finding them, having them die off without ever knowing me, without us knowing each other.

So I stay, and so I am Cuban and, like my sisters, live a life of struggle, *la lucha*, a life that would surely have been mine had I not been given lucky passage across the Straits of Florida many years ago.

I lock myself in the bathroom and pull a surefire fantasy from the mental file. I exhale my pleasure quietly, savoring it internally. Quickly, I shower and dress.

The hotel room is empty, Terence has fled.

The note on the bed sits like frosting on a cake of dollar bills.

On it is scrawled one word: *bitch*.

23

Jiggle. Jiggle. Metal pay phones scorch fingertips under a torrid sun. The stench of rotting fruit permeates the humid air, mixing with petrol leaked from forty-year-old carburetors.

"Camila?" I say into the receiver.

"*Chica.* What happened to Bounce?" she says in a chirpy tone. I swear Camila is enjoying herself at my expense. She's amused I've got an American passport and may, in less than a year's time, return to my homeland.

"He's got issues," I say with a sigh, explaining my recent encounter.

"Hmmm." She listens. "Insecurities, Oedipus complex, probably molested by his mom. Explains the breast smacking," she says perfunctorily. "I once had a man who couldn't orgasm unless he had a nipple in his mouth. All about the matriarch."

I roll my eyes. The Cubans love Freudian analysis. I'm more fond of Jung, myself, but the populace here thinks he's *déclassé,* so I change the subject whenever Herr Sigmund comes up. I've had enough penis as it is.

"Guess who came over last night."

"*Dígame.*"

"Señor Rafael Oro-Sabell." My heart stops. "He asked after you. *Ay chica,* did he think it was *extraño*"—weird—"how you left Las Vegas so fast?"

"What'd you tell him I said?" I practically shout.

"That his tongue felt like an iguana's."

"*Didn't!*"

Camila laughs. "You're right. I gave him your number."

"I'm going to kill you," I say with a huge smile.

"Richard comes when, tomorrow?" she asks. "He may be your best client yet. I'm superjealous, *mi vida*."

"God, if I *did* have a sexual relationship with him it would be so much easier."

"What, baby-sitting his teenage object of affection isn't glamorous enough for you?"

"I'd take a Canadian with mommy issues any day."

Camila ekes out her generous laughter as I watch toddlers in the park play with condoms blown up and tied at the opening. The only prophylactics to be had on the peso economy are imported from trading partners such as China and Vietnam. But a condom manufactured for the Asian set is sewn a little tight for the typically robust and unclipped *cubano*. The only thing the condoms are good for here are as a substitute for the children's balloons, which cannot be found in any store.

I feel a tap on my shoulder. "Gotta go," I say into the phone as Limón flashes white teeth and criss-crosses his dark hands. We air-kiss. Limón is in his early twenties and his yo-yo-yo, arm-swingin', dreads-floppin' braggadocio belies his cool, calculating self.

Despite the tightly controlled media in Cuba, Limón and his friends have picked up the Rasta look surprisingly well, and use it as a subtle signal of anti-governmental rebellion, as well as to hustle young European girls. Girls with a clichéd idea of tropical romance.

"*¿Qué bola?* It's hotter than a bank robber's pistol," Limón says, wiping the sweat that drips down his temples.

Limón and I have a little deal: he helps me with my search for my Cuban father, and I teach him American slang. Problem is, I don't know much current slang, so I've pulled out expressions I remember my Mississippi grandfather using. Limón won't know the difference, I figure.

Limón pulls me aside, into the shade of a colonial building in Old Havana. His mother says she named him Limón, the Cuban word for lime, because that's the type of citrus tree under which he was conceived.

Speaking of mothers.

Limón whispers to me in English, as he's determined to master my native tongue. "*Mira*, your momma lived in Miramar."

I raise my eyebrows. Limón hasn't delivered much, but what he has told me proves he's correctly informed.

"Limón, that ink ain't fresh. All American diplomats live in Miramar."

"*Mira,* I'll bet you don't know the exact street in Miramar." He precociously waves a scrap of paper near his face. I snatch it. On it is written an address, the same one Victor procured.

"Impressive. But I already have it," I said. "I just can't go there."

Limón taps two fingers on his collarbone, and I nod. Walrus. Although I can merely speculate as to why the G-2 man follows me, my instincts say it's best to derail him from the track of my investigation.

"I'll go over there as soon as I can," promises Limón. "Ask around, see if anyone remembers who worked in the house." I hug him in sheer happiness.

Then Limón's expression goes dark. "Word is you've been out nightclubbing. That ain't true, is it?" He gingerly knuckles my collarbone. "Nice *yanqui* girl like you . . ." He takes note as I study my nails. Then he whispers, "Careful. There's a crackdown coming."

"Crackdown?"

"Crackdown. Us on the street, guys with tourist girls, girls with their *yumas.* It started last week in Santiago, they've been arresting. Keep an eye out. You don't want to be eating rice and beans for three years."

I shake the cloud of dark news, furious that there's only one real way to make money in Cuba, and now they're putting people in jail for it. I step over piles of dog crap, as quickly as my flamboyant heels allow, and march home.

For there I've got a sexually active fifteen-year-old country girl with a world-class boyfriend, and I must teach her how to insert a tampon so that she may please him, and her family may eat.

24

I'm an expensive toy. An A-list plaything. A Ferrari 360 Modena Spider F1 with heel-toe downshift and four hundred horses. My engines are revved.

I'm sitting on the lap of an Armani-clad Italian TV executive from Rome with a wallet full of family pictures. I stick out my lower lip and pout until he agrees to call up a dressmaker. I playfully tap his nose and quickly calculate the outfit's worth on the black market. With it, I can make November's rent.

Camila's words are on repeat loop in my ear. *You're a luxurious trinket, a petulant muse, a status symbol to the man attached to the trappings of his class.*

"Be interesting and intelligent and very, very demanding," she lectured.

"Intelligent," I said. "Men hate that."

Camila flashed a knowing smile. "Wrong. What real men want," she elucidated in a whisper, as if her words contained the location of the next Rosetta stone, "are clever, witty, and charming women." She paused. "Who absolutely need to be rescued. Hero fantasy. Trust me."

I figure Camila's the expert, and so when I ask Aldo for a match in the lobby of the Hotel Melia Cohiba, one match leads to another leads to a Cuba libre and now, a week later, I'm his spoiled princess. Helpless. In need of rescue. A Rapunzel locked in a tropical tower.

I tickle Aldo's chin and lure him out of his chair, and we tumble into the king-sized bed in the middle of the hotel's finest suite. All *jineteras* know the Melia Cohiba is the prime place for a romp, as the island's few upscale shops are in the downstairs lobby and across the street.

Maintain an intrinsic connection between the bedroom and the bureau.
Thus far I've collected four pairs of Brazilian high heels—cheapo and
overpriced, but the very best of the island's offerings—three necklaces, a
purse, panties and bras, and a pair of white hot pants so tight they aren't
so much worn as applied, and never after breakfast.

A $100 handbag will fetch $30 in the street; a gold chain twice that. I'm
raking it in.

The Italian is under the sheets, his Cohiba filling the room with pricey
pollution. He's watching the fastidious tailor sketch a gauzy dress that will
expose more flesh than a bikini. I feign delight. Aldo suggests lace.

Then we are alone. Aldo drops his wallet on the night table, reclines,
and pulls me to him, to finish business. *Show no inhibition in any matter.*
I start at his neck and, with an awkward stride, work my way across
the terrain of his chest and over the softly covered hipbones and down
further still, until he groans in pleasure. I'm remembering Camila's instructions, that wild enthusiasm makes up for flaws in technique. Out of
my surprised mouth come "hmmms" and "oooohs," but despite my accel-
eration the only thing on fire in this room is the stub of his Cohiba.

Ferrari engine stalled. Sixty to zero in 4.2 seconds.

Aldo—frustrated and more than a little embarrassed—gestures for me
to leave. As I quickly dress, I see his wallet splayed on the nightstand next
to him, the faces of his wife and children peering out accusingly.

25

That the concierge believes me to be Cuban and not a foreigner would normally thrill, but I need to use the phone, and so I whip out my U.S. passport, useless though it has become in the four months I've lived here. From the lobby phone, I tell Camila about my pathetic performance.

"Can't get it up?" Camila says. "*Muchacha,* either you're worse in bed than I thought or he has major family guilt. Thing about Cuba is that it's the safest place in the world for a married man to have an affair. They control the entire situation. We girls can't afford to contact them, much less fly out for a surprise visit to the wife."

"No boiling bunnies," I quip, but the island's pop-culture barrier makes much of what I say fly over a Cuban's head.

"I don't know what's wrong with you foreign girls," says Camila. "I'm surprised any of you ever manage to procreate, much less marry. What kind of *mierda* do they teach you about men?"

"You wouldn't believe," I say.

"How many have you slept with?"

"Four. No, five."

"And before you came to Cuba?"

"That's including. Before and after."

Camila can't believe her ears. "Impossible! And this is normal? For a *norteamericana* your age?"

"I guess, I don't know."

But she's not listening. "*Que represión!* No wonder you're all so insecure. *Cubanas* are good at sex because they *like* sex. The power is in the enjoyment of it, not in the withholding or distribution of it."

The clerk motions for me to return the phone. "What should I do? I'm terminally *mierda*."

"Come over Monday, I've got an idea for some lessons."

I'm not sure what she means, but as I'm oh-for-three with the foreign men; I figure I need all the help I can get.

Who doesn't need any help is Modesta.

With supply greater than demand, it's typical for a crush of lovely *jineteras* to jockey for a lone, scruffy tourist. But Modesta traverses the lobby with a *yuma* on each arm, uncommitted, as if she hasn't yet decided which one will be lucky enough to pay for the night's affections.

When her gaze finds me, she hesitates, and then I'm placed in her recall. Irritated, she maneuvers her entourage in my direction, but I quickly exit the lobby, knowing I couldn't stand another humiliation in this hotel.

As I pass the jammed Habana Café outside the hotel, a *jinetera* working the line of single guys discreetly tells me my face is smeared in lipstick. A *gracias* is barely out of my mouth when I turn and practically smack into Rafael. He's more gorgeous than I remember, and a quick scan of the crowd tells me he garners appreciative glances from both men and women. The one holding his hand—a Canadian *yuma* in her midfifties with a frizzy perm—fumbles for a tissue in her purse, and dabs away my lipstick.

"Good night?" asks Rafael with a smirk.

As if it could get any worse.

The Canadian, who speaks little Spanish, asks who I am. Rafael introduces me. "Alysia. *Mi prima*." My cousin. I roll my eyes. Cousin is a euphemism for sweetheart, the lie every Cuban tells a foreign lover when their real paramour is present.

"No way I'm your cousin," I say in Spanish. "I'd rather die."

"You *could* be my cousin," says Rafael, enjoying himself. "But you'd have to return my calls first."

"I don't get it," says the Canadian. "Are you his cousin or not?" Rafael's eyes are locked with mine. "Sweetheart?" she implores.

"Ask her," Rafael says.

The Canadian woman turns to me, and in an English only we understand, beseeches some advice. "I'm not sure I believe anything that comes out of his mouth. How do you *know* if Latin men are lying?" she asks.

"If a Cuban male says anything more than once, it's a lie."

The Canadian looks up accusingly at Rafael.

"What?" he says defensively. "She's my cousin."

THE BUSY STREET along the Malecón is replete with sponge-painted Ladas, horse-drawn buggies, Russian motorcycles with sidecars, converted Chinese bikes rigged with chainsaw motors, and 1950s American classics with more natural curves than even a *cubana*. From among these choices, I scout for a peso taxi heading south.

Behind me, I hear Rafael's voice. "*Mira,* this one here is just business. When her plane takes off, I'm coming to see you."

I hold my breath and keep walking.

But nothing.

He only says it once.

26

"Dahling, I want her pussy shaved."

Richard is calling from England. He's to arrive in the evening, and I'm charged with having his va-va-voom teenage Caribbean princess toned down. No glitter. No *Flashdance*-inspired slashes in her jeans. He's sent in bags from Harrods: strappy heels, Yves Saint Laurent lipstick, and a tailored gown of red sequins.

Daya lives in a dirt-floored shack with fourteen cousins, uncles, and aunts.

"They do have such places, for waxing one's privates?" Richard asks. "Certainly, considering the hirsute nature of the Latin female." Richard roars with laughter.

Hair sprouts from every pore, but a *cubana*'s idea of shaving is stopping the blade midthigh. Many, when naked, look as if they're wearing biking shorts. Havana follicular fashion dictates *el cerquillo*, a bushy thicket that falls a few inches below the hem of a miniskirt. It's an unfathomable trend, and I resist the compulsion to offer its followers a blade and foam.

"We'll have it taken care of," I say to Richard, eager to hang up. "See you tonight."

I spend the morning at a lawless beauty parlor, my teen charge howling through the pain. When Daya's family invites me to lunch, and places me at the table's head as guest of honor, I'm nervous. What will they think of me, playing Mary Poppins to their thumb-sucking teen in Christian Louboutin pumps and a fresh bikini wax?

But my fears are allayed. Daya's grandmother weeps when she meets me, grateful for my tutelage. The dollars Richard wires Daya mean the family has won the *boleto,* and her neighbors don't hide their fascination with the round of televisions and stereos and dead pigs delivered to the crammed hovel.

Daya's mother—whom Richard refers to as *la tiñosa,* the vulture— takes me aside after lunch and presses a *carmelo,* a hard candy, into my palm.

"For Oshún," she says, indicating I'm to make a donation to the saint of love and seduction. "We pray today Richard will continue *resolviendo* our problems."

"Richard asked that Daya be waxed," I say, fumbling for a delicate way to tell her that his fantasies may be more pre than pubescent. Instead, she smiles and waves away any darkness from the warning.

"We're all so proud of Daya," she says, ignoring my comment. "Imagine! A real *millonario!*"

"Daya says she'd like to study architecture," I counter, "and that her dance teachers think she's talented. But being with Richard is distracting her from—"

"Daya's future is not in Cuba," she interrupts, speaking a bit too loudly. "An architect is hungry as a janitor."

Daya and her family are *palestinos,* the slang term for émigrés from primarily eastern provinces to Havana, the only city with *fula*—dollar— opportunity. Those wishing to move to Havana must first request a permit. But long waits and the usual rejection force those seeking a life of dollars to settle in illegally. For Daya's family, the potential for their daughter to snag someone like Richard is the very reason for their sacrifice.

"But the system could change one day," I say, knowing I'm overstepping bounds. "And then she will need a marketable talent, especially when the *culo*"—I grab my rear—"goes *suave.*"

Daya's mother shoots me a sad, pitying look—one seen often—and says I couldn't understand.

Each trip to Cuba, Richard takes several rolls of photos of vultures circling overhead, or feasting on felled rodents. In comic punctuation, and just before he leaves for London, Richard hands Daya's mother the pictures, along with a *gracias* and a large wad of cash.

Daya's mother is 4'10" in shoes, and so from my relative height I look down at her and sigh. Richard is wrong. What oozes from her depths is not manipulation or greed but pride. Pride that her daughter is succeeding in the most profitable career available.

LIKE THE ISLAND'S other residents, I find myself lost in the long stretches between eventful moments. Having empty hours to fill is not a phenomenon to which I'm accustomed, and the slow pace of things teaches me to live fully in the moment. In Cuba, a three-hour line for rice is *not* a three-hour line but a chance to gossip with neighbors and tell stories dreamed in the night.

With a glut of time, and anxiety over my future, the punishing sun does little to soothe me. What I quickly discover is the salving effect of movies. In Havana, nearly sixty theaters, many with 1950s facades and neon, run classic films from the U.S. and Latin America. Each film is carefully screened by the censors, and only titles with suitable politics are shown. But some of the best make the cut, and for just two pesos—about eight cents—a ticket may be purchased and an afternoon may be spent in the coolness of an old-fashioned movie house.

This is how I spend my days, how I spend my waiting.

Today, I'm at Cine Yara, at the busy La Rampa intersection. The long, sloping theater is empty of popcorn but full of cigar smoke. Cubans creep into the theaters in the middle of a showing and spend most of the movie chattering excitedly to one another.

But today, the show is *Bread and Roses,* a Ken Loach film about Mexican janitors in the U.S. attempting to unionize. In one scene, a woman breaks down crying, having admitted that she prostituted herself in order to help her family settle in to their new country. I realize something odd is happening in the audience: I turn around and see nearly every *cubana* wiping her eyes. A few minutes later, as if on instinct, I turn around again and in a seat a few rows behind me I see Rafael.

He's sitting alone, and he winks at me, and I want to think I see a tear in his eyes as well.

I turn around again a few moments later, but he's gone.

·   ·   ·

HALFWAY UP THE escalator at Terminal 2 of José Martí International, I realize I'm talking up a storm—to myself. Whirling around, I see Daya at the bottom of the escalator. I motion for her to hurry along, but like a mule before a stream, she refuses another step.

Daya, the hayseed in her Harrods red sequined dress, is sobbing. My tasteful makeup job has melted into a charcoal stream down her cheeks.

"What is *this*?" I demand.

She points to the moving staircase. "What is *that*?"

I sigh, and my patience returns. The nation's only escalators are inside the airport, and few Cubans have experienced the automated staircase. Daya is trying to be game, but she's too young and too unsophisticated for her assignment as Richard's love interest, even if it means her family can have a nice round of pork for many dinners to come. I clean her up and explain in detail the mechanisms of an escalator, and when we land on the second floor, I see a heap of tourists clearing customs and leaving for home, and it's all I can do to keep from bursting into tears.

27

*S*choolchildren in crisp white tops and mustard bottoms line up along the Malecón with flowers in their arms. When teachers give a signal, they flood the ocean with freshly cut oleander and bougainvillea.

It's Camilo Cienfuegos Day, and *habaneros* pay annual tribute to a popular revolutionary, a non-Communist, who died under suspicious circumstances in a Cessna that disappeared over the sea some forty years before.

Victor stands across the street, his arms loaded with fragrant flora. The hardliner revolutionary dumps them unceremoniously and signals for me to keep walking. I make my way slightly uphill, without looking back.

The sidewalk is covered with turtle shells, their bodies bleating for mercy in hot pans. Victor is twenty paces behind. We have to be discreet, and I'm praying he has information on my father. I step into an empty bodega.

A rusty scale sits on the counter, and a sign over the barren shelves reads: *Socialismo o muerte.* Socialism or death. With this bounty, the latter seems most likely.

"Are there any eggs?" I ask the shopkeeper.

"There won't be any eggs this week," answers Victor, sidling next to me. "The chickens aren't getting enough food, and so they're not producing."

The shopkeeper agrees with Victor and goes back to reading his newspaper.

"How much more food does the chicken need?" I ask. We are playing a *charada,* the kind of double-talk common in a land where what one says can land them in *agua caliente.*

Victor scratches his chin. "The chicken needs about a week's worth of food. Then there will be eggs."

The shopkeeper shoots us a strange glance.

"The chicken should know that it needs to produce," I say. "That people are counting on those eggs."

"The chicken knows, *compañera.*"

"Would the chicken be satisfied with a few scraps?"

"The chicken would prefer seed."

"*Coño,*" says the clerk, gesturing that he's trying to read. "Eggs next week."

"The chicken is worried," says Victor, "that the seed is *inventando* in the night, and the ill-begotten seed shall cause problems to the digestive tract of the chicken." I'm pretending not to be mortified that Victor knows of my new occupation, but my face turns crimson nonetheless.

"The chicken should not worry," I say, smiling at the confounded shopkeeper while discreetly slipping Victor a hundred bucks, "where the seed comes from."

"Perhaps," says Victor, fingering the bill. "But what incentive does the chicken have to produce on tainted seed? It could infect him. Make him ill."

Rolling my eyes, I hand him another hundred. "Those taking the seed in the night won't get caught."

"The chicken," says Victor, "is not so sure."

28

Toilet paper has disappeared from the markets. It's been weeks now. Those fortunate enough to stockpile the dollars-only luxury (made of recycled sugarcane and wood pulp, so it feels like sand) hoard theirs as if it's Lalique glass.

My landlord is blasé about the crisis and hands me a newspaper. It isn't for reading. This evening, I decide, I'm not going to be Cuban. I grab my passport from the closet and make for the nearest hotel bathroom.

I nearly trip over a figure at my doorstep. In the darkness, I'm confused, though hoping it's Limón with information on my childhood home.

But it's Richard who's waiting. He's frantic. Daya, he says, inexplicably dumped a Cuba libre over his naked body and took off without enough money for a taxi home. After my pit stop, a car drops us near Richard's rented apartment on the fringes of the old city. It's pitch-dark. On the west side of Parque Central, two sidewalk bars are alight, and Richard and I agree to scout separately and meet there in an hour.

On intuition, I wait until Richard disappears before heading directly to the bar, arguably the wildest joint in all of Havana. Musicians play bongos and maracas, keeping infectious time with the dazzle of their feet. Police fortify the saloon, awaiting bribes from the low-rent prostitutes and hustlers and *camajans* inside. I scan the room. It's filled with a farrago of creepy multinationals; the dregs of the world's sex tourists. The lumpen sort who could never get a decent date back home. Drunk and groping—with bored lingerie model–type *cubanas* at their sides, many of them barely in their teens—the men grab at female body parts as if they're souvenir-shop gimcrack.

"Gluttons," I mutter under my breath. The girls wear tight jeans and Lycra tops, their mouths lined in black and their faces blank. I wish I had enough money to pay every girl *not* to go home with the barbarians.

I think of the island's beloved orange-red flowers known as Cupid's tears. The bouquets bloom upright and are immediately swarmed by birds and insects who would steal their nectar. It's a short-lived frenzy: the flowers, once depleted, droop downward, and wither to the ground.

In the corner, my own Cupid's tear is sucking her thumb, sitting on the lap of a three-hundred-pounder. Daya leaps up and clutches me as if I'm her mother. I grab her by the arm and push our way through the crowd.

His voice is deep and honeyed, and I instantly recognize its owner as being out of place among the oddly shaped and intoxicated foreigners. Rafael is flanked by two German tourists, sunglasses masking their eyes and preteens gracing their arms.

Rafael thinks a moment before speaking. "I leave three, four messages for you, and nothing."

I put a hand on my hip.

Rafael continues. "What, the Cuban phone system is too difficult for you to figure out?"

"Yeah," I say, smirking. "All those buttons."

Rafael leans near my ear. "Maybe I'll come over and teach you how to push them."

My face starts to burn, and I wheedle Daya out of the bar.

"I know where you live," he threatens playfully, shouting over the top of the crowd. He doesn't see my smile.

As we leave, a policeman follows, hollering at Daya for his *mordida*. I throw a clutter of dead presidents in the ditch and it quells him.

I can barely pull myself together to scold her. I clear my throat and manage to look stern. "What the hell, Dayanara? You have a very nice and very rich boyfriend. One you are going to lose if you keep this up."

She pulls her thumb from her mouth long enough to tell me about their fight, that she needed money to get home and had been promised $20 for a few hours with the jiggle-bellied beast.

"Daya," I say. "Do you want to be with Richard?"

A shrug.

"It's your mother, isn't it . . . You don't have to do this, *tú sabes*?"

"Like you know," she says accusingly. "*Extranjera.*" Foreigner. I sigh. No matter how Cuban I've become, no matter how much I share the struggle with my kinfolk, I'm rarely granted the permission to sympathize.

"There may be a crackdown coming, Dayanara," I say sternly. "When it does, those cops won't just take a few bucks, they'll take you to jail. You hang out in a place like this and you are so busted. *Coño.*"

In Cuba, women with foreigners aren't arrested for prostitution. Instead, they're written up for other infractions—whatever fiction the police invent. When three delinquencies land in her police file, the girl is usually sent to prison. Hundreds of Cuban women are said to be in jail for having relations with foreigners, yet technically they're serving time for other crimes. Girls who work the sleazeball joints, the ones who behave like common prostitutes, are especially targeted by the police, who either demand a cut, a freebie, or both. I'm betting the petite ballerina is safer being with just one foreigner, with Richard. The government doesn't outright encourage these long-term liaisons, but certainly looks the other way at most of them, knowing repeat tourists, and those who wire money regularly, help boost a desperately sagging economy.

"You going to tell me what's going on?" I ask.

"Richard is cursed," Daya says quietly. Curses are the currency, the *moneda nacional,* in which many people trade, and are made formidable by Santería, a religion brought over by Africans and practiced, on some scale, by much of the population.

"Why is he cursed?" I ask patiently.

She whispers in my ear. "His *pinga* doesn't go down, it's stuck on up. He comes but he's still hard, and he does the *llello*"—cocaine—"and rum and he's *so old* but he's still *duro,* so I know it's a curse." She's wild-eyed now. "He wants it all the time and his *pinga* is never soft, so I poured a drink on it, to cool it down, but it stayed up, and I got scared." The teen dancer's thumb goes back in her mouth.

If she wasn't near tears, I'm certain I'd have howled with laughter. "Daya, have you noticed Richard take any pills?"

She thinks about it and fumbles in her bra. Daya offers a blue tablet, slightly damp from sweat.

"He wanted me to take one too. I spit it out when he wasn't looking." I explain to Daya the wonders of Viagra, though it takes a few minutes to convince her most of the world knows of its existence. Relief touches her face.

"You're crazy," she says, and then hugs me. Cubans rarely say "thank you" and I take the embrace to mean just that.

29

The U.S. Interests Section, designed by Americans in 1953, is a slick seven-story building on the Malecón. Its mirrored exterior reflects and refracts a Caribbean sun, formidably luminous, a retina-burning beacon of intimidation.

In 1961, during his final days in office, President Eisenhower withdrew the U.S. diplomatic corps from Havana. A few months later, under a nascent Kennedy administration, the Bay of Pigs was invaded by CIA-trained troops. In further polarizing relations, the following year, American spy planes photographed nuclear missiles at hidden sites on the island's northern shores, ones with enough range to obliterate America's Eastern Seaboard.

But optimism eventually prevailed. At the behest of President Carter—who'd ordered the embassy dusted off, debugged, and resettled after a sixteen-year vacancy—the corps returned under the protection of the neutral Swiss. Embassy functions were downgraded to a charge d'affairs level, which is where they remain today.

The newly arrived *norteamericanos,* having been long absent from Havana, were treated kindly yet with curiosity, and observed at a distance.

Common in Havana were those from the USSR, the island's patron saint and the bête noire of America. My mother remembered that lessons in Russian permeated the airwaves, and Cubans—natural linguists—proudly practiced the Slavic tongue in the streets and the markets.

The U.S. Interests Section opened in 1977 to little fanfare. John reported for work in September of that year and was charged with dispensing the ethos of American democracy to the Cuban public.

For John, it was the career move of a lifetime.

My mother, however, was less than delighted, believing John embraced the polemics of the job with too much gusto and with too little respect for Cuban sovereignty.

It was another of the many fissures in an already embattled marriage.

MY MOTHER FIRST met José Antonio under the yellow-and-red banner of the Spanish embassy, housed in an Art Nouveau palace in Old Havana.

The Spanish—newly reestablished in Cuba, and basking in a post-Franco glow—hosted the U.S. diplomatic corps' coming-out party on neutral territory. Russians, Cubans, and Americans attended. To dilute the combatants, the Spanish invited the Swedes, the French, and the Danish.

My mother wore a black cocktail dress, pearls that once belonged to her grandmother, and a fluid silk Spanish shawl she'd bought in Madrid. She believed the palace to be the most beautiful of all of Havana's inspired architecture, and turned to whisper the sentiment in John's ear.

But it was José Antonio who was listening.

Flustered by the unintended intimacy, my mother scanned the room for John, and not finding him, coolly accepted José Antonio's introduction. A Cuban translator who'd been stationed in Moscow and Africa, José Antonio was serving as an interpreter for his Soviet bosses. Hearing this, my mother stiffened and introduced herself as the wife of an American diplomat.

"Don't be upset," said José Antonio in a low and mischievous voice. "No one here likes the Russians, either."

What didn't need to be clarified, however, was the intensity of the physical chemistry between them.

Later in the evening, partygoers were seated in a semicircle around a slightly elevated wooden stage. A lovely, lithe flamenco dancer was illuminated by a single light, and accompanied by a master guitarist and hand-clapping percussionist. My mother's eyes were glued to the dancer's feet and the sinewy musculature of her body, one that responded with sensuality to the complex rhythms.

My mother felt his eyes burning her skin. She strained to see through the darkened audience and found José Antonio sitting directly across from her. Despite the dazzling artistry on the stage between them, José Antonio was staring at no one but her, a path obstructed only by the occasional blur of the dancer's ruffled, swirling red skirt.

DURING THE ENSUING months, my mother and José Antonio met accidentally nearly a half dozen times in galleries, at parties, and in restaurants. My mother refused to acknowledge the attraction between them, or the irrefutability of José Antonio's charm.

She carefully noted their encounters in her journal, and part of her secretly hoped each outing would bring another round of clandestine flirtation with the handsome Cuban. Her fantasies grew in proportion to the deepening depression of her marriage, which was slipping, a rung at a time, into oblivion.

On the nights John had promised to be by her side, my mother sat alone among palm trees and the heady, aromatic breezes of a Cuban night, starry-skied and voluptuous, a symphony of heavenly beauty put on each evening with the smooth perfection of a long-running Broadway show.

John was increasingly obsessed with his career, and worked all hours. My mother believed his ambition was partly rooted in shame, in the latent failure of his body to conceive a child. She told him it wasn't important. But in the margins of her journal, my mother etched the names of unborn babies: John Jr. for a boy; and for a girl, Alysia.

My mother rang in 1978 at a diplomats' New Year's Eve gala at the Hotel Nacional. She did so alone, as John had gone to Washington for work. My mother remembered arriving at the manicured grounds after midnight, and vowed to stay only a short time, making a brief social appearance before returning to the emptiness of her Miramar home. Slipping off her high heels, she pattered through the downy carpeting of green lawn, making way for the peacocks and antique cannons.

She sucked in her breath. The garden overlooked Havana Bay, lit by the warm, golden light from El Morro castle and the rotating brightness of the potent lighthouse on the cliff.

On this evening, she wondered how a woman in her prime, in a country that inspired poets with its air and mystical beauty, could find herself alone and unwanted by the man she'd loved most. Or how her life had become narrow and full of a yearning so palpable that it lived like a third person in their home.

But my mother knew that the Hotel Nacional on New Year's Eve held a historical precedent for change. Batista, she remembered reading, had spent his last minutes as Cuba's president at this very hotel, on this very night nineteen years before.

She was thinking this when she felt a hand under her elbow. Without looking up, she knew who it was, and knew she'd succumb to the Cuban at last.

My mother felt her back arch and her arms elongate and her gown flutter behind her as she dove headlong into the Havana Bay, receiving the warmth and the gold and the light. It was José Martí's words that preceded her supernal fall, in verses spoken by José Antonio, the man who would alter the course of many lives:

Todo es hermoso y constante,
Todo es música y razón,
Y todo, como el diamante,
Antes que luz es carbon.

All is beautiful and right,
All is music and reason,
And like the diamond, everything
Is coal before it's light.

30

n outstretched arms Limón holds furry brown chunks away from his six-pack stomach. Jesús, a dreadlocked Dominican who could easily be his twin, is egging Limón on.

"Drop the damned coconut already!" demands Jesús.

"Obí," says Limón, closing his eyes and summoning the coconut oracle. "Obí, tell us, is Alysia's father alive and living in Havana?"

He releases the fruit chunks and opens his eyes. All four pieces have landed rind-up. Limón pounds the wall and looks at me sheepishly.

"We need an expert," he says. "We'll have to ask my priest. I've no idea what rind-up means."

"A Magic 8-Ball could tell us," I quip.

No matter how often I tell Limón I don't buy his religious practice, Santería, or his trust in *orishas*—gods representing human attributes, a theanthropism similar to the practice of ancient Greeks—he's convinced his beliefs will provide clues to finding my father.

Limón's faith didn't help him in an earlier scouting of my old neighborhood. The mission was a bust. No one remembered a family of American diplomats living there two decades before. Limón did, however, confirm a figure-eight swimming pool next door to my supposed childhood home—a tidbit that matches the description in my mother's diaries.

"We Santeros communicate with ancestors," Limón says solemnly. "Isn't that what you want?"

I nod. Limón has been pestering me to visit his priest, and I agree to visit him. It can't hurt, I figure.

"We're not going anywhere until the tour," says Jesús, who's eager to begin our day, this crisp and bright December.

Limón scoops up the fruit shells and chews on the white meat while we scoot through Old Havana in search of a peso taxi. Limón confides later that Jesús, who approached him on the street, paid $3,000 for Limón's identity *carnet.* Jesús is spending a few weeks in Havana picking up enough Cuban slang and geography to fake his way through Krome Detention Center, where Cubans in Florida are processed before being handed a green card, with residency all but guaranteed after a year. Cubans are the only immigrants automatically granted this privilege in the United States. Mexicans, Europeans, and Asians must all fight their way through the bureaucracy in order to have a shot at becoming American citizens.

Jesús, however, has found a loophole. He'll use his Dominican passport to enter Florida on a temporary farmworker's visa. While in Miami, he and other friends who've bought Cuban identities will dump their real passports and swim along shallow shores off Key Biscayne, claiming they are Cuban rafters who've just floated in. Their purchased Cuban *carnets* will be offered to immigration as proof. I tell Limón it's an outrageous scheme, but he just shrugs and says it's more common than I'd think.

"West Africans, Venezuelans, and Spaniards," he says. "Some you see here are probably scouting for a look-alike Cuban's ID. Works, too. I just show up at the police station, claim mine's been stolen, and get another one. No problem."

In Cuba, there are few stores, and fewer still that advertise with a shingle or an awning or fluorescent lights. Yet everything is for sale, and anything may be purchased at any time—in the middle of the night, on holidays, during a category-five hurricane.

It's called the black market, but it is ineptly named, as black implies dark—and thus evil or sinister—and here it does not assume a morality. If all colors, when swirled together, make gray, then it's the true color of Cuba's market. Because everything from lottery tickets to laundry soap to a twelve-year-old's virginity can be had. All it takes is a whisper in the ear of a *jinetero,* or a mechanic, or a retired schoolteacher, and enough greenbacks to make it happen. And happen it does.

· · ·

AT THE INTERNET café, I make my written apologies to Susie and my friends, explaining away my tardiness with the excuse that a few minutes of e-mail access cost as much as a week's worth of taxis. Susie writes that she's worried about me, and doesn't seem to buy into my chipper inventions of my life here in Havana. She wants to know what I do with my days. I tell her about the movies and, today, regale her with stories of the dreadful chore of clothes shopping.

Anatole France wrote this: "Show me the clothes of a country and I can write its history." Perhaps the recent history of Cuba can be summed up by the women's-wear store near my home. In a shop window, only sizeable, polyester underwear is on display, and the unmentionables hang suspended on fishing line. The sign above reads: *No compre de prisa,* Don't buy in a hurry. It's this nonsensical reflection of the Cuban economy that forces me to shake my head. And as I do so, I'm stared at funnily, and the look is likely to come from a sexy, haughty beauty, swaying down the street in tight, sheer white pants with big, old-lady underwear bunched up underneath.

Cubanas possess a raw beauty, but without the sophistication and refinement that could be gleaned from a few copies of Spanish *Elle.*

I'm hoping these tidbits keep Susie's worry at bay. What I don't tell her is how I awaken each day hoping it will bring a visit from Victor, and the address of José Antonio.

Lying to her is the worst of it all.

"DON'T YOU WANT to say *hola?"* asks Limón, pointing to a middle-aged foreign man holding the hand of a teen *cubana.*

"No way in hell," I say, shaking my head and crouching in the cavernous back seat of the 1956 Ford Fairlane we've hired with a driver for the day. The floorboards reek of gas.

We watch the couple. Daya sports a bored expression, and Richard is so amped he's practically dragging her by the hand.

"Who has more fun, people or monkeys?" jokes Limón, quoting another of my grandfather's sayings and tapping on the window.

"We've got time to stop if you want to say *que bola,"* says Jesús, jumping in the back seat with a bottle of rum and a $10 marijuana cigarette that, as he soon discovers, is—quite literally—grass.

"Forget it. *Vamos.* Those two are like peanut butter and jelly," I reply, watching the couple fade into a crowd. "Fine together but after a few bites so messy and sticky and you need something strong to wash 'em down."

"Peanut butter?" asks Limón.

"You're kidding," Jesús says. "They don't have that here, either? Man, you guys are in for a shock when things change—"

"Never mind," I say to Limón, whose pride is visibly wounded. Like most of his countrymen, Limón views himself as erudite and sophisticated. Considering the high level of education here, it's a warranted belief, and Limón is one of the brightest people I've ever known. Whenever *extranjeros*—consciously or not—suggest the Cuban is less than worldly, hackles will be raised.

"It's like most of the stuff you don't have here," I say, trying to cool Limón down. "Overrated."

But Limón sulks just the same.

We spend the day sightseeing. A clinic for handicapped children. A home for Alzheimer's patients. A rural retreat—bucolic and relatively luxurious—for those with HIV. A beach compound for Ukrainians, Russians, and Belarussians suffering from the crippling and sometimes grotesque effects of Chernobyl. All are offered free of charge to the poorest of people.

Despite his antigovernment sentiments, Limón bursts with pride on our tour, needed to acquaint Jesús with the local culture. Limón's effusions give me the feeling we're paying for our peanut-butter comments.

"Unlike most of Latin America, we're not being run by a U.S. puppet government," says Limón. "And no other country has these kinds of benefits like free medical care and education."

I roll my eyes. It's an argument I hear all the time. "You mean, except Canada, and most of Europe," I say, but Limón's not listening.

"It's bullshit here," says Jesús. "You're fine if you're poor and sick, but what if you want to make money?"

"Money isn't everything," I say.

But Jesús ignores me. "I'm going to the USA to make money. Make lots and lots and lots of money. Join a real gang. Be like Tony Montana. Like Scarface, *coño.*" He shoots off an imaginary machine gun.

Limón shifts uncomfortably in his seat. In macho societies such as

Cuba's, women are expected to adhere to extreme forms of femininity, and men are obsessed with proving their manhood. A man's ability to provide financially for those he loves is the defining *latino* characteristic. A lack of avenues, legal or otherwise, for *cubanos* to make a living is the singular demasculinizing factor. And daily visions of their *cubana* beauties with richer, foreign men provide a fresh slap in the face.

"*Mira,* tell me really how people here feel about the leadership," says Jesús with a twisted smirk. "For my interview with the Americans."

"Ambivalent," says Limón, after a few minutes. "A few people hate it and a few people love it and most people love it *and* hate it."

As a *norteamericano*, I'm unaccustomed to the Latin way, that idea that opposing beliefs can be held simultaneously, in one human heart, without a need for a settlement. As a *cubana* now—as a *latina*—I try to open myself to the duplicities, and allow them to grow and coexist peacefully in my consciousness. But it's an adjustment.

Watching Limón quietly protest against the strictures with his Rasta dreads makes me wonder how he can be so ambivalent himself, particularly since he, a black man, is singled out by police more often than whites, and especially while careening about publicly with *blanca*-skinned foreigners.

"What do you think?" Jesús asks me. "About the government?"

"Not allowed an opinion," I say, miming a zipper crossing my lips. "If I say I hate it, I'm told my opinion doesn't count 'cause I don't *live* live here, and if I say I love it, I'm told I'm from *afuera*." The outside.

"Your country was also started by a revolution," says Limón, looking at me. "There were growing pains. Like here."

"Who was it?" I say, knowing it's safer to discuss politics in the abstract. "Camus? Who said the revolutions of the left and the revolutions of the right are barely distinguishable?"

"Yeah, Camus," says Limón. "The French guy, an interesting *hombre.*"

"Who?" says Jesús, looking confused.

"They let you read Camus here? I'd imagine he's almost a heretic," I say.

"Who the fuck is Camus?" says Jesús, flicking his cigarette out the window.

"*Pero,* you do know about—what is it, the butter of peanuts?" harrumphs Limón under his breath, shooting a victorious glance at Jesús.

Like most Cuban hustlers, and I'd never tell him this, Limón's clownish appearance conceals a book-smart knowledge he accesses easily and readily. He'd talk intellectual circles around an American frat boy and make a stimulating companion for the intellectual set. When I once told him how lucky he is to be so educated, compared to the citizens of other Latin countries, he dismissed me with a snicker. We're European and African, he told me, and comparing us with Mexico or Central America is all mixed up, like *arroz con mango.*

"I'm telling you, this shit here is fucked," says the hunky Dominican, taking the last word. "Could never live here. Never."

The Cuban system is loved. It's hated. But pride and fear—including a wariness of any alternate system—keeps most people from protesting too loudly.

As the day recedes, Limón and Jesús play a few rounds of soccer with survivors of the Chernobyl disaster, who have complimentary beachside apartments near Havana, where they rest in the warmth and are attended to by skilled physicians. Some have silent, invisible killers eating away at their cells. Others have tumors on their heads or backs the size of an Isle of Pines grapefruit. Their convalescence, a gift from the Cuban people, is given despite the political debt to Russia being all but extinguished. The small happiness, Limón tells me, makes their fragile lives bearable.

31

The Hill, *El Cerro,* is a working-class neighborhood famous for its petty thieves. There are no decorations to indicate the approaching Christmas season, as stringed lights and plastic reindeer aren't sold. In the warmth of winter, it hardly feels like the holidays anyhow.

With a half a year already behind me, I'm growing more frustrated by the lack of information about my family. I'm hoping the man inside this house will be my Santa Claus.

Limón knocks at the door, and we wait.

Limón's midnight skin is offset by stark white pants, shirt, and driving cap. Light beads of sweat cascade down his fresh face.

"What do you *mean* you spent all three grand already?" I whisper, incredulous.

He shyly ticks off his purchases from the sale of his *carnet* to the Dominican: a new washing machine for his mother; a *quince* party for his sister; a water tank that doesn't churn out rust; and beds for the family, who'd been sleeping on plank wood and blankets.

Although he's proud of his family contributions, I scold him for not saving part of his windfall for harsher days.

"*¿Cuál es el punto?*" he asks. "I can't put it in a bank *porque* they might connect the missing *carnet* to the cash. Besides, thieves can steal it or the dollar-store prices will, *ya tú sabes* . . ." He jacks his thumb skyward.

Limón isn't alone. Few understand the concept of a savings account. If money is around, it's spent. Parties, clothes, roast pigs. In a culture that doesn't put much premium on the future, *mañana* is left to be "resolved" anew.

A shy teenage girl answers the door and shows us in. It's the house of a famous *babalocha,* a Santero priest capable of communing with coconut oracles and dead ancestors. I try to resist my skepticism, but when I see the fresh bloodstains on the wall I'm overcome with doubt.

"Animal sacrifices?" I whisper to Limón.

His mouth says "Shhhh," but his eyes confirm. Doves and chickens dangle from the ceiling in cages, and the girl drags a stool to each spot, dropping seed into wooden tubs for the fowl. On rickety benches, we wait nearly two hours, and I drift into sleep on Limón's shoulder. He shakes me awake in time to see, through a dramatic parting of curtains fashioned from bed sheets, the fattest man I've seen in my second homeland.

His belly rests atop skinny legs, and a faded Fruit Loops T-shirt stretches a Tucan Sam into comic distortion over the beans-and-rice gut. I suppress a giggle, sensing Limón's deep reverence for the man.

The *babalocha* sits on the ground on a straw mat, his back supported by the blood-spattered wall. Limón and I sit facing him, in chairs. The priest calls on Eleggua, the opener of doors, the bouncer at the velvet ropes of the other world. Eleggua apparently believes us to be presentable, because the *babalocha* smiles and welcomes me.

"Each person is the child of a particular *orisha,*" whispers Limón. "The *babalocha* will ask who claims you. My guess is Changó." The frisky one, the god of fire and thunder.

The *babalocha* opens a red-and-black bag, and from it drops cowry shells into my hands. I'm instructed to shake them. When I return the dappled shells, he lays them on the ground, and records the configurations in a notebook. I sneak a glance at the paper and see him writing complex formulas of 1s and 0s. Binary code.

Limón had explained how Santería was a Yoruban religion brought to Cuba by the slaves from Western Africa. Cuban slave-masters wouldn't allow open practice of the religion, so the slaves syncretized the beliefs with Catholicism, the dominant practice of Spanish settlers, and adopted the saints as visible representations of the *orishas.*

Saint Anthony, for instance, represents Eleggua. And the Virgin Mary—the patron saint of Cuba, known as *la virgen de caridad de la cobre*—is the *orisha* called Oshún. Priests also teach the veneration of ancestors, who are said to offer moral guidance from another realm. Much like the Catholic model of communication, the priests approach the *orishas* through a mediator.

After a long, silent contemplation, the *babalocha* stares at me with a discomfiting calm. "You're the daughter," he says, "of Oshún."

"Oshún?" Limón is incredulous.

"The goddess of love and beauty," confirms the *babalocha*.

"*Imposible!*" stutters Limón. "Try again. There's no way, not this girl."

I shoot Limón a look and kick his foot. "Why not?"

"Oshún is the ruler of streams and rivers, and operates on a system of flow," explains the priest. "She represents fertility, is flirtatious, and a great dancer."

"That's why not."

A smile slips from the corners of the *babalocha*'s mouth. "Oshún welcomes you and has some work for you to do."

"Work? Sorry, unless it pays dollars I don't have time."

"*Ay, coño,* no joke," says Limón, shooting me a warning.

The priest continues. "Oshún says you've many difficult tasks here in Cuba, and she's proud of you. She promises to give you," he says, pausing and leaning toward me to whisper, "everything you came here for."

"*Que suerte,*" says Limón, impressed.

"But you have to change your approach in order to receive her spirit and guidance," the priest commands.

"Change my approach?"

"She wants you to stop thinking all the time." The *babalocha* reaches up for my hand and places it on my chest. "And start feeling. Oshún is the goddess of the river. Think of the rhythm of a river, and move into that flow."

"Rhythm of a river."

"'*Ño—any* rhythm would be an improvement," says Limón, still shaking his head.

"You're looking for somebody, someone close to you, *verdad*?" asks the priest.

Knowing Limón could easily have told the *babalocha* of the search for my father, I nod noncommittally.

"Her father," prompts Limón.

"Yes, the father," says the priest. "Oshún says your whole life your father has been closer than you think."

"Anything more specific?" I ask. "Perhaps a phone number?"

"Oshún says your father will come to you, Alysia, when the time is right. There's a strong female presence also. I see your grandmother, and an aunt, and some cousins. They've been calling out to you. It seems you've been placed under special protection, in spells cast by them." The *babalocha* pauses for a second, receiving information. "Spells they've cast in your favor since you were a child."

"Are these people—" I cough and start over. "Is this family of mine alive?"

He pauses again. "Yes, they're here living in La Habana. *Tan tan cerquita.*" So very close.

"*Chévere,*" says Limón with a somber nod.

"It seems," says the priest, "the rain which falls from your roof is the water they step in on the way to the market."

I feel a rush of excitement. This must be my father's family, and to believe they live close to my home is more than I can handle. I think of how my mother told me on her deathbed my father's family was waiting for me. But I don't want to believe the *babalocha*'s words. I feel only a slight thaw in my doubts.

"Anything about my mother?" I say.

"She's not living?" It's more a confirmation than a question, and he closes his eyes before I nod in the affirmative. "She is with you now, watching. She wants you to know her spirit can be felt most strongly here in Havana. Does that make sense?"

I'm still not convinced, so I ask another question. "Ask her for a sign, one only she and I will recognize."

The priest studies me a long while. The sunlight has gone from the room, and the doves and chickens rock slowly in their cages. A slight breeze blows the sheets along the wall, and I feel wind carry in a rare coolness. I rub down the goose bumps forming on my arms.

The priest concentrates, mouthing silent words, his eyes resting. I think of the 1s and the 0s floating in the air, expanding from code to consciousness and back to code again, and hope the science and earthy mysticism, with its powers rooted in herbs and stone, flowers and animals, will summon the psychic remnants of my mother.

His eyes pop open like a china doll's, suddenly wide and alert. I lean forward.

"Monkey baby," he says, not understanding. "A small monkey. That's what I'm told. Mean anything?"

Shrugging my shoulders, I turn to Limón and send a smirk that suggests it's all a ruse in the end. But suddenly the goose bumps return, and in the copse of memory I recall my childhood name, one that Limón could never know, a nickname I'd myself long forgotten.

Little monkey.

Frenetic now, I gasp and stand up, practically shouting. "Tell her I'm going to find him," I nearly shout to the priest. "Tell her I promise! I'll find him!"

"She knows," he says, smiling.

"Anything else?" I ask, practically begging.

"Your mother wants you to follow your heart. She made a very big mistake once by not listening to her own voice. She hopes you will not follow her down that path."

"Is there more?" I ask meekly. "That she said?"

"Just that—" His voice cracks. "Just that she's sorry."

32

*S*tanding at the intersection, I'm lightly rubbing a raw egg over my body. Careful not to crush its fragile shell, I chant for Oshún's guidance, Changó's protection, and Eleggua to get the whole message up to the right zip code.

Women sweeping the sidewalks are staring. Cars drive by slowly, and passengers toss bawdy comments. As instructed, I turn my back on the intersection and pitch the egg into the middle of the street.

Splat.

The priest had given me the instructions the day before, and I'm loathe to carry them out. Nearly everyone watching knows precisely what I'm doing, having practiced *macumba* before. Nonetheless, my face burns.

Accidentally, I crack the second egg on my chest, and embryonic goo drips down my tank top. I hear a muffled giggle from one of the balconies and sigh: I've eight more eggs to go.

"It's for protection," the priest advised. "You've made a few enemies, and you're about to make more." The only *enemigo* I can think of is Walrus, my shadow companion. But Limón is most worried about the priest's final pronouncement.

One that signals a time of unprecedented tumult for the entire country.

33

My arms wrap around Camila. Our bodies entwine. Hips glide together in rhythmic circles.

Then I stomp down on her toes and she jumps back.

"*Por favor!*" shouts Camila, pausing the salsa music and rubbing her beleaguered foot. "Are you certain the priest said you're Oshún's daughter? I mean, *chica*, your rhythm is *mierda!*"

Great, I think. First dance lesson and my spiritual lineage is already suspect.

"The only dancing I know is this," I say, bouncing like a hip-hopper and smacking my own rear.

"Don't ever," she says, horrified, "do that again!" Then, using a word devised for those who can't dance, she shouts: "*Patón!*"

Limón bursts into laughter. "Look at her all jumping around like a flea in a hot skillet."

Limón's been sitting in a corner writing identical letters of love and longing to *yumas* in five different countries. His Cuban girlfriend, Osanay, is helpfully pointing out grammatical errors. Under the pretense of true love—a story Limón spins anew for each foreign girl—the romantic grifter is angling for one of his lovers to marry him and take him out of Cuba.

Limón and his legitimate sweetie are smoking a stick of cow-trampled grass mixed with negligible amounts of marijuana. It's a rare drug in Cuba, as pro-government farmers in the lush interior guard against its cultivation. Drugs do, however, roll up on the beaches in bales, having been discarded by nervous drug-runners in boats and planes scuttling between South America and the Caribbean, or Central America and the U.S.

Limón tells me locals have formed alliances and claim strips of real estate along the coastline. Definitive lines in the sand. The precise point at which bundled drugs wash up determines which gang is the lucky recipient. It's an honor system that works surprisingly well, as drug-related violence is uncommon.

He also says the main narcotic in Cuba is cocaine, and its demand comes from both tourists and locals lucky enough to line their pockets with dollars. It's slipped covertly into the country on cargo ships and pleasure boats. But it's a dangerous game. Drug dealers, if caught, are harshly sentenced.

El Prado, a marbled walkway from the Malecón to the Capitolio, is a stroller's lane. But in the *barrio* west of El Prado, as any *jinetero* worth his salt knows, is where kingpins ply their trade. In the labyrinths of sectioned apartments and rooms and secret doors, police raids are rarely effective. The risks are profitable. An ounce of pure cocaine retails for $20 to $30, and *jineteros* resell it to their *yumas* at triple the price. One sale, and a hustler rakes in the annual salary of a hotel manager.

"Camila, take a rest," Limón offers as Camila winces at her foot pain. "I'll teach the guy part now."

But Camila shakes her head. The most accomplished *jineteras* are also the island's best dancers, and in Havana, music is serious business. A dancer's feet are an instrument in the band playing *cha-chá, mambo, casino,* and *danzón.* Knowing your moves is more than just art, it's also finance. Top *jinetera* dancers bring high rollers to clubs, and the musicians give them a cut of the night's profit.

"On the dance floor you're auditioning for the bedroom," lectures Camila. "All men know that a woman who can dance is *una buena hoja*"— great at sex. "So you have to know your moves."

Camila is prepping me for *jineterismo* home runs, but I can't help thinking my dancing moves may also serve to impress Rafael. He's been on my mind more than usual since I saw him yesterday, when I'd promised myself I would resume my habit of jogging. Though I'm thinner here than I've ever been, I've become determined to strengthen my muscles. My new profession requires that I can defend myself in a daunting situation.

Despite the emphasis on physical fitness, and the many athletes Cuba produces, few people jog in the streets or along the seawall, the way they certainly would at home. Runners are spotted occasionally, but are usually men, as women wouldn't be caught dead outside a track or a gym with less than enough paint on their faces to forge a Van Gogh. Despite the stares and *cubano* commentary, I decided the custom was hooey, and worked up a sweat along the Malecón.

Ignoring the catcalls, I focused on my breathing, and my legs, and the way they burned as I pounded over uneven cement, and the strength I was beginning to feel in my body and mind. When I felt someone pinch my rear, I whirled around, only to see Rafael in sweats sprinting alongside.

"Girl's got some *cojones* to run here," he said, smiling.

I was panting and sweating and paling in comparison to the sashaying *mamacitas* who were pursing their lips at Rafael. I pushed myself to go faster; he kept up with me easily.

"How long am I going to have to run after you before you'll agree to go out with me?"

"Why would I do that?"

"Because the way I see it, you may be a sprinter, but I'm going to win the marathon." To hide a smile, I ran even harder, but he jogged backwards, easily keeping pace.

"Tell me, how does it work on a date with Rafael?" I asked.

We slowed and nearly stopped at an intersection near Old Havana. We walked around, catching our breath and taking a stretch in the silence. I tried to hide my disappointment when he put a shirt over a well-worked stomach.

"Dinner," he said. "I make dinner at my house. You take a shower, put on a dress, show up at nine. *Oye*, how many Cuban men do you know who will cook for you?"

"Is that the tourist special?" I asked, realizing at once I'd blurted out an insult.

He retained his humored composure. "How about Saturday?"

But I couldn't, as Camila had a *yuma* coming into town, one she was certain would fancy me. I knew she wouldn't let me pass him up. When I told Rafael I was busy, he shrugged and squinted his eyes at the oncoming traffic.

"Say no all you want, *muchacha*. We'll see who's crawling at the finish line."

Finding a break, he set off to cross the busy street, leaving me to admire him dodging the heavy machinery.

"HOLA. EARTH TO Alysia," says Camila, holding up her arms. I give her my hand and drape an arm on her shoulder.

Even though I've relegated my *jineterismo* to the nighttime, ever since running into Rafael, I've made a conscious effort to dress with more *cubanía* in the day. Today, Camila and I are wearing corked platform heels, ultra-tight jeans, and silky crocheted scarves with tapered fringe, slung over our jeans and knotted at the hip. It briefly occurs to me that either of my known grandmothers would be horrified at my outfit, and even more so at the movement I'm forcing my hips to enact.

A real *cubana*'s hips undulate like a belly dancer's, another of Arabia's lasting imprints on Cuba, but my joints stubbornly won't detach from the upper torso, much less perform the required figure-eights.

Camila adjusts my posture and removes my arm from her shoulder. "Let's just get the feet down," she says, "and we'll worry about your hips later."

Jineteras troll for wealthy targets at sybaritic nightclubs like Johnny's, Macumba, and Casa de la Musica. Competition is fierce. The moment a lone male tourist walks in the door, a crush of *jineteras* descend upon him. It's a woman's chore to stand out from the competition. Dancing, Camila suggests, is the best method to display one's wares.

In this culture, I'm expected to be overtly sexual in my appearance and demeanor. But I'm also required to be aggressive, to go get my man, to engage my *yuma* in a romantic swindle. One that unfolds at hyperspeed, from the first glance to immediate sex to him buying clothes and proposing marriage and supporting the whole family.

In my own country, in my social circles back home, broadcasting one's sexuality with provocative dress or demeanor is frowned upon, as is an aggressive chasing of men. These things happen, of course, but where I come from, the art is in the subtleties. In Cuba, I'm adjusting to the extremes. Men are expected to be *men,* and women are expected to be *women,* and *jineteras* are expected to pursue *yumas* with the voracity of a firefighter squelching a schoolyard blaze. I've never felt completely comfortable with my womanliness. Here I've been forced to harness my sexual power, put it on display, and market my goods to those who can provide security. It's both liberating and terrifying.

"You believe in Santería?" I ask Camila as she tilts my chin upward.

"Of course, *mi corazón.* We all believe in Santería, more or less." She winks at me. "You know, you're not the only daughter of Oshún. But then, I've known all along we must be sisters."

The music begins and, despite Camila's confidence in me, I jumble every step. The *babalocha's* words spring to mind, and I tell Camila what he said about feeling more and thinking less.

Camila stops and pauses the music for the second time. "He said that?" she asks Limón, who nods.

"*De acuerdo,*" she says. "With the priest." Camila absently massages her neck, looks out the window, and then around the room. The walls are covered in nude and seminude portraits of her. Talented and love-struck Cuban artists have been painting Camila since she sprouted into her teens. Oils are barely dry on the latest effort, and Camila admires the accurate and flattering portrayal with the discrimination of a sommelier. Then she turns to me and wraps a cloth around my head, obscuring my sight. Limón raises a wan eyebrow. Music returns to a high decibel.

"Listen," she instructs. "Don't count the steps. Don't *think* about your moves."

"How can I not think?"

"Shhhhhhh. Listen. There's a soundtrack for everything in life—for cooking, for walking, for conversation, and especially for sex. There's a beat to it all, but you have to listen for it. Move to it."

For days, I listen, blindfolded, to Cuban music, moving my limbs and hips—ungainly at first but more certain as I single out the maracas and bongos, the *timbales* and *güiros,* and then allow them to blend together in the background of my mind. When the blindfold comes off, the feet find their place with little resistance. My hips begin to circulate, and a rough gracefulness appears. Camila claps her hands together in delight.

This *jinetera* hasn't won the derby, but she's definitely in the race.

34

The country that claims half my bloodline launches an attack on Iraq in March, raising the ire of most of the world. Cuban phone lines burn. A few hours later, switchboards alight at Radio Bemba—the word-of-mouth system perfected by gossipy *habaneros*. The news: nearly eighty journalists, librarians, and dissidents are rounded up and arrested in Havana. They would be given lightning-fast trials and sentenced—some to life in prison.

Limón's aunt, an antigovernment librarian, would receive ten years.

The next day, angry Cubans hijack a DC-3 Aerojet, place a knife to the captain's throat, and demand a ride to Florida. U.S. fighter jets escort the plane to a landing field. Many passengers and crew defect.

Eleven days later, a Russian-made Antonov-24 twin-engine is hijacked and lands in Key West. Half of its thirty-two Cuban passengers apply for asylum.

The next morning, locals hijack a ferry that glides across Havana Bay. It runs out of fuel just shy of international waters, and is towed back to shore. A forty-eight-hour standoff ensues. Passengers are eventually rescued.

The scuffle is documented on video and shown across the island on state television. Families crowd around their sets, and people without TVs peer through strangers' windows to view the odd encounter.

The police on the island snap their batons.

An island-wide crackdown begins.

No one does not feel the wrath of their king.

Four

35

Pink feathers. Ruby-studded pasties. Gold thongs and high heels and even higher kicks. Breasts and bottoms shimmy and shake. Chandeliers of fruit and fluff topple above sleek showgirls' heads.

The Tropicana nightclub debuted in the 1950s and is perfected nearly every night in the outskirts of Havana before a crowd of tourists, as average *habaneros* could never afford the tab. With no city lights or pollution to interfere with the night sky, the moon on wax or wane appears close enough to pluck. The outdoor revue is lit in pinks and peaches and crimsons. Falling stars streak overhead.

It's at the Tropicana that the annual Habanos cigar festival ignites. For an ambitious Cuban girl, it's an Elysian Field of the world's most freewheeling playboys and bachelors, all in Havana for a weekend of Cohibas and cognac and sun. The pluckiest *jineteras* gin up the fun and serve as the festivity's sensual bacchantes.

Camila introduces me to the business partner of one of her long-term boyfriends, Ignacio, a man who plies her with feathery Christian Louboutin stilettos, Balenciaga handbags, and Stephen Dweck teardrop diamonds for her wrists, neck, and ears. I'm not certain Camila understands these gifts are luxuries in any city, much less one of the world's most shambled.

The business partner, Reinaldo, is freshly shaven and smart in a turquoise silk shirt, white pants, and an iridescent leisure jacket courtesy of Armani. He's the kind of man who'd never look at me twice anywhere, much less in a country of *mulata* goddesses worthy of a Herb Ritts spread.

My stomach is tight and I'm panicking with insecurity. Camila must sense my dread, because she lightly taps my arm, as if to remind me of our earlier pep talk. I force a smile.

The four of us settle in front of the stage. One surreptitious signal from Camila, and the headwaiter rushes to the table, knowing she brings in the big guns and spreads her profit around. A snap of his fingers, and a bottle of Matusalem Gran Reserva—aged fifteen years, a rare specimen—arrives with chipped ice.

Under Cuba's previous regime, most women in the sex business answered to pimps and boyfriends and gangsters. Under the current regime, it's the women who are in charge, and capable of bringing in the highest salary. Considering the machismo inherent in this society, I can't help but feel sorry for men who have no equitable means of power. But if the revolution promised progress for women, it's been fulfilled in ways few would have predicted.

The Spaniards are in their late forties and exude a serene, immutable confidence along with an air of slight self-deprecation. It's an attitude embodied only by the self-made of incredible success. Camila's pillow talk had revealed the two are wildcat oil riggers with European financing who'd made their fortune off the coast of Venezuela.

Camila met Ignacio the year before, when he was in Havana negotiating for the rights to prospect in Cuban seas. In the midst of discussions, Ignacio suffered a mild heart attack. Camila bypassed his weakened artery, replacing it with a vein from his thigh, and he healed well.

But he never fully recovered from Camila's supernatural touch.

When the burlesque subsides, an emcee announces a Christian Dior fashion show. Knowing haute couture isn't even sold in Cuba, I snicker under my breath and excuse myself to go to the restroom. Reinaldo politely stands when I leave, but lack of eye contact confirms his boredom with me.

Taking a deep breath, and following Camila's sagacity, I whisper a tremendous compliment in his ear. Reinaldo smiles and steps back, as if seeing me for the first time. A whopper ego-boost is effective merely once, and best applied at the first meeting. Camila says no man, regardless of his accomplishments, is impervious to that kind of talk.

The compliment has to be preceded—or followed—by The Look. On Camila, The Look is dead-on, lower lip down, and shot through the barrel from over the shoulder. It's a half-turn to the right, left hand on the hip, shoulder forward maneuver that flatters the body.

When delivered by Camila, The Look is long and lusty and deep-freezes the air molecules floating between shooter and mark. The Look is the first lance thrown. The target, taken by surprise, is more than happy to be wounded.

A follow-up stare, he'll soon discover, is a few seconds away, after Camila first feigns brief disinterest. Returning her attentions, she'll hold her gaze for three beats, perhaps four, and then deliver the deadliest blow.

Target immured.

Antlers above the grill.

At Camila's insistence, I've been practicing my own version of The Look, but I'm certain I come off like a cross second-grade teacher instead of a voluptuous siren. Nonetheless, tonight, with Reinaldo in my scope, I squeeze the trigger. The bullet seems to ricochet a few times and then hit somewhere near Reinaldo's heart. Camila sends me an approving glance, but I know it's just beginner's luck.

Reinaldo doesn't take his eyes off me the entire night. Except once.

Modesta.

THE WOMEN'S BATHROOM at the Tropicana is flooded. In desperation, I slip into the dancers' dressing room and seek a toilet. Pasties are peeling off, and the lanky, slender ballerinas—the loveliest with *café con leche* skin and eyes the color of lime—are chattering excitedly about the clothes they'll model.

Jean-Paul Gaultier perfume—vanilla, orchid, and amber in a bottle sculptured like a woman's corseted torso—is the favored scent of a *jinetera.* It's impossible to purchase anywhere in Cuba, and its power lies in the intimidation, as its wearer broadcasts a past success with a returning, gift-bearing *yuma.* In this dressing room, the sexual wattage is overwhelming. When I find a toilet, I leave the door open a crack, to facilitate eavesdropping.

"Wish they'd just wear flags over their head," says one dancer.

"It'd be so much easier," agrees another.

"Swiss are the best."

"*Ay,* no!" argues a dancer. "Norwegians and Swedes are the best."

"She's right. Once you're in, the country totally takes care of you. Health care, education, housing, the works."

"Same in Canada."

"*Mira,* but Canadians are so *cheap*! I had one for two years and he barely took me out. Said my mom's cooking was so good there was no reason to leave the house. *Tacaño* just hoarding his *fula.*" The other girls laugh.

"Mexicans," says one. "Absolute worst. *Escorias.*" There's a wave of agreement.

"*Y mala mala hoja!*" says another.

"All saliva and sweat. Ick."

"There's only one or two *norteamericanos* at the festival this year," says a glum dancer. "That's what management is saying."

"*Ay,*" says another dancer, flicking her wrist to snap fingers. "Just because a few journalists got arrested last week and thrown in prison for no reason!"

The room is silent. Rarely do Cubans so openly express their political sentiments. A wind of quiet nervousness fills the room. I fasten my golden-yellow dress, the favored color of Oshún, and peek through the door.

Finally someone speaks. "Bunch of Yankee cowards. We need real men anyway!"

Everyone bursts into laughter. Exhaling, I slip through the room and find myself back under the falling stars, only to run into Rafael.

"So let me get this straight," he says.

His tan is darker than usual, and his breath smells of mint and mojito. Rafael puts an arm on the wall, where my back is firmly planted, and leans close. If I were a more talented *jinetera,* I'd shoot him The Look, but as the equilibrium drains from my body, it's all I can do to keep upright. I again think briefly of my mother, and how she felt whenever José Antonio was near. Anemic.

"*¿Que pasa?* You only date foreigners?" Rafael asks. "Every time I see you, it's with another *extranjero*. Going to take all the work away from the *jineteras*. Imagine if it gets out you do their job for free."

Ducking under his arm, I chortle nervously and try to walk away, surprised and grateful he hasn't heard about my part-time occupation, and knowing it can't stay a secret much longer. His hand stops me.

"*Oye*, Alysia. *La malcriada*." The spoiled brat. "You haven't returned any of my calls. Don't you know you're not Cuban until you've been *with* a Cuban?"

"Really."

"*Seguro*."

"Speaking of your work," I say. "Shouldn't you be out looking for your next victim?"

"Shouldn't you be out looking for your father?"

"That's not going so well."

"*Oye m'ija*, I know half the city. Perhaps if you'd let me help—"

She slithers up to Rafael like a cat on a tightrope. Her lips are Chanel red, and her thick, straight black hair is waist-length and swings over an impossibly hourglass body. A Christian Dior fringed black dress fits snugly atop a round stomach, tiny frame, and wide hips. The model looks at me like I'm a *jutía*, the tree-dwelling rodent of Cuba. I know her as the invidious Modesta, perhaps the most beautiful *jinetera* in all of La Habana. She places a protective arm on Rafael.

"Zip me, baby," she coos, arching her back and tossing a glance to her own behind. Her eyebrows are drawn like Van Gogh's birds on a distant horizon, and hover over slanted, almond eyes. Eyes that register severe irritation at my presence.

Rafael maneuvers the apparatus on her dress with one hand, and without taking his eyes off me.

Then, in rapid-fire Spanish, the woman tugs at Rafael's shirt and asks: "Is she *cubana* or *extranjera*?" Cuban or foreigner?

"She," says Rafael, "has not quite decided."

THE CHRISTIAN DIOR show begins to a track by the Orishas, Cuban hip-hoppers who've defected to Paris, and one of the country's most famous exports. It's a Santería-themed bash, and the music quickly gives way to live Afro-Cuban rumba. Dancers and percussionists deliver a wild performance, one with roots in slaves' communication through the beating of drums.

Dancers in fiery Changó costumes perform a trancelike ritual with jerky, and then fluid, body movements. Models strut the makeshift runway in French designer gowns and necklaces of doves' feet and colored beads. On the floor, cigar girls work the room, and tobacco connoisseurs send puffs of smoke up to Alpha Centauri.

A tall, elegant man sits at the table next to us, cuddling with a crush of Cuban beauties. Without subtlety, he dips the fiery end of his Cohiba in a tin of *llello*. Considering the number of military honchos at nearby tables, I'm surprised by his brashness. Then I recognize him.

"Camila," I say excitedly, pointing toward the table.

"Who's that?"

"You don't know? He's a superfamous and supermarried NBA basketball player!"

"NBA basketball?" she asks, as if I'm nuts.

"You know, the game," I say. "That guy's Mr. Clean, has a reputation for being a role model."

"That's dumb."

Scanning the room, I see another familiar face. *"Dios mío!* That one," I say, pointing to a full table where a man is being fondled by foxy *mulatas*. "He's an actor. Last year he signed a prenup that was huge news." But it's all chatter to Camila, who understands little of what I'm saying. In Cuba, there are no prenups, and a divorce costs $5 and takes twenty minutes.

"Where's the paparazzi?" I ask, half kidding, before realizing the stupidity of my remark. The U.S. embargo and its twin, the travel ban, keeps American culture at bay, and makes it unlikely *cubanos* will recognize boldface names, much less understand how valuable a photograph of them at this moment would be worth to the *National Enquirer*. At once, I'm reminded how so very isolated I am from the rest of the world, from the comfort of knowing how things work ninety miles to the north.

Reinaldo's hands bring me back to the moment, as he peruses my knees and explores my thighs under the table. Camila sends me a subtle wink of approval.

"You're so *caliente*," proclaims Reinaldo as I impishly accept a puff on his cigar. As he pays his compliment, I nearly gag on the smoke and cough so hard I'm forced to suck down a glass of rum. Camila's face goes from approval to incredulous head shake.

Her protégé is a jockey who can barely stay in the saddle.

A shivering male dancer is acting the *guaguancó* of sexual games between man and woman—seduction, surrender, and then rejection—and the cycle repeats again and again with different partners. Drumming seizes the crowd. It's a frenzied orgy of models and performers and saints and *orishas*. The final costumes are on display as models make a last turn down the runway. Modesta is clearly the most sensual in her saffron ruffled dress, and few in the audience can keep their eyes off the perfection of her face. Then she sets her sights on our table, first at me and, moments later, with a haughty smile and as the lights go down, on my new boyfriend, Reinaldo. As the dancers and models make their way through the crowd, sugaring up to the foreigners, the Cuban brass looking on approvingly despite the crackdown, I find a face between Reinaldo's and mine. It's Modesta, and she's practically straddling my *yuma*, delivering her own deadly version of The Look from atop his lap.

It's only when Camila signals for her to leave that Modesta moves on to a neighboring table. But not before a parting shot in Camila's ear.

"Tell her to stay away from Rafael," she warns. "Or *la jinetera norteamericana* has had her last *yuma*."

La jinetera norteamericana finds herself on her side, on the floor of a bedroom in a private house, a *casa particular,* while Reinaldo slams into her hard, and an acrid smell emanates from the stink of hundred-year-old tiles, propane in rusted pipes, chloroform in hyper decay. My revulsion is propelled by each thrust, and as he gets deeper, I realize we're experiencing messianic sex. Doomsday is all but guaranteed as I finger his tattoo of Christ on a cross and, as if in didactic response, he flips me on my stomach. There are apertures he's found that I hadn't known existed for sexual pleasure, and as he explores orifice after orifice, digging and pushing and consuming me whole, upon reaching his untrammeled goal, Reinaldo screams the name of his savior, and the louder he petitions the stronger his devotion, and on the floor his disciple is wishing for a prophetic end to all the madness.

When it's over, Reinaldo showers alone. I hear chanting from under the rush of water, and so I press my ear to the bathroom door in time to hear him plead forgiveness, and when he emerges, he's swathed in white clean towels and it's in this purity that he asks me to join him on his knees beside the bed of unholiness, to beg for enlightenment, and while I suffer his platitudes, I find my own prayer. One that enables me to survive, to find my father, and restore my faith.

SUNRISE, AND I still can't sleep, though Reinaldo has hardly stirred all night.

I sneak out of his room and join the fishermen on the rocks, hoping the morning's first heat will cool my nerves.

Somewhere in the distance, I later learn, shots rang out, and the bodies of three cocoa-skinned men crumple before a firing squad. Days before, they'd been convicted of hijacking a ferry, of trying to escape.

36

The neoclassical, nineteenth-century mansion sits behind royal palm trees and purple jacaranda in ritzy Cubanacán, near the former Havana Country Club. Andalusian tiles in blue and orange carpet the floors. Sunlight and salty air dance through the open shutters leading to a courtyard filled with hummingbirds and rare Cuban parrots.

Camila is inspecting each room and planning décor in excited stream of consciousness, her feet not once touching the ground. But her happiness would soon be supplanted.

The home is a gift from Ignacio, whose company has leased it indefinitely. Foreigners aren't allowed to own property in Havana, and Cubans who own their homes aren't allowed to sell them, either, although technically they may swap properties with other Cubans, a transaction that usually includes an illegal exchange of cash. I'm impressed with Camila's gift. Ignacio's permission to lease long-term demonstrates the massive investment he's making in the country.

Camila explains that her family will keep their Vedado apartment, but when Ignacio is in town, she'll live in the mansion with him. When he's gone, Camila will be in charge of looking after the house, and may live there as she pleases, although the home won't be remodeled and ready for months, long after my return to the U.S. I'm free, in fact, to leave in just fourteen weeks.

Camila confers with a gardener about the landscape plans and turns to me. "So what did Reinaldo leave you?"

"Pens," I say with a pout.

"Pens?"

"And hotel soap. Four bars."

She laughs. "He's coming back in two weeks. Don't worry, he's probably just testing to see if you'll be around when he returns. He wants to think he's in love. Have you been convincing?"

I shrug. My sexuality, I've realized, has become about the playing of roles. When I'm successful, and my *yuma* is happy, I experience an unanticipated surge of pride in my work. Foretelling the divine role required to please my *yuma,* without him having to explicate his desires, is the raison d'être of a *jinetera,* and the precise distinction between us and prostitutes. My playing the bad girl tempting the virtuous Reinaldo, as I did last night, as he expected of me, only proved my ability to intuit his fantasy. When I think of sex back home, I sense it's hardly different. Didn't my few boyfriends in the U.S. expect me to play a role as well? The one I projected in daily life, that of a somewhat wholesome Southern daughter, preppily dressed and attractive but not overly intimidating? This revelation emboldens me in my *jineteando,* as I realize there's an art to sexuality for any reason, for pay or pleasure or both.

"How's the sex," asks Camila, "with Reinaldo?"

"He's, um, very exploratory," I say, wincing. "I could barely walk yesterday. And he's got a Jesus thing going."

"What luck, *chica.* Religious types are the most fun. They let loose and get crazy during sex, the forbidden fruit, knowing they'll have to repent afterwards," she says with an incorrigible gleam. "Listen to Camila on this one, okay? It's all about binge sinning."

I'm not as enthusiastic about guilt, but there's no time to counter, as construction workers deliver Sheetrock and plaster through a back door. Like most materials, these have been stolen from government factories and stores and sold on the sly. Thievery is widespread in Havana, and I'm convinced by the rampant justifications of its practitioners that many are not happy with having to steal to get what they need.

"Are you going to marry Ignacio?" I ask Camila when the workers leave.

"He is already."

"He's married?"

She smiles as I flop down on a chair, dying from the humidity. "His wife's family backed his oil ventures and are still owners in his company. If they divorce, the company would have to be sold. He and his wife are not romantic, they have an arrangement." She gingerly wipes hair from my brow. "I'm sure I'm not the only cinnamon in Ignacio's chocolate."

"Doesn't that bother you?" But I know her answer will be the same as that of the workers when attempting to justify their stolen goods. It's not the preferable way to live, but basic needs are met *a lo cubano,* as Cubans are shockingly clever at skirting penury and quixotic rules.

"Ignacio and Reinaldo will be living in Havana on and off for the next few years," Camila announces.

"You think I've a chance with Reinaldo?" I ask Camila.

"No pressure, but if you can hook him, he's a gift from Oshún. You wouldn't have to worry about resolving your situation."

Being able to look for my father full-time would be a dream come true. Earlier this morning, Victor had stopped by my landlord's home to tell me he was closing in on an address where my mother went to visit José Antonio. It's the same promise he's been feeding me for months, and I'm feeling distraught, as if waiting for my own Godot. But no one seems to have any advice except to engage in the national pastime: hanging out. Waiting to wait. Waiting for nothing and waiting for everything.

Camila's tears interrupt my thoughts. " 'Mila, what's wrong?"

"*Cariña,* I don't know." She wipes away the dampness and attempts a smile. "It's just that I'm overwhelmed. Thirty-three years old and I have it all. Everything I wanted I worked hard for, and now I have it. Look at this place! It's amazing!" The house is beautiful, but nearly unlivable by Western standards, with ceilings caving in, and paint five decades untouched. But I know that she means she has it all—all that's attainable for a Cuban.

"What else is there to do?" she says. "I've got the career, the men . . ."

"Babies?" I suggest, yawning from the heat.

She looks at me a long while and bursts into a fresh round of tears. "Impossible," she says, patting her stomach. "All the doctors say so." It will take Camila many more weeks before she confides in me about the brutal incident with a *yuma* during her teen years, one that left her scarred and incapable of bearing children.

Knowing the society's emphasis on motherhood—the highest attainment of femininity—I'm sad for Camila for the first time ever.

• • •

IN THE AFTERNOON, I send off my monthly e-mail to my friends. I'm crushed to learn that one is engaged to be married, and I've yet to meet her fiancé. I also try not to feel sorry for myself when I learn that my brainy best friend, Susie, has aced her foreign-service exam, and will be leaving Washington soon for her first assignment in Ghana.

My inbox is bare of any e-mails from my father in Washington. My anger has softened some, and part of me still hopes he will change his mind, and offer help.

To avoid thinking about my other life in the U.S., and convinced my mind is melting in the sun, I use my student *carnet* to gain access to the university library.

There's no air-conditioning, but I find a stillness in the small spaces and stacks of books. I read about pre-revolutionary Cuba and the words of José Martí, scouring his verses for insight into the Cuban soul. In all my travels, I've never encountered a formerly colonial people with such a sense of entitlement and pride. It makes me love being Cuban. But only in reading the poems of the turn-of-the-century writer and statesman do I begin to glimpse the profound sense of history my people possess. And their perennial struggle to be free.

FIRST-RUN MOVIES ARE snatched off satellite, rapidly subtitled, and shown on Cuban TV free of charge to some 11 million citizens. Hollywood filmmakers have no recourse. It's one of the few benefits of being quarantined by Uncle Sam.

Camila and I are in the middle of *The Quiet American* when she shuts off the sound, her eyes refulgent and wide.

"There aren't any *jineteras* in your country, are there?"

I'm taken aback by her question. "Well, there are mistresses."

"Tell me about mistresses," says Camila, her attention rapt.

"Mistresses are like permanent girlfriends, usually to married men, and the men put them up in apartments or pay their expenses or buy gifts."

"Do these women play *una estafa*"—a swindle—"like *jineteras*?"

Camila is sensitive about the subject, so I try to frame my answers diplomatically. "Some women will only marry men who are rich, whether or not they love them. So yes, I guess if you're American and you'd only marry, say, a rich finance guy in New York, or a successful movie guy in Hollywood, then that's pretty much just like a *jinetera*."

"Are there any differences?"

I think about it for a moment. "If you lived in almost any other country," I say, "with your brains and your looks and work ethic—"

"And my education."

"Precisely, being a doctor. A surgeon. Well, you'd have been able to buy yourself this house without ever having to sleep with anyone you don't fancy. You'd have a choice. You could be a mistress or not, but there'd be a hundred different ways to afford what you need or want. You wouldn't have to fuck any old geezers for it. Unless that's your thing, of course."

Camila bursts out laughing. "It's not like here, is it." She thinks a minute more. "So the girls who *jinetean* in your country, they can't respect themselves so much."

"How do you mean?"

"If you have an opportunity to make your own *fula,* why would you rely on someone else to do it for you? Why not just do it yourself and find a man who you really love?"

I nod, and Camila thinks for a moment. "Ignacio said something that bothers me. He said we Cubans don't understand that our government does everything to keep the American embargo in place, as a way to control us. Ignacio said this like I was stupid!"

"What did you tell him?"

"Nothing, *mi vida*. He needs to feel important and all-knowing. But it really irritates me when *extranjeros* think we don't understand our own situation."

As always, when it comes to politics, I don't say much, as my *de afuera* views are generally dismissed. But Camila takes my noncommittal nod to mean I'm hiding information.

"That settles it," says Camila, standing up. "I'm going to leave Cuba." I stare at her a moment, in shock. "*Mi corazón!* Not permanently. I'm just ready to visit another country. Knowing you makes me understand less about how things work out there, and I need to go see for myself, to connect the dots."

It's only the most educated and politically suave Cubans who are allowed to travel abroad temporarily, and it sometimes takes years of planning, but I know Camila will pull it off somehow.

When Camila asks me what I miss most about my country and my former life, I can't even think about Aunt June, or John, or my friends whose e-mails are a highlight of my days. I open that window only a crack and let myself feel the breeze of mourning for small things. A spoon's first tap on a crème brûlée, the inky stain on fingertips from reading the *International Herald Tribune,* and Chesterfield Lights, my irregular and sneaky habit. Even though I've been incredibly fortunate to be taken in by Cuban strangers, and they've become my family, I miss more than anything the people in my life who know my history and my past, and to whom I don't have to explain myself. I also miss having a date. A normal dinner out with a regular, semi-nerdy college boy my own age. One who'd laugh if I ever conjured up a bêtise such as The Look.

37

A miserly pall has been cast over the streets of Havana. The police force has seemingly tripled overnight. Under the new uniforms are farm boys freshly shipped in from the Oriente, the nation's eastern region, and put on counter-*jineterismo* patrol.

My Cuban friends just shrug and say they'll deal with the springtime crackdown. I've no energy to worry about *guajiro* cops, because it's Walrus who tirelessly follows, if not anticipates, my every destination. Many times, having thought I'd shaken my perennial tail, I round a corner and there he is, like a puppy, waiting anxiously and smoking a *puro*. Everyone advises me not to speak to him, for fear of further inflaming his dubious interest in my Havana wanderings. But today, I'm feeling brash and wanting to visit my childhood home without Walrus on my tail.

"*La princesa*," he says, standing up from the perch he's taken up across from my home.

"Why are you following me?"

He laughs a long while. Only *extranjeros* get to the point so quickly, without first developing a rhythm of conversation.

"Should I be following you?" he asks, puffing on a *puro*.

"Am I in trouble with the authorities?"

"*Tranquilo.* If you were in trouble with the authorities you wouldn't have to ask that question."

"So what are you doing then?"

He jiggles a sweaty arm over my shoulder. "Let's just say, *princesa*, there are people out there who want to know how you're faring. Let's just say it's protocol, following certain *extranjeras*. Special *extranjeras*."

Nodding at the horizon, I think for a few moments before looking Walrus square in the face. He's sweating from his pate, and his skin is acne-scarred and reddish. I can't help but feel sorry for him.

"May I ask a favor?"

He shrugs.

"Take the rest of the day off. There's somewhere I need to be."

He laughs. "Nice try, *princesa.*"

RAFAEL'S 1956 BEL Air Chevy in brush-painted green motors up to my landlady's door, and the driver lays on the baritone horn. Rafael's Chevy is further proof of his *jineterismo* plundering, as few Cubans can afford the luxury of car ownership. A good portion of the rural population, in fact, has never even ridden inside one.

Instead, most wait in long lines for packed buses, known as *guaguas,* or are forced to ride camels, the two-humped train cars lugged by flatbed trucks. In the stuffy, crammed containers the riders suffer pickpockets and roaming hands on body parts. The joke is that a ride on camels, known as *camellos,* is like an R-rated movie: there's swearing, sex, and crime.

Rafael toots the Chevy again and kills the engine. It's early morning. My mother's diaries are out, and I'm conferring with the map that hangs above my modest desk. Little red stars are drawn over the places I know for certain: the U.S. Interests Section, where John worked, and the hospital in Centro, where I was born. The third star is scrawled tentatively over the home in Miramar, one that Victor believes I lived in while young, and where I'm afraid to visit in case Walrus, my perpetual companion, follows me there and links my Cuban family to me or my illicit nighttime dealings.

It seems a futile effort, staring at this map. Victor had sworn just yesterday he would have my father's address locked up by April, now a mere few days away. But I am losing faith.

A sweet redolence fills the room, and I feel a rush of energy in the staccato of his footsteps on the stairs. Rafael wears khakis and a ribbed white tank top that shows off his massive shoulders and arms. Arms I could easily climb into for safety. He hands me a potted plant blooming with pink flowers.

"There are seven hundred varieties of orchid in Cuba," he says. "This one's special."

"How so?" I say, unable to meet his eyes. What I love about Cuban men—as opposed to many back home—is that both flowers and dancing are considered to be macho interests as well as feminine.

"It blooms for only one day. And today," Rafael says, "today is that day."

I touch the tender leaves and breathe in the fruity scent.

"One day," he repeats.

"That's a short bloom," I say coolly, too shy to meet his stare. Rafael takes my hands and pulls me out of the chair.

"One day together," he says. "*Muchacha.*" Rafael's is the rare kind of charm that provokes envy and frustration in many who know him, or who want from him, and it's his entitlement that makes me reluctant to give in. I shake my head.

"I've got work to do—" I motion to the map.

Rafael says Camila has phoned him and told him about Walrus, and how I'm afraid to visit my family home in the event he follows me there. I can tell when he says this that he thinks I'm being ridiculously paranoid.

" '*Ño,*" he says. "We'll go to your house together. I've a plan to lose the G-2 *caballero.*" His scheme to outwit Walrus sounds feasible, and so I relent, grateful for Rafael's help.

As we leave, my landlady, under her yellow, sallow skin of depression, shoots me a smirk, one that suggests my handsome suitor is more interested in my passport than my heart. She reminds me in a stern voice that there are no visitors allowed.

EAST OF HAVANA lie long stretches of *playa* and tourist hotels, and further still, empty beaches, the water pristine and calm. Limited investment in Cuba has preserved much of the island's fragile ecosystems and, away from resorts and crowds, the country remains lush and heartily in bloom. Rafael stops his Chevy near a deserted section of the beach and we swim four hundred yards into the sea. My mask is leaky and fills with water, and just as I start to get nervous about the distance from shore, an oasis appears through the foggy lens. The reef is massive and shows no signs of human detection. It's as breathtaking as any tourist-magnet underwater park in the Yucatán. Yet we're the only ones diving, and it feels like a discovery worthy of Cousteau. We spend the morning chasing eel and barracuda and brilliant yellow and blue fish around pristine brain coral. Back on the beach, Rafael and I rip into mangos with our hands, chattering like the blackbirds in trees above.

Finally convinced Walrus has not followed us to the lonely outpost, I suggest we pack and head for my childhood home. I'm nervous and excited about seeing the place I lived in the first year of my life.

The home's occupants confirm what Limón discovered: no one remembers a towheaded Yankee girl and her American parents having lived there so many years ago. We make the rounds to the neighbors, all of whom invite us in for coffee or orange juice. As exhausted as we are, and even though I'm constantly looking over my shoulder, Rafael pushes me on, to every door on the street, to ask everyone and anyone what they know. In the end, it's nothing much, but I feel victorious nonetheless.

At my doorstep, Rafael leans in to kiss me, and the passion I feel is strange, and I realize it's because I'm not pretending or forcing myself to have false urges. Panicking, I wonder if I've forgotten how to have an authentic romantic experience. But I've little time to think, because his mouth lands on mine and it's no less dazzling than our first kiss in the crowded disco nearly eight months before, and as I leave him behind and return to my room and my papers and my map, my mouth on fire, I know that I've complicated my life in a way I never intended.

38

My bikini is on the hook.

I'm in the bath. It's a luxury, and I linger longer than necessary. I think about my family's house in Miramar, the flowers that wind around columns, the latticed patios and Spanish mosaic tiles. It failed to elicit memories when Rafael and I found it yesterday in the evening darkness. I'd been just a toddler when I lived there, if it had indeed been my house. What settled it, for me, was the scent. A deep breath, and the notes resonated, convincing me that somewhere in Cuba I belonged.

A smell that said home.

I step out of the bath, dry off, and grab what I think is my underwear, but there is a surprise new set of lingerie on the hook. It's a ribbed white tank and tightie-whitie briefs. Men's. Puzzled, I stick my head out the door.

"Wear it!" barks Jaap from somewhere in the darkened room. I'm nervous now. Being a *jinetera* to grateful tourists—men who wouldn't necessarily have access to young flesh or exalted passion back home—affords a certain inviolability. I may not have the material upper hand, but I have the emotional one.

Until now.

Jaap is Dutch, and in the days we've been together he's been seemingly harmless. Now he throws me to the bed, his aggression unusual, and as I'm regaining my wits, he flops next to me. He flicks on a light, grabs for me, strong, and pulls me on top, his muscled legs wrapping around my back. I look down, stunned, at a black bra fastened around his chest, its empty cups flapping sadly, and then he whispers, "Take me, you bad, bad boy," before deftly pulling his erectness from a corner of lace panties and plunging inside me, through the slit in my briefs, ordering me now to move missionary-style, my legs straight back, while I pump up and down, awkwardly, painfully in my apprehension, my unreadiness; and yet with teenage enthusiasm he howls and squeezes his nipples, and releases himself, clutching greedy handfuls of my ass, groaning with pleasure, making a man out of me. I roll off, feeling dizzy. His breath slows, and he reaches for me, asking me if I liked it like that. I figure if he wants me to act like a man, there's no need hanging around and cuddling.

While he watches, I find his wallet. Facing him, I deliberately count seven hundred Euros and stuff the bills in my new briefs. I pull on a pair of his khaki shorts and cinch the belt.

"Go ahead and keep my bikini," I say, walking out. "It'll look better on you anyway."

CAMILA COMES OUT of the operating room in scrubs, in triumph because of another successful heart bypass. The doctors and nurses are the best in the hemisphere, yet from the outside the hospital looks squalid, like a Harlem crack house. Inside, Camila signals, and goes to change.

A few blocks from the hospital, we perch on the Malecón, smoking cigarettes and basking in the sun's final rays. Across the street, the light reflects on the U.S. Interests Section, and I briefly wonder which office was John's.

I imagine my stepfather, obsessively working through sunsets, ignoring my mother, leaving scope and space in her heart for a man like the Cuban who fathered me. I wonder about José Antonio—wonder what he would look like, his laugh, his face, the *sonrisa* that touched my mother.

"You're thinking about him again!" accuses Camila, breaking the silence. "Any news?"

None, I say.

"You'll find him, don't worry! Have faith in Radio Bemba," she says. "If your father's alive, you'll meet him. And when you do, promise you won't be wearing that nutty men's outfit."

I sigh and tell her about my afternoon.

"It's dominance, silly!" she exclaims. "Don't you understand? Who has it and who doesn't is crucial in matters of sexual play. Eighty percent of men are dissatisfied with their current lover. They're embarrassed to ask for what they want, too worried about what their wives or girlfriends will think. To be a good lover, you have to let the men believe that you're talking them into what they, themselves, really want to do. Give them what they want, and don't make them feel like a *pato* or a sissy for it."

Next to Camila, I feel like a miserable fraud of a Cuban girl, my romantic instincts unrefined and my sexual tastes sophomoric.

"Suggest that your bra or your high heels might look really good on him," she says. "Or that he needs a spanking. Take your clues from his reaction."

"What, you let a guy wear your panties and he'll be faithful?"

"He'll never stray."

"Camila, why didn't you become a psychologist instead of a heart surgeon?"

She thinks a moment, then replies, "They're both the same thing, *mi vida*. You open up the heart and poke around."

39

"What's the news?" I whisper.

Victor and I are hiding in darkened shadows and heavy drapes to the right of the stage at García Lorca Theater. Built in 1837, the theater was once considered the world's most astonishing. Now it's held together with netting and wire.

It's opening night for the National Ballet's rendition of *Don Quixote*, and all two thousand seats under the dome and grand chandelier are filled to capacity. In attendance are janitors and dignitaries and government *jefes*. Tickets, for locals, sell at a proletarian ten pesos, about forty cents.

In Cuba, ballet is serious business. Under the revolution, the National Ballet has become world-renowned, its only dark cloud the consistent defection of its dancers on world tours. *Don Quixote,* as are most of the prominent ballets, was choreographed by Alicia Alonso, the legendary and nearly blind octogenarian dance great. She's melded Cuban moves—a collision of African and Spanish dance rhythms—with classical training perfected by the French and Russians.

Despite the dancers' undisputed brilliance, this close to the stage I make out snags and runs in ballerinas' tights, their pink shoes stained dark from wear.

"It's the crackdown," says Victor, shaking his head. "It's becoming too dangerous to access your files."

Because of the crowd, and his coworkers who comprise it, I'm surprised Victor has chosen this venue to meet. But he assures me the razzle-dazzle of an Alicia Alonso effort is perfect cover.

"How dangerous," I inquire, "is retrieving those files?" I'm wondering if Victor's recalcitrance is a way to procure future graft, or whether the secrets of a U.S. State Department family from two decades before are truly under heavy guard.

As Don Quixote slays dragons onstage, Victor answers rapidly. "Everyone is suspicious of everyone. Divisions are reorganizing, department heads changing. I'm having trouble not arousing attention."

"Is it money?"

He nods, and I sigh. It's always money, and while the dancers pirouette in my peripheral vision, I lament that my own knight-errantry is becoming so costly. I hand Victor half the Euros from yesterday's caustic encounter with the cross-dressing Dutchman.

"This will open more doors," Victors says, folding the bills into his jacket. "When I phone you next time, don't call me back. Just know a message from me means we'll meet the next day at four P.M. in the courtyard of the university, on the bench by the tank. I will have your address."

"I'm so frustrated, Victor, I can't imagine why this takes so long."

"At four P.M., by the tank."

"How do people live like this, all this waiting?"

"The tank at the square. Remember that, *compañera*. You must promise you will not try to contact me," says Victor, wiping his brow.

I nod, but he makes me swear, saying his livelihood is on the line.

"Two weeks, *mi vida*. Just give me two weeks, and we'll know where José Antonio lived," he says, gently kissing my hand. He quickly exits, and I see him a few minutes later, in the balcony, taking a seat next to his wife and daughters.

For a few moments, I watch the ballerinas and their rendition of *Don Quixote,* and after a while my mind wonders to Walrus, who is undoubtedly waiting outside, and then I start to wonder if I, too, am tilting at windmills.

40

My mother stood naked in front of the three-quarter-length mirror. Her reflection was partially obscured, as most Cuban mirrors are faded from age, the coppery matter underneath peeping through instead. She turned to view her body's blooming profile and stare at a new roundness.

It meant trouble, for sure, but she vowed to put feelings of guilt and regret on hold. Thinking that way, lectured the doctor, wouldn't be good for the baby.

The baby.

She could barely contain her glee at mouthing those words, over and over, until she finally dressed and met John downstairs at the breakfast table. The house was bustling with gardeners and maids—the employees bestowed upon diplomats—and so she announced the news right there, to all of them, believing that in their presence John would opt for a reaction that would fall in line with his persona, one crafted to be career-advancement suitable. Calm, confident, and with all the emotional tremor of a flat line.

But that morning John broke the mold. Hugging his wife, with rare tears in his eyes, he ordered champagne to be iced, at seven-thirty in the morning, if only there was sparkling wine to be found in that Soviet-run city circa 1978. My mother searched John's eyes for signs of cruelty, or at least irony, and, seeing none, realized John believed himself to have been capable of having children all along. That somehow he'd willed himself fertile.

But the excitement of impending fatherhood wore off quickly. After a few weeks, John again turned to a favored solace. His work. My mother was set adrift and left to deal with her pregnancy alone.

Not entirely alone.

The revolution had made a eunuch of the Catholic Church. Guilt about sex, extramarital or not, and its consequences, was eradicated along with the religion's power. So it was no surprise that when my mother announced the news to José Antonio, he was nothing but thrilled.

"Is it mine?" he asked, his eyes shiny and hopeful.

"Honestly, I don't know," she replied.

"No importa." Not important. "It's part of you, and so I'll love it." And then he'd demonstrate yet again his affections for my mother. José Antonio continued doing so until just before she gave birth to a seven-pound baby girl in December 1978. Nearly a year after they'd begun their affair.

My mother had never known such happiness. The regret and guilt she'd promised to confront was pushed further down the pike, though she was aware of its existence. Like any bad debt, it was racking up high interest, and capitalizing.

As I grew, she became more brazen about her extramarital activities. Phrases like "going for a long walk" or "I'll be at the market this afternoon" thinly disguised her time with José Antonio. Part of her hoped John would tackle her in the driveway and demand she return to him, return to *them.* But he never did. He let her walk out of the house with me in her arms and come home late in the day, each and every day, for nearly another year, saying nothing of my mother's behavior.

Saying nothing.

41

Friday power lunch at The Grill, in one of the booths near the entrance, is the Hollywood equivalent of Saturday dinner, back of the room, at Havana's El Aljibe.

Green tablecloths flutter in the breeze under the palm-thatched, open-air eatery. Recorded *son* from Compay Segundo booms over speakers, and waiters command the affairs of the room in tuxedoed splendor.

Drivers zoom up a ramp to the maître d' station and drop their passengers. A *cubana* with smarts has intentionally chosen a seat on the right side of the car, so that her practiced exit—in usual painted-on attire—is a choreographed effort in lissomness, as she's aware her maneuverings are being witnessed over chicken à l'orange by every patron in the scrutinizing room.

Tables are scrummed together, and bodies in close proximity are electrified. Camila and Ignacio hold court in a coveted corner. Reinaldo and I exchange greetings with the couple and settle in. My friend wears a silk sheath in baby blue, and I'm in a pink spaghetti-strap tank and jeans. Reinaldo's cross-and-savior tattoo peeps through a vintage rayon Hawaiian shirt.

I'm genuinely happy to see Reinaldo, who returned the day before, and just two weeks after our date at the Tropicana. Today, I'm optimistic about my chance to snare him long-term, and find myself relaxing in his presence.

My mother wrote in her diaries about having dined at El Aljibe with John. In the days before her furtive affair began, she'd often see José Antonio here, and they'd share a conspiratorial smile at the great fortune of having met, unexpectedly, yet another time. I look around the restaurant, wondering where they sat, and what they were wearing. Did José Antonio raise his glass in toast to her from across the tables? Did a humid breeze swirl around them, generating the kind of voltage palpable here right now?

But I don't have time to contemplate the past, because I'm captivated by the present. A quick study tells me this is no ordinary restaurant, and I count three types of social arrangements prevailing at El Aljibe.

First and predominantly are aged and potbellied foreigners with *cubanas* in their teens and twenties, ranging in shades of skin from bitter mocha to the Madagascar orchid that produces vanilla. The generation gap may prove thrilling in bed, but the permanent silence between most couples says it doesn't transcend into conversational efforts.

Several tables are filled with the second type: the wealthy and connected of enigmatic residency—diplomats and syndics and bureaucratic sycophants.

And the third type are emigrants who've returned home to shower their relatives with gifts and, in doing so, prove their foreign successes. These prodigal sons pick up the tab for ten or twelve with the affected casualness of one sporting a Red Sox cap at Yankee Stadium. Their families pretend in equal measure; pretend not knowing that in order to pay the bill themselves, they'd have to save one peso a day, every day, for twenty-eight years.

But it's the demimondaines with their foreign boyfriends that most fascinate. Nature cannot explain these couples, though the bottles on the table will. At El Aljibe, when a bottle of wine or imported scotch is emptied, it's not removed by waiters but, rather, left on the table as evidence of a diner's wealth. In Hollywood, power lunch can be full of quiet anxiety in surmising the liaisons formed at other tables. In Havana, *cubanas* and foreigners, too, scan the room, their eyes lingering on tables sporting the most beautiful women and the most expensive spirits. Narrowed eyes wonder: Is my girlfriend as beautiful as that foreigner's? Is my *yuma* as rich as hers? And thus the social scale is weighted and adjusted by everyone in the room. Malcontent is either buried or born.

Camila pours another glass of the Condado de Haza 2001 Ribera del Duero. Our table is littered with the $55 bottles. Camila whispers in my ear to stop looking around and pay attention to Reinaldo. I reach over, halfheartedly, and pat Reinaldo's knee, but I miscalculate and smack his crotch instead. Reinaldo winces and Camila slinks into her chair.

It's no wonder he's sensitive. Upon Reinaldo's return to Havana the previous night, we've had eight bouts of intercourse, though I use the term loosely, and he's been threatening all evening that we'll be "making love" yet again before we sleep. This isn't your mother's sex. This isn't married-for-five-years sex, either. This is girl-on-top, thrash and wreathe and glissade—but no screaming, as Camila says it's juvenile—while he lies on his back, hands clasped behind his neck, Christ tattoo bared, eyes rolling back in anticipation of his little death and the attendant resurrection. In the perversity of my recital, I feel pleasure myself and tell him he's the greatest, the absolute best ever, that mine, too, is a rapturous release and may we thank the heavens together for our reunion. This is performance-art sex. This is *jinetera* sex. This is how a *cubana* is supposed to fuck.

If you read the brochures.

"IT'S LIKE COLONIALISM all over again," Camila had said on the phone after my marathon with Reinaldo. "Except this Spaniard is conquering Cuba one *chiquita* at a time."

Whenever I study a new language, I first must relearn the rules of my native English. In fact, it's only when studying another tongue that I've come to understand the fundamentals of my own. And so it's in learning to reside in Cuba, this conglomerate of socialism and dictatorship, that I grasp what it truly means to have lived under the banner of capitalism. I left America for the construct of Cuban Communism and found myself in the most materialistic, possession-obsessed land in the hemisphere, and the scene at El Aljibe astounds me.

As I'm thinking of Havana, my city that dangles off the Tropic of Cancer, I stare at the vulgar display at our table and notice the whole room is fixated on our four chairs. On Camila and her date and Reinaldo and me. But somewhere, I sense a dangerous set of eyes probing me, and with the practiced affections of a *jinetera* (mouth slightly parted and chin held high), I turn casually to the left, and then to the right. But I smell her before I see her. Nose the scent of Jean-Paul Gaultier on the woman he adorns: Modesta.

Modesta is known as *la superturistica,* as she's notorious for her many foreign lovers, and Camila had warned me to stay far from her.

Instinctively, I crouch as she nears.

Modesta comes replete with her own lore—one that serves to intimidate me even further. Like many girls whose dinner plates were empty each night during the *periodo especial* in the mid-1990s, Modesta headed to the beach resorts to join those selling themselves nightly to tourists. Bartering their flanks for a string of beads.

Modesta was arrested at fifteen after having solicited an undercover cop in the heavily guarded tourist fortress of Varadero, a miles-long strip of sand and all-inclusive hotels. Modesta spent four months in a women's reeducation camp outside Havana before crafting her escape.

Reeducation camps for prostitutes and *jineteras* are whispered about in the Havana underground. Cuba certainly doesn't have a monopoly on punishing sexually active teenagers. When I hear of the reeducation camps, I'm reminded of the nun-administered, hard-labor camps in twentieth-century Ireland, for pregnant and promiscuous teen girls. Punishment of a young woman's sexuality is common throughout histories and across international borders, and yet, somehow, Cuba's publicizing its young beauties as a tourist attraction counters its harsh way of dealing with those suspected of delivering the goods.

The story goes that at around four in the afternoon, when the girls were ending their punishing day of cutting sugar cane, Modesta stripped herself of the prison uniform, rolled her body in mud, and slithered her way through damp fields. She was barefoot, as prisoners weren't allowed shoes, to reduce their chances of escape through the harsh, rural landscape.

When dawn broke, she'd progressed to a Havana suburb, her feet raw, the mud—dried, and hardened, and then cracked—flaking off like pieces of a jigsaw puzzle.

People watched in shock as the nude girl, with bloodied feet and curves worthy of a verse by José Marti, made her way down the streets as if on a directive from the saints themselves. Likely, a few dozen people viewed the spectacle, but, in the years after the incident, it became seminal. The sworn witnesses grew to a couple hundred, then several hundred, then thousands—the Cuban Woodstock. It seems nearly every male in Havana, when asked, will take off his cap, place it on his heart, and stare into the horizon, whispering the name of Modesta, the *jinetera* who walked into Havana that day the same way she came into the world.

It's her mythical status that frightens me most. I want to hide, I want to keep my nose to the ground and sniff the trail of my father without interference. Judging from the expression on Camila's face as Modesta approaches, I know my wish won't be granted. I look up. Neither Modesta's eyes nor mouth are smiling, and hatred courses through the air. Modesta leads the *jinete*. Modesta is an expert marksman with a lance and bow.

"Stay away from Rafael," she whispers in my ear, "*jinetera norteamericana.*"

IN CUBA, THE cockroaches are big enough to saddle and ride.

I'm watching one of Germanic strain skirr across the hardwood floor in the mansion home of our host, an oversized man in a cream suit and hat who's taking his stylistic cues from Havana's 1950s gangsters.

Borrowing also the thug mentality, he has transformed his rooms into hourly rentals used by some of the loveliest *jineteras,* all of whom will cut him in on the action.

It's the first time in my nine months in Cuba I've seen anything like it, like a brothel. Before the revolution, brothels were rumored to number in the hundreds. But those houses of ill repute were eradicated when the new guns tramped into town in 1959.

Sex in Cuba, until the crackdown, has been anything but organized, and bordellos have been out of fashion for forty years. In a snap, the crackdown changes this—maybe for a day, maybe for longer. It's ironic that the policed streets are less safe, subjecting women to brokerage through boyfriends and pimps. In a society desperate for money, and an ingenious population hell-bent on surviving, it's no surprise.

When a car's radiator cracks, a real Cuban knows to pour table pepper down the pipe. Pepper withstands heat. It settles into the fissures, melding the damage together until the next crack appears.

Whatever happens, Cubans find a way.

· · ·

WHEN I WAKE up on the couch a while later, Reinaldo's fellow oil big shots are laughing over Cuba libres and lines of cocaine. Our host fingers the pharmaceutical-quality powder and places it inside his eyelid.

There's a Dutchman at my side, or maybe he's from Belgium, I can't remember, though I'm trying to keep it straight now that in the wake of the Iraq war the division of European states seems more distilled—France is good, as they refuse to join, and Spain, Reinaldo's homeland, is not. Except for Reinaldo, allies of the distant war in Iraq won't get my time or attention. Which is fine, because many Europeans have no interest in my skin tone. They want their beauties dark, with pronounced African features.

Frustrated middle-class tourists from places like Holland and Italy and England come to Cuba not just for sex, but for sex with black women, with beguiling *negritas,* to restore some idea in their minds of the way things should be, that females must be cleaning, doting, sucking, submitting, and that had colonialism not gone awry, the darker-skinned would be in their place, as their inferiors, as their toys of pleasure and capitulation.

My skin is light, and so I attract a less audacious man. Or so I thought.

When Modesta enters the room in her saffron ruffled Christian Dior dress, she stares at Reinaldo until his eyes find hers, and she discharges a devastating version of The Look. I tug at his arm and suggest we leave, but he's not listening. My chest heaves with anxiety. Camila promised that Reinaldo would be my biggest source of income, and I can't afford to lose him. To lose Reinaldo means to lose time.

But to keep him may mean losing other things, far more important.

Modesta's feet cross symmetrically in front of each other as she oozes toward my prize. Reinaldo is entranced and ignores my pleas to leave, and nothing short of physically hurtling myself between the two will break his concentration, and even when I attempt this, it comes out as an awkward maneuver, calculated and ineffective, as Modesta steps around me and behind Reinaldo and drags her long fingernails down his neck.

"You are the man I've been looking for my whole life," she whispers convincingly.

Reinaldo allows her to take his hand and lead him from the couch toward a bedroom. He stops and turns, as if not to forget me.

"Come, Alysia," he says, his face drunk on greed, and when I shake my head instinctively, in horror, he comes back for me, taking both my hands and insisting: "You're going to love this."

The bedroom is full of luscious antiques propped up with plywood. Modesta wastes no time. Melodious inch by melodious inch, her dress is stripped off her exquisite shoulders and down to her waist, and when I turn to leave, Reinaldo grabs my arm.

"Your turn," he says, indicating I, too, am to undress.

Modesta is triumphant. I cringe and curse silently, considering my few options. I'm a bull in the ring with a star matador. I stand no chance, and when I look at Reinaldo I consider his lack of munificence with me, and wonder if he's worth it, worth this.

"So he's not buying you things," Camila had mused earlier that day. She was in front of the mirror, trying on the lacy Prada underwear Ignacio brought from Europe. The bra's cups were too loose, and Camila smirked, making a crack about Ignacio's optimistic nature. "Well, you can't complain to him."

"We've had sex nearly twenty-two times, and the only thing he gave me was a hickey," I complain, pulling back my shirt and displaying my gift. "So don't tell me I can't whine."

"Directly," she clarifies. "*Mi corazón,* you can't complain *directly.* Men want to believe certain things about themselves," she says, sitting me down. "They want to believe they're powerful and attractive and generous. Especially generous."

It dawns on me what she's getting at. "You want me to tell him I think he's generous, don't you?" I say, exasperated.

She lightly pulls my chin. "Tell him he's the most generous man you've ever encountered. Tell him you're *so* happy he's generous because you despise a stingy man, and are glad he is anything but."

"He'll know I'm lying!" I protested. "I can't say that with a straight face. He's cheaper than Jack Benny."

My obscure reference does little to derail her advice. "Just tell him. You can get anything from him if you employ this little trick, *te lo prometo.*"

In this brothel, Modesta's calculations register on her face, and the skilled matador signals with a wave of her red *muleta* that she's just one move away from driving the knife into my skull.

Modesta believes I'm going to chicken out and exit this room, leaving her with the spoils. Myself unsure, I think about how I've not yet employed Camila's tactic on Reinaldo. Reinaldo, indeed, may be a prince under his frog skin of stinginess, and I want a chance to find out. I think of my mother, of the risk she took to be with José Antonio those many years ago. Then I send a telegram heavenward for an appetizer-sized portion of the strength she held.

My dress goes down. There's little charm to my move, but my breasts are now bare, and Modesta, licking her chops, begins to lower her dress around carved hips. Her long fingers slink down Reinaldo.

My dress, too, falls to the floor, though with considerably less charm. Determined, my lips find Reinaldo's neck, and when Modesta whips off his belt, I move for the buttons on his shirt, and then she has his pants around his ankles and her mouth and hands begin their trained maneuverings. Reinaldo grabs at her hair like it's the reins on a thoroughbred and moans in pleasure, and not to be outdone, I find his mouth, but he wants to keep it free so he may broadcast his delight with Modesta's craftsmanship. He motions for her to move, and then my mouth finds him, but the pressure drops steadily and, despite my ebullience, my boyfriend can take no excitement in my ministrations. I'm thrust aside.

Modesta slays the bull.

In triumph, she pushes Reinaldo on the bed and, sliding over him, her arms thrown skyward, she jockeys like an Olympic equestrian, pausing only to sidekick my dress into the hallway. I close the door on them all— on Reinaldo and his tattooed Christ and his Mary Magdalene—and wonder if I'd only employed a twist on Camila's tactic and told Reinaldo he was a monogamous man, and I was so glad he was a one-woman kind of man, the only kind I admire, I wonder that maybe if I'd said that, I'd be able to hold on to his affections.

I'm bawling at Camila's house—humiliation more than hurt—and the neighbors chatter excitedly about my losses, about my miscalculations, about the extraordinary lack of talent possessed by this girl, this unlucky one, this *norteamericana* looking for her father, and how it's *una pena* that I'm from the land of great cars and great freedoms but very, very bad sex.

42

*A*s I'm traipsing back from the auto mechanic's with my collection of high heels, a teenager greets me with a *bonjour*. Absently, I return a salutation in French. Then I realize it's the third time this week I've come across a Cuban Francophone.

At home, I dump my stilettos on the bed and inspect them. The auto mechanic had melded the slick soles with spare bits of tire. I'd done so at Limón's insistence, as I'm constantly tumbling from my artificial heights. My knees and elbows are banged and bruised, and the neighbors refer to me as *la yanqui que no puede caminar en sus zapatos*. The Yankee who can't walk in her shoes.

In my neighborhood, I'm rarely referred to by my first name. It's always the Yankee who can't find her father, the Yankee who can't go home, the Yankee who can't carve a chicken, the Yankee who can't *chupa* a tourist's *pinga*.

When I hear French being spoken again a week later, this time by grownups in the park playing hopscotch, I'm too shy to inquire. I remember my mother having written that in Havana, nothing is ever as it seems. I leave it at that.

Days later, I'm watching two small boys dressed in the blue shades of the ocean goddess Yemayá. They're peering into a neighbor's house where a TV is blaring, and the two are singing French phrases in unison. Unable to stand the mystery any longer, I ask them about it. The boys look at me as if I'm the stupidest foreigner in Havana—a common reaction—and point to the TV.

French lessons, they say. The whole country is learning it this year, out of solidarity with France's abstention from the Iraq war. I think about my family and wonder if—in one of the kitchens not so far away, where chickens are being roasted and rice is being boiled—José Antonio is practicing his verbs and whiling away time until his daughter happens upon the trail of breadcrumbs leading to his home.

This is what I'm imagining. This is what sustains me. This from the Yankee who can't learn that in Havana, nothing is ever as it seems.

43

Bliss is $6 a glass at El Floridita, the famed Hemingway bar on the western tip of the pedestrian-only strip, Calle Obispo. Outside, the saloon serves as a western gateway to Old Havana, the section with skinny streets and plazas and colonial wonders under restoration by the United Nations.

Inside the bar is cool, Old World grandeur, and it's no wonder El Floridita was once on a short list of the planet's great watering holes. Bull's-blood curtains hang from the walls, as do crystal chandeliers, Arabic stars, and black-and-whites of the famous and notorious who've sashayed through its shuttered doors.

A Canadian *turista* asks if I'll pose on the lap of the Hemingway statue, a bronze figure hunched over a slab of the bar reserved just for him. Rolling my eyes, and feeling like a zoo monkey, I comply. She tips me a dollar.

It's dark and barely crowded once the Canadian cruise-shippers empty out at dinnertime. I'm sitting at the bar, my Hemingway daiquiri served in a martini glass filled with an alchemist's elixir of rum, grapefruit juice, maraschino liqueur, and lime. Once it's sucked down, all that remains is shaved ice, and it shimmers under lights like cut diamonds.

Leonel and Chico are the chief *cantineros,* and when they're not polishing the dark wood bar or slipping hard-currency *propinas* into their tuxedos, they're speaking four or five languages with the guests and each other. I've never paid for a drink at El Floridita, and I'm not allowed to tip, either, and that's been the house mandate since my first visit with Aunt June two years before. It's a wildly generous gesture from the *cantineros,* as "drinks on the house" rarely translate into Cuban. Whenever I'm in El Floridita, it seems like a modern outpost, an oasis in the *barrio,* and I've marked the place on my map as a favored sanctuary.

El Floridita's barkeeps have the snappiest job in Havana and are paid far better than engineers or lawyers. Leonel and Chico both hold PhDs in engineering, and practiced their trade for several years before being rewarded with the lusted-after slots as rum pullers. Hotel maids, tour guides, and taxi drivers are, in fact, the best-paid legal professions in the country. Many who hold them consider themselves lucky, and have typically given up previous careers in accounting, management, and dentistry.

I'm hoping Leonel and Chico are the kind of good souls I'm shortly to inherit, if I ever find my Cuban family. I'm answering the bartenders' questions about the search for my father as Richard and Daya show up for dinner. We've barely exchanged greetings when I feel a mouth brush against my ear.

"*Muchacha,*" whispers Rafael, "two million people in Havana and I'm always running into this one."

He's with two women in their early forties, probably English and certainly very drunk. They pull him away from me, out of the bar, and Daya gestures from the crowded dining room.

"Don't think you're getting out of me making dinner for you," Rafael says, walking backwards and sporting a cocky grin.

I smile despite myself and take a seat at the table. Richard and Daya avoid their usual pantomime and speak only to me—one in English and the other in Spanish.

"Dahling, please tell Daya her table manners are atrocious, and I'd like you to give a dining lesson," says Richard, leaning back in his chair.

"I'll show her at home," I say, confounded. Her table manners seem fine for a country girl suddenly thrust into a life of luxurious restaurants and nightclubs.

"Now," he instructs. "Show her now. She eats like she was born in a barn."

When I translate for Daya into Spanish, she ingests her thumb and looks away.

"Isn't that adorable," says Richard, beaming. Then he gestures toward her table setting and instructs me again to teach her properly.

"You tell him I'm not doing anything more until he gives my mother the money she wants," says Daya, her dark eyes flashing in anger.

"She says she'll be happy to learn but she's a bit tired now," I say to Richard. And then, to Daya, I ask: "Your mom is pressuring for money? I thought she was going to leave you alone about it."

"What about what I want?" asks Daya. "There's more to love than—" She picks up the lobster in butter sauce by the tail and waves it around. "Or this—" She pulls at her backless crepe dress. "If I'm going to *mamar* his *pinga* three times a day, I think he should give money for my whole family. I don't care about lobster or fancy restaurants or mojitos. *Mira*, I want him to help my mother." Now she speaks directly to Richard, loudly, as if his problem were volume and not fluency. "We need a wash machine! We need new plumbing!" Then she turns to me. "I won't eat any more twenty-five-dollar lobsters. What does he think, I can sell my shit?"

"Oh, Lord," grumbles Richard as the customers begin to stare at our threesome. "Do translate, I should know what I'm dealing with."

"Daya, you don't have to sleep with him, you'll get by without his money," I say, ignoring Richard.

"*Ay,* Alysia, *mi vida,* how many times do I have to say you will *never* understand?"

Richard pulls me back into the conversation with a tug on my forearm. "While we're on the subject of improvements," he says, "I'd like to talk about why it's I that must always initiate sex. Could I have an explanation? Also, do clarify, is it possible to have one's menstruation twenty-three straight days? Or would that require hospitalization?"

Before I can translate, Daya interrupts. "He calls my mother a vulture! Every time I say *dinero, por favor,* he says, what for, for *la tiñosa?*" Then, to Richard, she yells: "Now he calls me the little vulture. *La tiñosita, la tiñosita,* that's all I hear. It's not funny!"

A jovial Richard interrupts. "It would be more pleasant, really, if I didn't have to practically beg for my pleasures—"

"What did he say?"

"What did she say?"

But neither await my translation.

"What I want to know," says Daya, "is if he's going to marry me or not. I need to know right now." She punctuates by banging her fork and knife on the table. "I want. To go. To England."

"No, dahling, that's not exactly an improvement in holding your utensils," cracks Richard. "Now you're chucking a strop."

"ENGLAND!" shouts Daya.

"Ah, England. That's a word I understand," Richard says to me. "Tell me, do I have 'imbecile' written on my face? She doesn't want to be with me in Cuba, imagine she'll want to in England, where she's free?"

"ENGLAND!" shouts Daya again. "*Boda.*" Wedding. She hums the bridal theme.

"My wife in London wouldn't be so amused," he says, laughing.

I relay this information to Daya, wondering how on earth I found myself in this situation.

"Your *wife*?" It may be the only English word Daya understands, and her eyes flare. *Cubanos* are the most jealous folk in the world, and it's an attribute I find irritating and puerile. I've refused to include it in my own *cubanidad,* but Limón tells me I'm not truly native unless I can muster *celosía* when my love interest is threatened. Daya, however, proves her bloodline.

"He has a wife?" she asks, seething. The waiter cautiously sets down our desserts, three flans framed by whipped cream and soupy caramel sauce. Daya looks at her plate a moment and demurs.

"Tell Richard I'm ready for my table manners lesson now."

"Twenty-three straight days, imagine. Does she appear anemic to you?"

Shock cuts me off midtranslation. For Daya picks up the plate of flan, lifts it above her head, and slowly tilts the ceramic. Sauce dribbles down her face and into the crevices of her designer dress. Lifting her chin, she accepts the juices and the creaminess until the flan is all but down her throat.

My hand is on my forehead. Chico from the bar is wiping glasses and shaking his head with a smirk. Richard takes a long, cool drag of his cigarette before turning to me.

"Well, translator," he says, a slow grin spreading across his face. "Suppose you're going to tell me that this is Spanish for 'Where's my high chair?' "

44

Deep in the night, a hand covers my mouth. I wake up with a man on top of me. It's Limón, and his eyes are wild. I sit up and hit him hard, on the arm.

"C'mon," he says. "I need to crash here tonight."

"What's *wrong* with you?"

"Look, I've been busier than a one-legged man at an ass-kicking contest," says Limón, coolly reciting one of my grandfather's sayings. He lights up a hand-rolled cigarette.

"How'd you get in here?"

"I get in anywhere."

"My landlady will kill you first, then me," I say, pulling on jeans and shooting an anxious glance toward the door. "What have you been busy with anyhow?"

"They arrested my aunt," he says.

"Arrested?" I can barely speak. "*Dios mío.* For what?"

"For being a librarian," he says, his eyes flashing anger. I stare at him. She runs an independent library, with antigovernment books. I'd forgotten. What he doesn't say is that his aunt may have been paid by anti-Castro groups in the U.S. to foster rebellion.

Limón exhales out the window onto a warm breeze carrying the unmistakable scent of the world's most heady tobacco. He hooks my arm. "I was *fleteando* the streets with a *yuma,* and the police ordered us to stop. Me and the *yuma* ran like hell straight here."

"Great! Fucking great, *cabroncito,*" I say, flicking him on the head. "I'm not in this house legally, and you *know* I can't get in trouble. They kick me out of this country and I've lost my chance to find my father."

"*Ay, monita,* that's why I'm here. A woman I met near your parents' old house in Miramar called me."

"Who? What'd she say—"

"*Tranquilo, loquita,*" he says, fumbling for a scrap of paper in his pants. He reads from it. "She says she remembered a woman who might've worked in your mother's house."

I can't speak. I reach over and bear-hug Limón. Finally, some information gleaned independently of Victor. If it comes through, it's the best lead yet.

Limón continues. "Did you go there last week, with a *cubano*?" I nod, telling him about Rafael. Limón thinks a moment.

"Did the G-2 man follow?"

"Not sure," I say. "Don't think so."

"You're not coming with me," he says as I protest. "Whatever I find, I'll come right back here with it. Perhaps we shouldn't be seen together."

I feel as if I'm a perpetual teenager in Cuba, that we're all perpetual teenagers, the children of an overly strict father, one dodgy and out of touch and not sensible in his dealings. People here are forever sneaking around, forever on the sly. I'd never known what it was like to lose my freedoms, even while my parents served in other countries when I was a child. It never occurred to me what tight controls would feel like in everyday life.

Havana, a breezy city full of liveliness and music, fights the drab atmosphere the government attempts to impose on the sensuous city, as if it were Pyongyang and not a tropical port. The constant insistence that war is imminent is meant to keep Cubans in line and temper the merriment. But rather than sculpting a believable sense of danger, the affected intimidation, at least for me, comes off as Monty Python slapstick. Officials with stiff, blow-dried hair and freshly ironed fatigues walk sternly among joking, bright Cubans in sparkly cosmetics and Lycra, their eyes twinkling.

Just when I'm about to agree Limón should scout the contact alone, a middle-aged Mediterranean man in moss-colored linen pulls himself onto my windowsill and swings his long legs over the ledge and into my tiny room. Limón turns his back as the effeminate *yuma* fires up a menthol cigarette.

"You can't imagine how uncomfortable it is out there," he says, brushing imaginary fluff from his shirt. "You don't mind if I step in a bit?" He points to Limón. "He loves to keep me his big, bad, dark secret."

Limón won't meet my eyes.

"Alysia," I say, introducing myself, and kissing each cheek. "Sorry, didn't know you were out there on the ledge. How long have you . . . How long have you and Limón known each other?"

"I've been coming back to Cuba for Limón for—what, baby—two, three years now?" he says, smiling. The *yuma* is amusing and, under different circumstances, I'd say I liked him immediately. But not with the police looking for the couple.

When the door knocks, my heart sinks, like that of a young girl caught with a boy in her room, and even though I'm grateful it's just the landlady, her furious rant sends Limón and his lover seeking a quick exit. I don't want to upset Limón, as I know he's going to retrieve information about someone who'd worked for my mother.

I follow them, wanting to tell Limón it's okay, that I understand, that although he's not homosexual—or even if he is—I know what he's doing for money because I do it as well.

But he leaves the house without looking back at me once, his enamored *yuma* traipsing after him like a pet Maltese. Not even the *yuma*'s conviviality can put out the volcano that has erupted in the center of my landlady, who is tapping two fingers on her skin, a silent damnation of Limón's dark skin color, and scolding me, asking how dare I bring a *chardo* to her house. Racism is not supposed to exist in Cuba, it's alleged to have had been eradicated. But we both know the truth, that black people here, like in most places, are treated with extreme prejudice.

45

*A*t first, I thought you were a *tortillera*." A lesbian. "Because you don't wear earrings." Rafael tugs at his own naked lobes.

"A lesbian," I say, shaking my head. "Four-inch heels, tight dresses, gold chains all over, and you think I look like a lesbian because my ears are bare?"

"A woman with no earrings means she loves women."

"Ridiculous macho *mierda*."

Rafael laughs. *"Eso es Cuba!"*

"Speaking of women," I say, cautiously bringing up the subject. "Your girlfriend Modesta doesn't like me much."

Rafael smirks. "She's not my girlfriend. We used to be *marinovios*," he says, using a word indicating a couple who lives together. "But she's nuts, really *loca*, has it out for all foreigners. You should stay away from her."

"Modesta said the same thing to me about you."

Before he can reply, a commotion of exclamations and whistles emits from his living room.

Under a ceiling of stars, we'd been lounging on the patio of his apartment overlooking ocean waves we can hear better than see. After several of his offers to make me dinner during past months, I've relented, and met Rafael at his home. After the first course, however, we'd been interrupted by neighbors waving a home video. The tape was shot by a Cuban professor who'd experienced a rare trip abroad, to San Francisco. Rafael had the only VHS on the block, and so they gathered in front of his TV.

But it wasn't the Golden Gate Bridge captivating the audience. It was a grocery store. They huddled over the set, transfixed like cavemen at a campfire, as the cameraman grazed the aisles of a California supermarket, scanning from top to bottom, lingering on fourteen types of mustard. Dozens of eggs, explained the mesmerized narrator, in brown and white and organized in sizes small to jumbo. Milk in several percentages of fat. Sugar in artificial and cane, raw and refined, confectioner's and superfine.

I've rarely seen so rapt an audience, and the multitudinous plenty of my country shames me. I slink back to the patio and seek out my favorite constellation, Orion's Belt, the one my mother taught me to look for whether we were in northern Africa, in Europe, or back home. It's under the same Orion's Belt, I think, that people both scramble through the day and drive their SUVs six blocks to the gym. The same Orion's Belt that shines down on my lost family.

Rafael brings us rum. "Camila says you only have three months or so before your year is up in Cuba." I nod. "How's the search for your father?"

My smile suggests all's well, but in reality I'm filled with longing, and fighting off irritation with the Cuban bureaucracy that hinders the netting of intelligence. While I wait for Victor, I imagine that each man in his midfifties walking the sidewalks could be José Antonio. Anyone who could meet his description is studied as I search faces for hints of my own features. It's driving me crazy.

"I know something about fathers," he says quietly. Rafael is wearing a black silky shirt that offsets his Galician face. He lights up a Hollywood cigarette, and the tip glows in the darkness like a firefly. "Mine, like yours, was a translator. He insisted we learn three, four languages when we were young."

"Don't you have a degree in linguistics?"

He nods. "All it's good for is hustling tourists. In the early 1990s, during the *período especial,* tourism really started up, supposedly to save the economy. Before that we hardly saw tourists. I didn't speak to a foreigner, really, until I was twelve or thirteen." He pauses and takes another drag. "You want to hear this?"

"*Dale.*"

"My father started to go crazy. There wasn't any food, and he had us four boys, all of us growing, and we were strong, real strong, even without enough food. My father went into the woods and caught *jutías* and we ate them. Rodents. Tasted awful. My father would always give us his portion, so would my mother. They were so"—he uses the Cuban symbol for "skinny," a pinky finger—"so *flaca*. He wasn't eating, and watching us boys go hungry, it played with my father's head. Started to slip, go crazy. I never told him, but I went with the tourist girls when I was thirteen. First one was an Italian, about thirty-five years old, and she took me all over, to discos and restaurants I'd never been, and you know, it's only recently that I've been old enough to think about how . . . how *extraño* it was. Me thirteen and she thirty-five . . . Well, at the end I stole all her money, and I brought a stack of Italian lira to my mother, and then I'm sure my father started to suspect, and it was all too much, he went mad. He traded the lira and bought food for us, but he wouldn't eat food bought with the lira. After a while, he just shut down, he wouldn't eat a thing at all. One day they say he walked into the ocean. He didn't swim into it, he walked and disappeared into it. He was a swimmer, a great swimmer, *mira,* he taught me to swim, and I'm a lifeguard."

He pauses and studies the sky, and I hold my breath, not wanting him to stop.

"I was in a hotel when he died. In Varadero with a tourist, I was fourteen and *singando* her brains out for money but it wasn't going to matter, because my father wouldn't eat anyway. I was happy with the women then, even though they were so old, *ya tu sabes.* I enjoyed feeling new sheets and seeing my first buffet—imagine a buffet in a time like that, *dios mío*—and not having to worry, just for a few days."

At this, he stubs out his cigarette and continues. "He didn't write a note, my father. He didn't say good-bye to my mother or us boys or anyone. He just walked into the sea, walking straight for Miami. Like if he could take one step after another he'd arrive there somehow, and there everything would be okay. When I came home from Varadero that night, I didn't sleep. None of us did. We thought maybe he'd drowned on accident, and we played out the scenarios. We couldn't believe it. It wasn't until the next night any of us could sleep. When I crawled into my bed, I felt something at my feet."

A self-conscious pause. He continues. "You're sure you want to hear this *mierda*?"

I lean and touch his forearm.

"There was this thing, there was something in my bed, at the bottom. I felt around, it was this . . ." Rafael pulls a thick, 24-karat gold chain from around his neck, one that ends in a long cross in the middle of his chest. "It was my father's—he was never without it. Never, it *never* came off. But he'd put it in my bed. Not my brothers', not my mother's, but mine. I didn't show anyone that first night, I just held it in my hand and curled around it, like it was him. I knew it would give my mother peace, some-how, to know he'd done it intentionally. But I couldn't tell her right then. I kept it a secret that night. I needed my time alone with him. My father left this to me, *m'entiendes,* his only real possession, it was like he was saying. He was saying . . . he knew what I was doing, where I'd disappear to and why, and how I'd get the money from the old women, and that it was all right, he didn't hate me for it."

The giddy neighbors erupt on the patio, still swapping exclamations of incredulity. It's nearly an hour before the rowdy crew leaves, and amid the din Rafael and I exchange secret, bittersweet glances. When we're finally alone, he motions me to follow him into his room.

"Let me show you something," he says.

Carefully, I sit on the edge of his bed. He picks up a shoebox and gently shakes off the lid. Then he hesitates and replaces it on the shelf.

"No puedo." I can't.

"Lure a girl into your bed and you won't show her the goods?" But my joking doesn't dissipate a somber mood.

"Mi corazón, promise you won't be mad." He's shy and his hands trem-ble when opening the shoebox he'd been holding moments before. Kneel-ing above his bed, Rafael gently dumps its contents onto rumpled sheets.

They fall everywhere, like angels from the sky. Sweet cherubic faces lying in a mosaic on that bed in that small apartment in that small town outside of Havana. *Girls.* His girls. The foreign women he'd romanced, banged, chiseled. *Extranjeras* who fell for *la estafa.*

Polaroids. Snapshots. Portraits. There are tacky bleached blondes in G-strings smiling seductively. Plain ladies with hopeful smiles and legs crossed at the ankles. Aging women, time having claimed their beauty.

He goes through, one by one. Naming names. A week. Ten days. A month. Italians. Canadians. Spaniards. Return visits over one year, two years, five. Cash they'd given him. Gifts and offers of marriage and escape. Undeniable and physical evidence, these photos make it impossible to wish away the past.

He looks at me expectantly but I can make no comment, wondering if I'm to reveal my own recent history and the nighttime duties I've undertaken. He must interpret my hesitation for pity, because he falls into the bed and rolls on his back, atop the photos, crushing them, and looking up at me.

"Don't ever feel sorry for a Cuban. We're smarter than the *extranjeros*. We let them believe they have the upper hand and are in control. But it's really the Cubans who are in charge."

Extranjero versus native. It's a distinction crucial to all *cubanos*, and I wonder how, in his private mind, Rafael sees me.

"Will you marry one?" I ask.

"My brothers are all here, in university and *jineteando*. We've all promised my mother we'll never leave. This is my country." He raises a fist. "I want to live in my country, *coño*." We don't speak for a few moments as Rafael meanders through the private corners of his mind. Then he pulls me into focus. "What about you? Are you going to marry one of those rich boyfriends you always seem to have?"

I'm chilly in his room, suddenly conscious that we're on the bed together.

"*Dios mío*," I say, checking my wrist. "Five in the morning."

Rafael motions me outside, onto the patio, and we sit and listen to the cacophony of birds reporting the sun's imminence. There's an uncomfortable silence between us, as I'm taking in what I've heard. He studies me with a mixture of defensiveness and vulnerability and so I go to him, settling onto his lap and curling myself into his chest. Thinking about his father and his life of *jineterismo*, I press close to his heart, as if to compress the wound. I feel his father's cross and chain dig into my ribs. Rafael's arms engulf me and soon our breathing is in sync, like lovers', and it's this way that we find ourselves hours later, stealing some peace, the sun blessing us anew, a son and a daughter left alone with the ghosts of their fathers.

46

*A*t the fruit stand near my home, I'm stocking up on peso *guayaba*, petite bananas, tomatoes, and my favorite, *mamey*. Produce, when available, is cheap and organic and scrumptious. Despite the sparse quantity, the state overstaffs the corner market, and the workers have little to do other than drink peso rum and contribute to the barrio's Radio Bemba.

"How much is the papaya?" I ask.

All the men burst into laughter.

"*Otra.*" Again, prompts the clerk, gesticulating.

"*¿Cuál es la mecánica?*" What's the deal, I ask, exasperated, and holding up the fruit. "How much is this papaya?"

"*Mi vida,* I don't know how much your papaya goes for," he says. "But that there *fruta bomba* in your hand is twenty-five pesos." The men are nearly doubled over with laughter now.

Limón tells me later that papaya means pussy, and my face turns eggplant. He tells me I'm not paying attention if I can be here almost nine months and still not know this. I vow to walk the long way home from then on.

MY BAGS ARE on the curb. My landlady won't open the door, but tells me through colonial wood and hinges that I'm no longer welcome, that my friends are scum, *dientes de perros*, that the neighborhood-watch types have been grumbling.

She took a month's rent the night before.

I sit on the curb and look around. The air is thick, different. More pungent. A discomfiting silence permeates the normally chatty streets. Absent are the hucksters and girls in too-tight Lycra. Discos have been shuttered. Cubans soliciting foreigners are being arrested.

The world may be crying for jailed dissidents, but everyday folks here have more immediate concerns. Namely, the police. And how to fly under the radar.

As I drag my luggage from one illegal rental to another, to Camila's house a few blocks away, I watch a bemused Walrus chugging behind, wondering what trouble his charge has managed now. Camila convinced me it was no bother, but I know a foreigner living without a permit in a local's house can only cause problems.

But my real sorrow is Victor, whom I'd sworn not to contact, and who will not know how to find me now.

After I send a quick e-mail to Susie, I find myself wandering through the domed Capitolio Nacional, the former house of senate and representatives. Inside its palatial walls lies the nation's centerpiece—a revered diamond in the floor. The diamond is covered by thick sheets of glass, and a bronze goddess nearly sixty feet tall oversees its safety. The jewel marks the very heart of Cuba, the zero point. From it, all distances in the country are measured.

Today, I climb the steps and seek the diamond, hoping it can demarcate not only distance but also time. It's a gemstone, and it's a crystal ball, and within its remedial powers are answers to questions of space and time. What is the distance faith travels? What is the distance of my determination?

Tell me, where and when will I find my father?

Tell me the distance of a daughter's longing, the distance from the zero point to the temporal and spatial coordinates of discovering the street where my family lives. For the rain that falls from my roof is the water they walk in on the way to the market.

Tell me the distance.

47

The Syrian banker clutches his chest and tumbles from the podium. The audience, comprised of Cuban economists, gasp collectively. Their speaker arrived in a Soviet-era ZIL limousine, but leaves in a Cuban ambulance.

Camila tends to Farouk's corrupted heart at her clinic. After a few weeks, and probably a bit longer than professionally necessary, she releases him. Under her care, he's developed another affliction, a psychosomatic one, and his symptoms signal an attack on the same organ.

Farouk is in love.

"Stockholm syndrome," says Camila, blowing triumphantly on her nails.

Ali, his sidekick, is less convinced of my charms, but agrees the four of us should burn through the candle of a Havana night. The days, lately, are too hot for anything but sleeping.

"To drink?" asks the waiter. We're in a basement Latin jazz club on La Rampa, awaiting the live music. As the men order Cuba libres, Camila watches me slyly, to see if I've developed chemistry with my latest charge.

"My guess is you're having a mojito," says Camila, speaking to me in the code we use to describe our dates. Liquors and mixed cocktails rate highest, beer and peso rum measure in at the wrong end of the scale.

"Last night," I confide, "I had a Cristal beer. Never, ever again am I going to drink Cristal. Made me belch. From now on it's at least, at *least*, a mojito."

"That's what I love to hear," she says.

The waiter is irritated. "Want a mojito or what?"

I study my date and rub my chin. "Perhaps a mojito."

"She's having a Hemingway daiquiri," chimes an optimistic Camila to the waiter.

"Same for you?" he asks.

"No, no, *mi vida*," she says mischievously. "Make mine a rum, fifteen years."

"Ooooh," I say. "That good, huh?"

She waves a hand near her cheek and winks at the waiter. "Cool it with some ice, would ya?"

The band arrives and soothes with classics. Latin jazz would never have formed without the amalgamation of Cubans and Americans. Ragtime and rhythm and blues would not have existed without the influence of Cuban music. I think also of the other great Cuban contributions to American pop culture, such as top-paid baseball and movie stars. Using its educated labor force, Cuban research companies are busy unscrambling the mystery of a cancer cure. I wonder what further brilliance could erupt if the freeze between our countries could thaw.

But I've little time to ponder because I'm attending to the droll Ali. He tells me he's Moroccan, from Rabat, and not Syrian like his boss Farouk. Ali proclaims that I, as a Cuban, should enjoy the privileges of living in a country that provides vaccinations, enjoys a near-perfect literacy rate, and schools its children, even the farm kids, at least through ninth grade.

Then he invites me up to his $445-a-night suite.

The Hotel Santa Isabel, a former eighteenth-century palace overlooking the sumptuous Plaza de Armas, is the country's most luxurious inn. I pretend not to understand Ali's rough Spanish, so as not to snicker over the irony of a lecture on gratitude from someone living in spacious rooms, with marbled walls and 600-count Egyptian cotton sheets.

Instead, I pull him toward me and slip off the Hermés tie and the Ralph Lauren suit of a poor country's top businessman. I'm white, so the sentry assigned to the hotel's lobby accepted Ali's $40 handshake and I was cleared to the top floor. If my skin color came in a darker pigmentation, I'd likely not be allowed inside the rooms of my own country's showcase hotels, regardless of the heft of a *yuma*'s bribe.

Fueled by the confidence of a few Hemingway daiquiris, I push Ali down on a silky couch and, with my back to him, provide a flirtatious preview. Nervously, he prattles on about his country while caressing my bottom.

To tell Ali that I've been to Morocco would be to belie the fantasy he's paying for, the invention that I'm an exotic *cubana* and therefore naïve of world affairs. It takes all my skill to hang, fascinated, on his sophomoric diatribe on international politics.

He needs to shut up, so I move down on my knees, and as I go in for the kill, he pushes me back gently and snaps off the light. Then he stands up and, at the bed, rips off the top sheet.

"*Habib*, would you," he says, his face illuminated by the golden lights that hang like angels over the Plaza.

"Yes," I say. More of a question.

He hands me the sheet. "In my country, a woman does not have relations until she's married. Women who have sex before marriage are prostitutes. Once she's married, if her husband leaves her, no one will marry her, she stays alone or becomes a whore. No one will marry a used woman."

Uncomfortably, I'm wondering where this is going. He continues. "This is a different culture, yes, but I do not want to think of you this way."

"Hmmm." As he wraps the sheet around me, I've got one eye on my pile of clothes and the other on the exit. "When I was young, there was a woman I wanted to marry, but my family wouldn't allow it."

"Did you marry her?"

"No, she was my heart, but I did not disrespect my family. I never violated her, so she could marry another. But we did share delicious nights," he sighs. "Something about you reminds me of her."

He drapes the sheet over the back of my head, like a raincoat, the top covering my head and hair, and draping over every inch of skin. No ankles show in my makeshift djellaba. He pulls me near.

"Tonight, you make love like a Moroccan virgin."

First it's the knees. I bend them and lie on my side, as instructed, and with hotel lotion so runny it's almost water, he lubricates himself and pushes in and out of the crevice created at the joint. He moans in pleasure. Then Ali aligns my arm to my side and holds it firmly against my body as his cock shuttles in and out of the hollow space of my armpit. He works his way clockwise around my figure, taking a pit stop in my mouth, until he hits six o'clock, and then he hesitates and inserts himself between the thickest part of my thighs and, just as I feel my legs beginning to sting from the rubbing and agitation, I force myself to stay still, as he's in his own private Moroccan lair, fucking on his virgin, excited by the technicalities of social law, the bending of rules and of skin, the Berber and French and Spanish and Bedouin blood that crosses in her, and when it's all over and he's sheepish, he reaches into his suitcase and slides 24-karat gold bangles up my arm. I keep waiting, expectantly. For something. But then I'm granted clarity. A Moroccan woman's virginity is more than protecting the sacred few inches of real estate that no man but her husband may explore. Virginity to Ali and his kind is about a man's insecurities over a woman's gratification. To know no other man has brought this woman to orgasm—that's the certified definition of virginity. It's not about physical territory as much as emotional, as he doesn't want to look in his wife's eyes and wonder if someone else was more skillful in granting her pleasure. He wants to know she could never compare and contrast.

Ali's virgin was no virgin; she'd certainly been violated. But not pleasured, the poor girl. Perhaps my own international relations are the spiritual commiseration with women under draconian sexual law. For the only pleasure Ali will give me is leaving on the morning plane. That, and the gold on my arms, which will fetch enough to help pay for more weeks of living and looking.

48

The *guajiro* cops are birddoggin' me," laughed Limón. Nervously. "People really do say that, in your country? I'm starting to suspect it's all *mierda*. Because the slang you teach well—it's a funny thing. None of my *yumas* seem to know what I'm saying."

"Perhaps they're not the hippest of *yumas*," I suggested, suppressing a giggle.

"Told my *yuma* that another girl was flirting, you know, giving me the hairy eyeball," he said. "*Coño* if she didn't think I was crazy."

"Someone gave you the hairy eyeball?" I asked, fluttering my eyelashes and clicking my tongue. I thought about my grandfather, who suspected until his final day that most women fancied him.

Limón laughed and I laughed, and I remember laughing because it was the last time Limón and I shared a giggle. In fact, it would be among the last handful of words we'd ever exchange.

But I didn't know that then.

What I knew was that Limón—in an unsolicited confession—swore an adherence to heterosexuality despite my protests, my saying that it was none of my business. That his sexuality, like everyone's, I was learning, was impossible to define and wasn't immutable. Like all of our thoughts, urges, and beliefs, our sexuality is up for grabs right until our last heartbeat.

But Limón didn't hear. In Cuba, he explained indignantly, *pingueros*—gay male prostitutes and, literally, *pingas* looking for *pingas*—are permitted to retain their machismo in a sexual encounter with another male under a few conditions. Those being that they are the *bugarron* but not the *maricón;* the giver of pleasure, but not the receiver; the top, but never the bottom. Yet the truth of the conversation was bigger than Limón admitted. In these desperate times, even the guardedly macho are venturing into humiliating acts of homosexuality, as foreigners on the hunt for attractive *hombres* provided an irresistible demand to be filled by those not normally gay.

Limón quickly changed the subject to the one I was dying to discuss: news on my family's whereabouts.

"The woman I met with in Miramar knows your old cook. She worked for your mother the whole time she was in Havana," he whispered, triumphant but cautious, as most Cubans believed their landlines to be tapped. "She hinted she knew José Antonio."

"You have an address?" My voice was calm, but my brain had exploded. I couldn't wait to tell Susie how right she had been.

"Let's meet at Colón cemetery in four hours."

When I hung up, I felt happier than I could ever remember.

TO ENDURE THE wait, I slip into the nearest movie house, the Charles Chaplin. A new local film, *Suite Havana,* has been released, and I get the last free seat. The audience is restless, and as the film opens, it becomes apparent it's without dialogue. The camera follows ordinary Cubans through their lives. It lingers on faces as they eat a tired meal of rice and beans. Hospital workers double as transvestites in a tourist show. A doctor dons a clown suit and unhappily entertains children for a few extra pesos. The Cubans are shown grim and fettered as they "resolve" their way through their lives.

As the movie ends, few eyes are dry, and the crowd applauds gravely.

Even in the dark, there is no escaping the light.

THE YEAR IS 1901 and a woman dies in the act of childbirth. Her baby is stillborn. With its tiny corpse between her thighs, to symbolize death at birth, the woman is entombed at Colón cemetery in Havana. Over the years, her husband faithfully visits the grave, and in doing so he devises a ritual and adheres to it determinedly. First, he knocks on one of the tombstone's four brass rings to announce his arrival. Second, he places flowers on the tomb. And third, he walks backwards until the headstone is out of view, careful not to turn on the grave of his beloved, out of respect.

Several years later, her corpse is exhumed. To the astonishment of the gravediggers, the woman's flesh is intact, and the baby has found its way into the cradle of her arms.

In the wake of this revelation, the woman attains the stature of a deity, and becomes known as La Milagrosa—the miraculous one. For the next hundred years people make a pilgrimage to her grave, believing her to be the granter of miracles and a protector of mothers and children.

I'm standing in line with flowers for La Milagrosa, awaiting my own try at a request for deliverance. An answered prayer from a saint who looks after wayward children.

It's nearly my turn. I watch as people knock on her grave, leave flowers, and pray for their own personal miracle. Like her husband, the seekers leave walking backwards, never turning away from the tomb of the granter of gifts.

A young boy nudges me. I'm up. Slowly, I knock at La Milagrosa's tombstone and, kneeling, place flowers at the mother's grave. Silently, I whisper the name of my father, José Antonio, and plead for direction in the wilderness of this vast city. I slip a small map at the base of her tomb, in case she needs to consult the streets for preciseness.

I'm about to back away when I hear my name yelled, and the voice carries such urgency and tumult that I whirl around. Limón runs toward me, his hand held by a young *yuma* with orange hair and refrigerator-white skin.

Close behind are two policemen in formal blue, sweating in their uniforms, their eyes locked on Limón. When they reach him, Limón is ballistic, flailing and shouting and scanning for me as he's dragged back toward the street.

I'm shouting no, please no, and then I'm shouting why, and I'm frozen on the spot, and the Cubans in line behind me are captivated by the theater. Except for the little boy. In his saint's colors of red and black he's pointing at the tombstone and looking frightened.

"You've turned your back," he says, his eyes wide.

And he's right. I've turned away from La Milagrosa.

Tears are streaming down the face of the Danish backpacker, the latest victim of Limón's romantic grift. She doesn't know why Limón is being arrested, and I don't have the heart to tell her it's because he likely reached the third warning in his file—the third encounter with police in the accompaniment of a *yuma*. Or who knows, I say.

In Havana, things are never as they seem. My own mother told me that.

After we phone Limón's family, his *yuma* and I return to the cemetery and look for the possibility of an address of the woman who cooked my mother's meals so many years ago. I inspect the ground for a slip of paper, hoping Limón had the wits to drop it somewhere for me to find. But on this cold earth, covering the one million dead below it, there's nothing but dust and, exhausted, I crouch between chunks of aging marble.

I pull my knees into my chest and watch the day fade. In the gloaming, headstones turn opalescent. In the foreground, a line of hopefuls are queued before La Milagrosa—including Limón's *yuma*, who's petitioning for his safe return, her eyes swollen and incarnadine from tears.

Forgive me, La Milagrosa, I whisper. Forgive me for turning my back on you. Forgive us that in this life it is miracles that we must seek, and in seeking miracles, we sometimes destroy our own integrity. Destroy what we consider precious.

Above me is a statue of an angel, a finger held to her lips so she may hear the whisperings of the dead. I sit underneath her, sadly accepting that another link in the mystery of my father's whereabouts has been severed. Like the angel, I, too, am listening to those buried and pray their secrets will spring forth and change the course of the living.

49

Mortimer Bardenfeld loves his super-yacht. No matter the actual location or year outside, inside it's always the same as the time and place the boat was born: Miami, circa 1985. He pays untold sums to keep the Feadship staffed and running and docked in the world's great ports. Still, the hot pink drapes have faded to a cool pastel, and the mirrored ceilings in the staterooms have turned orange with rust.

Even the faux pelican ice sculpture has cracked its dainty leg. But Morty doesn't care, he thinks everything looks beautiful.

Morty, of course, is blind.

Camila is his longtime girlfriend, *la mujer* in his Havana port, but as she's gone loopy for the über-rich Syrian, I've been nominated to make her excuses and occupy the yachtsman during his week in Havana.

Uncle Morty—he insists his "girls" address him as Uncle—loves Marina Hemingway. It's Cuba's prized marina, and one of the only smartly maintained places on the island. Long concrete strips reach like fingers into the sea, providing safe harbor for sailboats and motor yachts, many of them American flagship.

"Ah-lo, gorgeous!" The South African captain slides open the amidships door and gestures grandly for me to enter. With a wink, he points a finger in his boss's direction.

Uncle Morty moves gracefully about the salon. I can't help but admire the old guy. Born poor and with a degenerative eye disease, he'd worked his way to Wall Street, trained in mergers and acquisitions, and then spread his tentacles into businesses around the world. His blindness had given him a poker face that terrified competitors and clients alike.

Though Uncle Morty's money grew exponentially in the nineties, the eighties were his kind of decade, and he pined for them. And if the eighties were his time, Miami had been his place. Miami had reacted to Morty's egregious crimes with a wink and a shake of the maracas under a festive sun, thanks to a conspiratorial band of lawbreakers and lawmakers. Morty was in the thick of it, the orchestrator of trafficking. He set up webs of offshore corporations, complex tax structures, fake export-imports. Gym bags crammed with dirty cash were cheerfully counted and stashed by bank tellers on Brickell Avenue. Glorious days, he tells me. Lawless days. People getting rich. Very, very rich.

Then the crash. A district attorney under pressure decided to make Morty the first consummate white-collar criminal to be run out of Miami, a dubious distinction in a dubious township. "It was time," Morty explained. "The streets were paved, and schools were built. A city had been born." Illegitimacy gave birth to its legitimate heirs. And Morty's arrest crystallized the moment of transition.

In a quiet deal with the district attorney, Morty traded threats of massive prosecution—crimes that carried hard time—with a promise to never, ever again set foot in Miami-Dade County. Unless he fancied handcuffs. And not the velvet-lined kind, either.

Heartbroken, Morty commissioned a yacht to be designed and built in Miami as homage to his beloved city. *Dithy Ramb,* technically, is one word, but Morty found two carried more stature, and deemed it thus with a stern face that said no grammar queen was going to fuss him about it.

Dithyramb, traditionally, is a dance of Bacchus, the Greek god of drink and wine—your typical frat fellow's main mentor, and Morty's main muse. If Miami the mistress was leaving him to become Miami the wife, if she was going legit, Morty would carry her 1985 memory, her air and sea and sand, in his pocket with him. A pharaoh's tomb. One that would ply the seas, preventing nostalgia by keeping the past alive in the hermetically sealed world of expensive plastic.

I fingered the pelican's fractured femur and sighed.

When launched, the captain told me, she was one of the one hundred biggest luxury boats in American waters. Today, she's a rundown relic with many more super-yachts stretching well beyond her 126 feet.

"You smell lovely," Uncle Morty says. "You've been touching orchids."

Kissing his cheek, I flump down on a purple couch while the stew collects drinks. "You're amazing," I say, always awed by the precision of his senses.

Uncle Morty and I have spent a few hours alone together every day for a week. There's been no sex. ("Camila is my true Caribbean lady," he'd said. "My old nambycane sure misses her.") Considering Morty's advanced age, I'm extremely grateful for his sexual loyalty to Camila. Morty and I have, however, been emotionally intimate—far more so than with any of my previous *yumas*.

Each evening begins with dinner on the aft deck. It's the best food I've had in Cuba, and after the series of gourmet meals and top-shelf wines, I feel a softness return to my body. (Cuba is generally a dieter's dream, as transportation is scarce, dancing is its pastime, and food, in its banality, is without appeal.) After dinner, Uncle Morty and I converse under the stars until late at night, the thick X-crossed dock lines easing out and gently tugging back in.

Uncle Morty asks me to describe the constellations and, in exchange, he mesmerizes me with passages from his long and decadent life. In our first hours together, he'd pegged me as an American and waited patiently until I was ready to tell my story. I'd spared him no detail of my ten months in Cuba thus far. Tonight is our swan song, and Camila swears he'll pay me for our weeklong courtship, sexless though it has been.

"Last dinner," says Morty as the stew takes our plates. "We're pulling out tomorrow for Gustavia."

"What I would do to go to St. Bart's."

"Glad you mentioned it," says Morty clasping his hands over a walking cane. "I'd like to offer to take you with us, as I know you can't leave by traditional means."

Surprised, I consider the option.

"I know you're looking for your family here, but if you'd like, I believe we can arrange for a stowaway. Of course you can take your passport, and I'd have my plane fly you from St. Bart's back to the U.S. If that's what you want, Alysia."

I'm overcome, knowing Uncle Morty risks the ire of the Cubans in taking me out of the country. I also know that if I leave with him, and violate the terms of my visa, I likely won't be allowed back here at a later date. Briefly, I fantasize about a juicy steak au poivre in St. Bart's. I imagine myself afterward flying to Washington, being greeted by friends, and recovering from the whole ordeal. But I don't let myself indulge too long, because I know I must stay. I've come too far to quit.

"You'll find him soon," he says. When the stew leaves, Uncle Morty unveils his second idea. "I'm a businessman and as a businessman, I'd like to make a proposition. I'm going to give you a thousand dollars."

A thousand dollars. More than enough to pay Camila everything I've borrowed. But I can't accept. "No way, Uncle Morty—"

"Don't interrupt!" he says sharply. "You've given me your time and I always compensate people for their time." Truth is, talking to a fellow American has been a godsend, and I refuse again.

"What I want is a few hours together," he says. "Down in the stateroom."

"No, I can't take your money. And," I say, smacking his leg lightly, "Camila would be very jealous if anything happened between us."

Uncle Morty raises his cane in the air and snorts. "Alysia, sheesh. Can't make an old blind man happy? You've told me about your life down here with the tourists. If you go with these tourists, why not me? Tell you what. You consider the thousand dollars a grant, and your time with me friendship."

Reluctant, I can barely muster the image of Morty naked. But I know a thousand dollars will buy me more time and information. The old man *is* safer and kinder than the majority of *yumas* I've faced.

I think about John, and part of me is certain that the man who raised me—the diplomat who understands precisely how things work in the world—knows I'd have been forced to take up the oldest profession in order to live. John would conclude there'd be no other choice. Perhaps he didn't think I could handle anything so squeamish. Perhaps he believed in a day or two I'd phone him back and call off this fruitless search. But I don't want to do this. As tempting as a luxury-yacht ride out of the Havana underworld may sound, I'm resolved to prove John wrong. To prove to him, and to myself, that I understand what is important in this life.

•   •   •

UNCLE MORTY SETTLES his gentle frame on the pink-and-gray bed-spread with embroidered palm trees. I run my hand over the faded cloth, nervously, not wanting to offend the man who's become my friend. I'm grateful he's blind, so he can't see the sour look on my face. I fear the taste and feel of geriatric flesh.

Uncle Morty folds his dinner jacket over a chair, his chin stretched high. I, too, look up, half expecting a disco ball dangling underneath the ceiling's mirror. Uncle Morty is calm and relaxed. I'm wondering if it's kosher to suggest Viagra, or if I'm expected to perform miracles.

"You don't have to be nervous," he says.

"I'm not nervous!"

"You cracked your neck," he accuses, pushing the PLAY button on a cassette deck. Although we're in Cuba, it's not Latin music that blares from tinny speakers. Frank Sinatra and Count Bassie croon "Fly Me to the Moon." To it, I'm asked to remove my clothes.

Slowly I begin undressing. Though he is afflicted with blindness, I can't shake the sensation that Uncle Morty can see what everyone else cannot. My thoughts feel invaded by his prying sensory perception, and because of this, I'm unable to call on the memory of Rafael to get me through. My top is off, as is my skirt. Bra and panties now.

"Keep going," says Morty, his directing finger shaking slightly.

Taking a deep breath, I unhook my bra. A thousand dollars is a million in comparative economics. Down goes the underwear. Morty's face beams and radiates in my presence, like Mercury before the sun. I lean over to take his hand, but he shakes me away.

"All I want is for you to dance," he says. "I won't touch you. Just dance like no one is looking." Relief floods my face. I slowly move to Frank and the Count and lose myself in the strangeness of it all.

Morty tells me I have a beautiful body. "Beautiful," he says. "But you dance like an American. You may want to work on that if you are to find success at your new profession." Shaking my head, I manage to crack a smile.

For an hour or so I sway before my blind date, seductive in my own skin, feeling the adulation of a man who appreciates my spirit, and reveling in the new pleasure that if you're open, you can find connection in the most unlikely of places.

Morty roots through a nightstand and slowly counts ten hundreds, and throws in a few more for good measure. Then, fumbling in the drawer, he comes out with a prize. A thin gold chain is slipped around my wrist. The bracelet will become the only piece of jewelry I refuse to hawk.

"Bon voyage," he says, happily satiated.

On my way out, Uncle Morty's chef is in the galley, spreading creamy American peanut butter over toast. He watches me stare as my thoughts shift to Limón. The chef offers me a sandwich and I decline, instead asking for the whole jar. A get-out-of-jail gift for the inmate, a gesture based on a hopeful wish that Limón will be released. And when he does, he'll have a taste of what he's missing.

50

My first dance teacher was my grandmother. As it turned out.
She favored earrings with faux gemstones, unfashionable but available, and always clip-on, as her own mother believed piercings to be disrespectful of one's maker.

She made cakes, massive constructions of inedible density, topped by baroque whips of frosting in pinks and yellows. She gave hair barrettes the shape of lambs, belly-baring shirts and shorts, and diaper pins fastened into the mouth of a smiling, happy plastic pig.

They were the gifts of an impoverished family. Impoverished of money but *rico* with love. Crazy love.

On Wednesday afternoons, my mother would leave me with her, so that she and José Antonio could find solace in the government-sanctioned love hotels—*posadas*—for ten pesos a day. A thoughtfulness of the revolution for those who suffered in crowded environs.

My mother's was the most claustrophobic. At home, she and John had all but stopped speaking, and he made no attempt to hide the nature of his preference for long hours in the office.

My mother made sure I spent Tuesdays with my father. Wednesdays were for my grandmother. And every other day, in chunks of time stolen from her chores and duties, my mother would escape the heat and confusion in her own home, and take refuge in José Antonio's. I know now that she must have kept his address and last name out of her journals in the event its contents were disclosed. But in the safety of the future, where I reside, I regret her lack of detail, which would have illuminated the path to my family's home.

Though the visits with my Cuban family were short in duration, they proved long in happiness. This is what my mother wrote. She took me there for dance lessons. For *frijoles* and *leche*. For the special affections one can only find in the arms of a grandparent.

My hair, when I was a young child, was blonde. She described this in her journals. Alysia's hair is blonde, but with earthy undertones, like the rich and fertile soil of Cuba itself.

John looks at this hair, this dirty-blonde hair. He looks at this face with its roundness—one that springs enigmatically from two parents with features of distinct sharpness. My mother dismisses this discrepancy, but it's because she won't look him in the eye that he further suspects. And when this happens, she feels an infringement upon the hours of freedom in the daytime. She turns every few blocks or so, turns to see who, she fears, is following. He is following, whoever he is. But when she looks, she finds no one, and so she blames guilt, she blames the repression of facts, she blames the likelihood of parentage.

She knows her one-year-old daughter is half-Cuban.

Perhaps John knows now, as well.

51

*C*umulus clouds rocket through the afternoon sky, reaching for the stratosphere, and, failing, give in to gravity's pull, unleashing a damnation of rain.

Crystals on a chandelier have long been replaced with plastic ice-cream sticks, and they tinkle in the wind, attracting a thin condensation. Drops land on my head as I lie in the space Camila fashioned as a bedroom for her *norteamericana* guest. One who'd spent the last night with Morty and was sleeping late.

Outside, on the streets, puddles form and eddies swirl down gently sloped streets, washing away the felled pollution.

Thinking of the *babalocha,* and how he'd promised my family walks through the puddles left by rain, I soon find myself near my former land-lady's home. It's there I spend a wistful afternoon watching people. Wondering if each woman who walks by could be an aunt, a cousin, a niece. Or maybe one of the men walking past is José Antonio himself.

Perhaps these folks are my family's neighbors. Perhaps they are part of the informal exchange among friends. With them, do they, like all clusters of neighbors and friends, swap eggs for lightbulbs, fresh fish for bathtub rum, a screwdriver for scissors?

Breaking my thoughts, a tiny dog struts up and eyes me sweetly. Dogs in Cuba are said to bring good health to the home of their owners, and most are petite and *dulce* mutts. With a patchwork-quilt coat, this one curls around my feet. He is dirty and collarless, and he licks my toes.

The stores don't carry commercial dog food. Pooches are fed table scraps or, in lean times, boiled *boniato,* or sweet potatoes. Protein, in any form, is a humans-only luxury. This diet does little good for sidewalks and parks—not to mention canine longevity—and many bear the ribbed look of an anxious supermodel.

Rubbing his ears, I realize this little one is also unfed, and I peel bits of fruit from my produce sack.

"Whaddya think, fella. Should I just call Victor?" I ask the dog, who cocks his head at me. The mutt plunks his chin down on my feet and sighs.

Victor had made me swear I wouldn't contact him, but as he doesn't know my new location, or where to deliver news about my family, I've little choice but to risk his anger.

The dog follows me home. I leave him outside Camila's house with a bowl of rice and beans.

"There's a boxing match at Kid Chocolate tonight," I tell Victor on his work line, my voice trembling in anticipation of his wrath. "Middleweights from Santiago. I've got tickets, it starts at eight."

There's a long pause. "Wrong number," he says, slamming down the phone.

At eleven o'clock, I'm sitting in the bleachers, my olfactory senses on overload in the fetid arena. It reeks of sweat and the raw garlic the boxers swallow holistically. Two hours, three hours, and still, Victor is nowhere to be seen. My chin slumps into my palm.

Knockout, and spectators shuffle outside. Convinced I've lost my connection to Victor, I glumly swing my legs over the bleachers. It's then I notice a tourist eyeing me. He's wearing a baseball cap, a "Pork Fat Rules" T-shirt, and tight cutoffs. I'm certain it's a tourist, as no middle-aged *cubano* would be caught dead in shorts. He approaches, but I'm in no mood for working the *jinete* tonight. Taking a back route through old Havana, I nearly slip on discarded mango skins.

As I make my way deeper into the midnight tenderloin of central Havana, the corner police thin out and then disappear altogether. I'm no longer in tourist territory, but the hefty man follows behind swiftly, his feet sure of his path. It hits me: *The man is no tourist.* The moon is Havana's only light source, but my cover is blown, as my white skirt and shirt reflect its luminosity, like the black-light rays in a darkened club.

Ahead, candles flicker in a boisterous room. A party has emptied onto the streets, and I slip inside. In the corner of the small apartment, a San-tería pile of dolls and candies and honey-drizzled pumpkin slices nest among candles and herbs. I feel a touch on my arm, and turn to see my pursuer.

"*Coño,* what itches you?" he says, wiping his face. He puts his hands on his thighs and catches his breath. "Making me chase you." I must look scared because he broadcasts a smile. "*Tranquilo,* Victor sent me."

"He's angry?"

"*He* isn't, but woman, I've never seen anyone walk so fast in my life. Victor said to look for *rubia* tourist. For a second I thought you were a *cubanita* and I'd followed the wrong *bollo,* but your big-city walk gives you away."

"Scared the *mierda* out of me. How do I know you're Victor's friend?"

"*Oye, mami,* he paid me twenty dollars to meet you."

"Right."

"*Mira,* he said you'd reimburse him the twenty."

I roll my eyes. "Oh, *definitely,* Victor," I say, pulling some *fula,* some *fe*— faith, the new slang for money—from the interior of my bra and handing it over. Partygoers begin to notice us now, and Victor's charge pulls me down the street, insisting on walking me home, so as to relay my new ad-dress.

"Nice and slow now, *mami,*" he pleads.

"There'd better be news," I say, trying to sound tough.

Good news, he says. Victor has found the address where my mother would take me to visit my father and his family.

Good news—no, great news. Life-changing.

Great news until he tells me I must wait another two weeks before Vic-tor feels safe enough to pass it along.

Waiting, and waiting to wait, are the most common forms of torture heaped upon the Cuban population. I must wait because there are things I don't understand, because nothing is as it seems, because under the patina of a unified revolution is chaos, and so I slip him my new phone number and slip further into the night, waiting because I am Cuban, and that is my burden.

52

Three A.M. in Havana, and all my Russian gangster boyfriend can talk about are his suits.

"Versace is for the small men, for the *brodyagas*. Me, I forgot Versace in nineteen-ninety—what, five?—you know, when Gianni was shot in Miami. I was twenty-eight, twenty-nine. I heard the news. I go home, I take off Versace, and I say no more suits from him. No more Versace. He was a good man but he is bad luck. Executed in front of his house." He unleashes a string of Russian curses. "Everyone thought I had bad fashion to drop Versace. But I said you are crazy to wear the clothes of a dead man."

Our limbs are entangled in the soft cushions of Havana's hippest cigar lounge. I'm conscious of how my body reclines, and am twisting my torso and legs to their most complimentary, with Sasha's eyes my lens. I'd rather be back in the U.S., wearing sweats and sitting cross-legged on the couch watching college ball. But Camila is my internal guide, and so I pose.

Sasha is burning his way through a Punch Churchill and the story of his life, a feat fueled by Bolivian marching powder, seven-year Havana Club rum, and the intense interest of his *jinetera*.

One who has been to Moscow, but never on his tour.

"Now, only a *chajnik* wears Versace. Only a *chajnik* goes to St. Moritz and drives a BMW. Me, I go to Klosters. Drive a Mercedes S600. I drive Mercedes, yes, but soon I order Rolls-Royce Phantom. What do you think, black or silver? Silver I think." Sasha takes a long drag of his cigar and shoots a coded glance to his aide de camp, a bulky Russian who's guarding a walnut-paneled door that leads to the entrance.

Sasha is a boyish thirty-seven, with light hair and long, slender limbs. Dark circles underscore his steel eyes but don't detract from a natural handsomeness. The arcs are likely caused by his inability to relax fully, even in sleep. Lately that's been in my arms.

As I've fallen under the spell of his vampiric schedule—rise at dusk and sleep after toast and eggs at sunrise—I've come to know the intimacies of a Havana night. It's been a blessing to avoid the daytime bustle of long lines, lung-clogging pollution, and the depressing vision of a tattered city. But in the luscious nights, the appearance of stars—sharp and lustrous over an unlit city—is the only confirmation that we Cubans are not alone in the universe. That we're connected, indeed, to the outside world. The night says this. The day, however, speaks of loneliness and a longing for a lifting of the curtains on the world stage. When the embargo does end, when Havana is electrified like Seoul and rebuilt like Berlin and demonized like Miami, the day will be filled with a spirit of commercial purpose. Nostalgia, my island's only product now in copious supply, will dissipate under the stage lights.

"You," Sasha says, his fingers dancing up my inner thigh. "Me. We make arrangement."

Twirling my light hair around a finger, I ask what he could mean.

"I come back for you. We make arrangement. You need money, to help your family, yes. I can help. *Kroshka*"—little one, his amorous name for me—"what do you say I send you money. Perhaps each month. I come back to visit, I know you're waiting for just me."

Lest the help of a *yuma* seem altruistic, I've come to know retainers as a tool of control and power over the recipient. But still I'm shocked he's suggested a deal this early in our tryst.

Sasha and I have been together a week, ever since he saw me on the Malecón and ordered his driver to pull over. Although he believes our meeting to have been the intersection of fates, in reality I'd been waiting by the road and, upon seeing the Mercedes approach, one likely carrying a wealthy foreigner, I stepped in its path, working on gut instinct. I dropped my handbag and pulled back to the curb, tumbling on the sidewalk, as if by accident. The driver came to a screeching stop and jumped from the car to see if I was okay, and I brushed it off, apologizing for my absentmindedness and blotting the blood from yet another skinned knee.

When I saw Sasha fetch my handbag, it was a *coup de foudre,* or so I told him, flashing him my amateur version of The Look.

It's my longest and most successful *jinete* stint yet.

"We set up a bank account then?"

"What do I have to do for it?" I say, calling up Sophia Loren but delivering the line with all the sultriness of Shirley Temple.

"*Kroshka,*" he says. "Promise to never lie. Women who lie—" Sasha hits a sour note. "Okay?" I shrug coyly and look away. Camila would tell me to take two beats. Sasha rakes my hand with his and, after a slow, tense moment, I kiss his lips and say it's a deal. He is mine and I am his.

"I've always wanted Cuban girlfriend," he says in his broken English.

And I've always wanted to find my father. But that bit I say silently. I also say silently how much I miss Rafael, and how it's his face I imagine each morning at the hotel when the night's opiates have run their course through Sasha's veins. I pounce on top of him, hellcat, returning his heart rate to its former speed, grinding on my beast, jockeying, concentrating on his delectation, pronouncing mine to be genuine, and proclaiming this fucking to be the best ever. In my mind's eye, Rafael's etched face is plastered on Sasha's like a Halloween mask. It's the only way.

Sasha is on again about the suits, and I allow myself to glow in triumph. Finally, I think, I've secured a winning *yuma,* one who will send remittances so I may stop *jineteando* for the two months I have left in Cuba. And in just a week, if all goes as planned, Victor will hand me the coveted address of my family. It's a victory, and I'm savoring my accomplishments. As I should.

Sasha takes my hand and places it on his jacket.

"Take a look at this suit. Helmut Lang. Elastic wool. These shoes: Gucci loafers. No socks. Even winter in Moscow, I do not wear socks. They say, Sasha, you are crazy, but I am fashion. Nowhere on my body is purple and pink and yellow like wagtail. Those *babushka*-killers in Moscow buy clown suits with big money to impress the shop clerk one second. But not me, I think about fashion. High fashion. I tell my girl, don't wear fishnet stockings every night. Every night with the fishnet. So boring, Madonna *Like a Virgin.* It was good, you know, back then, but in Moscow, they don't want to move on in fashion. They are stuck when 1989 happened." He pauses and takes me in, as if for the first time. "You would not know, of course, you are Cuban girl." Then his voice lowers and he pulls me toward him on the buttery leather couch. "Beautiful, beautiful Cuban girl."

Although I've not corrected Sasha's belief that I'm clueless as to the outside world, I've demurred in revealing the truth about my life. I imagine the look on his face if I tell him about my past, the countries traveled, the country clubs and diplomats' parties, all that expensive education. With my foreign boyfriends, I briefly wonder at their reaction if I could only tell them of my true history. But I never do, knowing there'd be anger and outrage for my nefarious deception.

Part of a *cubana*'s allure is her perceived—and real—lack of worldliness. Foreign men relish the role of bon vivant, and also the notion that a *cubana* is forever ingenuous, an empty vessel to be filled with his own inarguable viewpoints.

So I let Sasha believe I've lived in Havana my whole life. I'm certain, in Moscow, or New York, or Munich, I'd have no chance of attracting him. Sasha's interest in me stems from the idea of my being Cuban and of having a romance with an affectionate, easily jealous, fuss-making *latina* stuck in a time warp. I'm a wall piece in the museum of innocence. Easily bought and traded for trinkets.

SASHA AND HIS buddies are in Havana for several weeks. Lying low, or so he says. Sasha cryptically suggests they're sitting out a storm of retaliation from rivals in Moscow. Havana is the perfect hideout: remote, racy, distractive. And with nary a gun to be had.

That a crush of wealthy, dissolute Russians are on the prowl has not gone unnoticed among the *jinete*. The imagination of Havana's most enterprising women has been excited by the *novi ruskis* who love to exercise their capitalistic jurisdiction, who check the time on Cartier tank watches, and who shop conspicuously for antique Bakalowicz crystal.

Even a crackdown won't upend this kind of good time.

At dinner, Sasha and his fellow playboys cock their pinky fingers and bow before plates of cocaine. Afterward, alone or in groups, we prowl through dark streets in rented Mercedeses, scouring the city for its few hot spots, the ones alighted by tourist dollars, in discos and restaurants and cabarets only the very rich can afford, as the best of Cuba is available exclusively to foreigners and those rare few with freewheeling currency.

Most *jineteros* believe that in the rest of the world, if they can just find someone to marry them and take them out into it, their lives will be a permanent holiday. That tourists party every night and relax beachside in the daytime convinces most that this lifestyle is the norm for those from *afuera.* Tell a Cuban how hard people work in the Western world, and they don't understand.

"There's a joke," Limón once told me about the population's employer, the government. "We pretend to work, and they pretend to pay us."

"You think the rest of the world is the same way but with higher salaries," I scolded, and his shrug confirmed the myth.

"What was your job?" he asked.

"I'd just finished school, remember?"

"*Jineteando* is your first official job?"

We laughed together. "The plan *was* foreign service, if I scored on the test. If not, then consulting," I said, perhaps too wistfully.

"Consulting?" he asked brightly. "Tell me about that." I loved the way Limón conversed as artfully as he drove. Reacting quickly. Steering the lumbering machinery effortlessly around potholes and avoiding crashes. What style, to maneuver our talk away from feeling sorry for myself. From missing my comfortable life.

"Consulting. Well," I answered. "You have clients, you listen to their needs, resolve their problems, make them more powerful. Like *jineteando.*"

"Like *jineteando.*"

"Yeah, but without the cute outfits."

SASHA SNAPS ME from my reverie with his fingers, but it's the cigar barista he's summoning. He chooses a few Diplomaticos No. 2, empties the bottle of seven-year Havana Club, and nods as his friends walk in, puffing on cigars with ring sizes 49 and up. The Russians are flanked by the latest round of *jineteras,* all of whom arrive in a gust of Jean-Paul

Gaultier perfume and jeans so taut they need to be washed with Valium instead of soap.

Cell phones, as is the trend, are clipped to the women's belts and dangle dangerously close to pubic bones. ("Talk about dressing to the left," I once said to Camila.) Fashion accessories, fundamentally, the phones are otherwise useless, as connection fees are beyond a mortal's reach.

"La jinetera norteamericana."

I hear her voice, but I don't want to believe it.

When great boxers size each other up, it's with an appreciative eye for stature and aplomb. But rarely does a lightweight become rattled by a heavyweight. With divisions as safeguards, they're not to compete. But for Modesta, divisions don't exist, and I'm thrown into the ring with the mightiest. My jaw locks at the sight of her towering over us on the couch. Sasha pauses midsyllable, taking in the mythic curves of her body and a face with the precise symmetry of a work by Da Vinci.

"What did she say?" asks Sasha quite slowly, turning to me. "Did she say you're *American*?"

When Rafael steps next to Modesta, he delivers a customary greeting of a kiss on the cheek, first to her and then to me. My internal organs freeze. Rafael's eyes radiate fury—again he's found me cozy with a foreigner. Yet he offers Sasha a gentleman's handshake.

Rafael introduces himself as a translator to Sasha's fellow gangsters, and the two chat briefly. But my Russian's eyes remain transfixed on my face.

"Did you"—Sasha points his cigar at Modesta—"did you say Alysia is American?"

Modesta smirks. Rafael pipes in. "She might be part Cuban, but I'm starting to doubt it," says Rafael cryptically. "*Oye,* I have to get something for—" He gestures toward one of the Russians.

"You're *American*!" screams Sasha, jumping up so fast I fall into his impression on the couch. "You *lied* to me! You said you were Cuban—"

"Sasha, wait. I'm both!" I plead. "I'm both! I'm—I don't know, it's hard to explain." He's pacing now, his pallid face nearly red. The group has hushed and everyone is staring. Modesta glowers, unflinching.

Sasha seethes. "You said you would never lie. I am to *pay* you to be with me. You said you do not lie." He addresses the room. "The cunt lies. I *pay* her and the cunt lies!"

Then Rafael says it quietly, stealing no thunder from the Russian. It's a slow realization, an accusation that springs naturally. More shock than malice. Rafael says this: "You're a fucking *jinetera*."

A corner of Modesta's lip curls in triumph.

Light gleams off the Havana Club bottle as Sasha swings toward my head.

One-two punch.

Knockout.

Five

53

There is no pain medicine at the hospital, not even aspirin, so the boy nurses wet my throat with peso rum and stitch up the mess on my head with thread and needle. I'll be fine, but they're keeping me overnight, in case of concussion. I can't feel anything. The real damage is internal, and hemorrhaging. Wondering if Rafael will ever forgive me. And how I'm going to get home.

Modesta carries a pungent bundle of mariposas and an expressionless face. She tosses the flowers at my feet. I have no idea why she's here, and I'm terrified by her presence. But I resolve not to show fear.

"Radio Bemba says Camila is away."

"They don't know where she is," I reply coolly. Camila's mother is sick with worry too, but I don't tell that to Modesta.

Modesta rips open the window, lights a Marlboro, and perches on the second-story ledge. I wish I could push her out.

The heady perfume of the mariposas nearly sets me adrift into a sleep the nurses forbid. From the window, a fresh burst of tropical breeze is soothing, and fuses with Modesta's burning cigarette. On an island that grows the world's greatest tobacco, imported Marlboros are inferior but expensive, and a *jinete* status symbol. Leave it to Modesta to light up in a hospital.

From the streets come deep rumblings—a collective susurrus of anger in this poorer section of town over the ferry hijackers' deaths. My nemesis, on her second cigarette, hears them, too, but doesn't say a word. I'll wait. Newly unemployed, I've got all night.

Finally, she speaks. "When I was seventeen, I married an Italian. He charmed my mother. I wasn't so *enamorada* with him, but I didn't want to work Varadero anymore. He made such promises. Never date an Italian, they're the worst, *tacaños*." She tosses the glowing tip out the window. "I lasted three months. It was a small village near Naples, he was into some kind of crazy work, the whole neighborhood was nervous around him. Actually, they hated him more than they were nervous. I think I knew he was a bastard. But here, we were starving here. *Período especial.* I caught my grandmother eating a paint peel—imagine seeing your *abuelita* so hungry she eats paint."

I have no clue why she is relaying this. Out comes another cigarette. With nowhere to go, I wait until she's worked through the tobacco. It's another long while before she continues, and I'm fearful of falling asleep in her unsettling presence.

"The Italian said I could go to university and then we would have babies and a new house, and I could send money home. There was none of that. There was a house. But I wasn't allowed to leave it. I was his wife but he sampled me to every one of his *comemierdas* friends. Everyone had a taste. *El sabor de cuba.* Sometimes it was two at a time, or three. I snuck out of my own driveway in the trunk of a Fiat owned by a boy too stupid to be afraid. I made it to Spain on twenty dollars and it took me two years to earn enough *fula* to see my mother again. When I did, she made me swear I would never leave Cuba."

"Lucky me," I mutter in English.

But she's not listening. "When I returned I studied architecture, and came out with the highest marks. I have a medal for it, from Havana. Not metal, though," laughs Modesta. "It's a wood carving. Six years and I get a wood carving. But do I have a job? Yes, *a* job, but not a *real* job. I roll an eraser from one end of the desk to the other, and then back again. I was hired to relieve my *papalón* supervisor's boredom and give him someone new to jerk off to. In Havana, there's everything to construct, no? So many plans to be made for the future! But we have no materials. We have nothing, and it's all thanks to your embargo." Angry now, she stares out the window until a calm overtakes her.

Strangely, it's under these harsh fluorescents that Modesta's riveting features become softer, less superhuman. Until my arrival in Havana, I wouldn't have been able to put myself in her skin, but now I understand all too well her fugitive's tale. I find a strange fascination—and perhaps a comfort—in knowing that a great beauty, such as hers, is no insurance against acts of God.

Modesta goes to light a third cigarette, but changes her mind. I'm hoping a nurse will smell smoke and boot her diamond-cut ass.

"I'm with Sasha now," she says casually, rubbing wayward ash off her thigh. Her eyes lift to check my reaction.

Lightly, I touch my wound. "May I suggest you stick with beer. In cans."

Modesta laughs. Then a long pause. Eternity. "What happened last night was unforgivable. I don't feel good about myself."

My head nods slightly. So this is why she's come to see me. Probably the most apologizing Modesta's ever done.

She goes ahead with the third cigarette, lights it, and allows her lids to shut briefly and accept the comforting breeze. Another long silence in a night filled with them.

"I never knew my father, either. I would do anything for him, if he were alive."

My eyes start to close and I feel myself adrift.

"The other thing Rafael told me last night," she says and then backtracks. "He—we, we put it together after what happened. What I knew and what he knew, about your father. And everything. Rafael's not angry."

"Liar."

She flashes her *yuma*-winning smile and flips her long hair. "*Claro,* but I know what he thinks, *mi corazón.* He doesn't keep a grudge. Don't think anyone's ever—and I mean *ever*—said no to him before the way you have." She leans in, excited now. "*Dios mío,* he nearly *killed* Sasha after . . ." Modesta taps her head.

"Oh my God!" I bolt up, but the pain comes now and knocks me back down. "Oh my God. He fought the Russian? Is he okay?"

"They roughed him up a bit and threw him in the alley."

Closing my eyes, I feel my heart racing and then a warm hand presses gently on my chest, calming its speed. My mother. The heat climbs from my chest to my neck and my face, to my tender wound. "I sure know how to pick 'em, right, Mom?" I want to say this aloud, so my mother can hear. So we can laugh together at how weird the journey has been since it began twenty-four years ago in this very hospital.

But it's Modesta who speaks. "Rafael and I have a history, you know. We won't work, but I don't like him to have anyone else."

"You Cuban drama queens are the most jealous people I've ever met. You'd be jealous of a *cucaracha* in a tutu. My God." Now my head hurts bad.

She smirks and lights yet another cigarette off the glowing end of her third. The silence we share is torture.

"Sasha's a fucking drag, no? His *pinga, coño!*" She makes a small space between her thumb and forefinger. *"El palo de gallo."* Penis of the rooster. "It's so *chiquitito*. How'd you even know when the thing was in, anyway?"

"And the suits."

"Por favor. It's one thing to *wear* them, but does he have to *talk* about them too? What, he's critiquing for Russian *Vogue*?"

After a few more Marlboros, Modesta leaves the safety of her perch and nears my bed. Hesitantly, she allows her fingertips to graze my forearm. I don't want her near me—she's seen me naked, she's seen me botch a blow job. I've seen her curl her thighs around a cock wet with my saliva.

"I don't like you," I say.

"A street that has two lanes, *mi corazón.*"

She looks at my bandage, hand hovering to touch, then retreating, as if she feels my mother's protective presence. She makes for the door. At it, she turns around.

"I get off work when? Sunrise?"

"Sunrise, eggs, toast, sex, clock out," I say, ticking them off.

"I'll be back with aspirin and a car at nine. We need to get you home."

It's then I recall the Santería priest's words and his long-ago warning to be aware of those who would do me harm. Long before Modesta may return, with my hand carrying the weight of my head, I sneak out of the hospital and hail a taxi home. The driver agrees to take my shoes instead of the fare I don't have.

54

"You can take the girl out of Morón, but you can't take the Morón out of the girl."

Richard laughs uproariously at his own wit. He's calling from London. After a spectacular breakup, he said Daya have reconciled and he'll be flying back to Havana in a few days.

Daya hails from Morón, a dusty way-station in central Cuba. She's reunited with Richard under the condition that he meet her family there and announce his intentions.

I'm groaning at the thought of elegant Richard in backwater Morón. He asks, "You will come with us, won't you?"

Grateful for a break from sex work, my market-worth down to zilch with a swollen noggin and stitches, I agree to the overnight trip. With Camila gone and Victor's meeting still a few days away, I'm climbing the walls.

"You've got yourself a translator," I say, sensing I'll regret this. "Anything Daya needs to do, before you arrive?"

"Tell her to slide down the banister and warm up my dinner."

TURNS OUT CAMILA left a cryptic note for her mother, saying she was leaving, but failed to mention for where, or when, or if she's to return. The neighbors huddle in the family's salon during afternoons, comforting Camila's family. Her *jefe* phones regularly, his voice full of concern for his beloved director. Everyone is baffled at this unprecedented disappearance. I ask if the crackdown could be responsible, but neighbors assure me in low whispers that Camila is indeed untouchable. This gives me small comfort, and so I go to Rafael's house to determine if he knows where she might have gone.

I figure it's a decent enough excuse to show up at his apartment, and a pretext to apologize in person. He's been refusing my calls since the night with the Russians last week.

"He's asleep," says Rafael's mother, shrugging. She takes in my bandage. Her face softens, and she slips out onto the porch and closes the door. I think about her losing her husband to the sea and madness, and I smile sadly.

"*Mi cariña*," she says, inspecting the bandage plastered on my head. "*Que pena.*" What a pity.

"Tell him I'm sorry," I plead. She nods, and promises to deliver the message and my gift to Rafael, a bottle of Havana Club rum. After I leave, I realize it's the same brand Sasha employed across my skull.

I can't seem to do anything right.

At the Internet café, Susie's expected update is conspicuously absent this week. Reading about her life and work in Ghana—a playing-out of my own life, I imagine, had other choices been made—has been one of the main bright spots in my life. I know she's busy and adjusting to her new role in Africa, but I feel lonely nonetheless.

Leaving the Internet café, I hail a peso taxi home, and the 1958 Rambler American blows a head gasket. In the corkscrew stilts that have become part of my *cubanidad,* I waggle the four miles home.

At Camila's house, worry has taken up residence, and the concerned faces of neighbors and friends rotate through the rooms. At the porch, the spotted mutt is waiting, and I feed him my own dinner of beans and rice from the kitchen of Camila's mother. The kids in the neighborhood have named him Tito, after a famous Latino musician, and Tito seems to believe I belong to him.

He's irresistibly cute, and I hold him up near my face. "Promise you won't love me and leave me," I instruct Tito while he licks my nose. Missing Camila, and uncertain if Rafael will ever forgive me, I'm feeling very alone.

Disappearing, around here, is endemic.

Unless you count Walrus. He whizzes by in his smoke-belching Lada, waving hello.

THE ROAD TO Morón is full of potholes followed by spacious freeways that end abruptly, and dozens of kilometers from any village or city. On the lonely stretches of new pavement, we pass few cars but several bouncy ox-and-carts pulling sugarcane and pineapples. Leathery-skinned cowboys squint behind the reins.

The freeways' billboards of propaganda grow more hostile the further south we travel from Havana. Stormy graphics demand an end to the American "blockade" and declare a rancor for its *enemigo* to the north. For my other homeland.

In the countryside, leafy vegetation springs from famously fertile soil, the green so dark as to be nearly black. This panorama is eventually replaced with a parched and dry interior. The early summer sun beats harshly and stings our throats.

At its entrance, a sign welcomes us to Morón. As if that's not sufficiently hospitable, visitors are greeted with the spectacle of the town mascot at the main entrance: a giant rooster poured from concrete. Daya tells us the village is named for a song about a rooster who continued to crow, even after it had been defeathered.

"That's one tenacious cock," quips Richard, snorting laughter through his cocaine-addled nose.

He'd arrived in Havana the night before, and by our midmorning departure, Daya had employed her mother's savvy and already procured several items of new clothing.

"My alter ego, if he could talk, would say this: Richard, your girlfriend finds a dressmaker and buys four outfits before breakfast? She's not from Morón—you are!" Though she speaks no English, Daya senses when the joke's on her, and a swollen thumb returns to her mouth.

Morón is poor and dry, and its Radio Bemba—traveling on lower frequencies here—rapidly delivers news of the *habaneros'* arrival. Within a few brief moments, our car is surrounded. Daya is Morón's prodigal daughter, returning home with her walking, fifty-something lotto ticket, a gift-producing golden hen, and she beams at the collective envy and pride and hatred. Hers is a true immigrant's homecoming.

Daya's father turns out to be a revolutionary hardliner with firsthand tales of long-ago dissidents brewing war in the Sierra Maestre mountains. Because of this, and Richard's substantial age, I'm certain there will be problems in his approving Daya's boyfriend. I hold my breath while the father sizes up the disparate couple sitting hand-in-hand on a little wooden bench in the humble room.

Richard catches my eye, and I do my best to keep up with the translations. When a young, dark-skinned woman walks by, Daya stops her and introduces us. She can't be more than nineteen or twenty.

"*Mira*, my father's wife," Daya says. "She's his sixth."

"His *wife*?" says Richard, incredulous. "That's his *sixth wife*? Well, dry your eyes, I've no worries at all."

By the end of the night, the father is back-slapping Daya's boyfriend, the two fast friends. My stomach turns at the whole scenario, as it does with much of what happens in Cuba, and I keep looking around for someone to validate my unease. What kind of father pimps out his teenage daughter? And to a man his own age? I must be the only person alive who feels this may be wrong somehow. As it would turn out, I am not.

YOU KNOW SHE staged this in her mind, planned ahead. Schemed. Every insult or slight against her was going to be rectified tonight.

It's only her naïveté that prevented her from knowing the police wouldn't stand for it. No big-city export was coming home and rubbing her new wealth in their faces. Not when it was counterrevolutionary wealth.

Wearing the gifts Richard brought from London, Daya looks stunning in a tomato-red, halter-top gown by Carolina Herrera. One that contrasts beautifully with her greenish-brown skin and greenish-brown eyes, as if the soil and foliage of Cuba had infiltrated her mother's womb.

It's the only disco in town, dirt-floored, and open-skied, and full of teenagers posturing with their Chinese bicycles. She dragged that Carolina Herrera through the mud, dragged the boyfriend, too, and I could hear her silently tick off the malfeasances. The boys who'd cheated, the girls who'd talked dirt. They all parted, *gaujiros* in shock, as she waltzed through the crowd until she arrived at the foot of its elevated stage. It was there that the young dancer unleashed the sublimation of her Havana-trained moves. Richard beamed at his young love. The crowd gaped.

Cops took her by the neck.

Richard and I spent the night before an unsmiling police commissioner.

Trips were made throughout town to confirm the story. That Daya was sleeping at her father's, and not in the tourist room with Richard two blocks away, where her suitcases were discreetly tucked away by landlords before it could all be proven false.

Regardless, Daya was issued a written warning, ostensibly for being underage at a disco. A rule until then never enforced.

Richard believed the infraction to be inconsequential.

But Daya and I knew the truth. That the record meant she'd been caught carousing with a sex tourist. Two more in her file, and she'd find herself cutting sugar cane in the countryside.

55

*S*lowly, my feet ascend the eighty-eight-step precipice of white-stone purity leading to the neoclassical platform at the University of Havana. Up here, the ocean's breeze erases the street pollution, and the country's top students stride purposefully through celestial grounds.

Under Batista's regime, his gun-slinging thugs and army weren't allowed on the sacred site. The campus, instead, was deemed a safe haven for all, including gangsters, political troublemakers, and the maniacal.

The university is no longer a protected zone, and all must be well-behaved here, like anywhere. Yet I'm certain its former political neutrality is an unconscious reason Victor chose the grounds to stage our final meeting. One where he promises to deliver the address of my Havana family—information culled from discreet and classified sources and papers "misplaced" by the power of my blood money.

Perspiration mars Victor's face as he sits nervously on a cactus-shaded bench next to an armored tank parked permanently in a corner of the campus's main square. Under copper-and-cream pillars, I await his discreet signal and then slide next to him. Part of me feels guilt over tempting Victor with the cash he desperately needs, knowing he's risking, or believes to be risking, social and political consequences for his classified snooping.

"We are surrounded," he announces, and I feel a sudden fear, "by philosophy—" He points, as I relax, at one building after another. "And law, and mathematics, and history, as contained in those buildings."

Victor pulls out a sliver of cardboard from his pocket and hands it to me. No one would dream of wasting an envelope or a whole sheet of paper on one small line of writing, no matter how momentous the words. Even wood pulp is a luxury in my homeland.

On the scrap, the following is written: *Calle M, Number 3051.*

The Santero was right. If it's indeed my family's home, then it's just a few blocks from my former house. And only two streets away from where I live now with Camila.

"What if it's wrong, what if they've moved?"

Victor mops his forehead with a hanky. "I know you only have two months before you leave. But I've gone as far as I may, in good conscience, in helping you. I have a family to protect. If your father is not there, then I'm sorry. Our business together is done."

"Thank you," I say, kissing his cheek. "I'm sorry you . . . I'm sorry about the risks." Folding the bills, I slip him the last few precious hundreds earned by dancing for Uncle Morty.

But Victor flashes a stoic smile and shakes his head. "You think we do everything just for money?"

"Take it," I say.

In response, Victor puts his hand on his heart and quotes José Martí, a habit of conversation shared by many Cubans.

" 'Men of action,' " Victor recites, " 'Above all those whose actions are guided by love, live forever. Other famous men, those of much talk and few deeds, soon evaporate.' "

Before he can finish, I'm dashing down the steps, away from the protection of philosophy and logic and mathematics and history. Toward my future and my family and the unknown.

56

The old clock on Avenida Quinta reads eight P.M. Much too late for my mother and me to be returning home from our day at the beach with José Antonio. John is expected back from the States within the hour, and my mother is irritated at herself for losing track of time. There are precious few minutes to shower away the sand from our outing, or the signs of affection from her lover, José Antonio.

In the taxi, she removes my Santería beads of protection. At our mansion's entrance, my mother slows her walking to a standstill. Where the house should be buzzing and warm, she finds it deserted and cold, lights off, the staff gone. My mother is mystified, as she'd instructed them to prepare a welcome-home dinner for three.

The handwriting in her faded diaries becomes elliptical as she describes what happens next.

With me on her hip, she cautiously explores each room, switching on lights and radios. As is her custom, she kisses and presses two fingers to the lips on the framed photograph of President Carter.

Slowly, she climbs the stairs. It's not until we arrive in the bedroom that she places me on the ground. John's suitcases sit open and unpacked on the dresser. On her bed—on their bed—is a single telegram. It's open. On it, she reads the words destined to change the course of our lives.

It's addressed to John, and it's from Washington, dated nearly two months earlier. It reads:

REQUEST FOR IMMEDIATE TRANSFER ACCEPTED, PLEASE
VACATE HAVANA POST AND REPORT TO WASHINGTON
DC ON MARCH 10, 1980

The day's date, she records, is March 6. Four days from their expected
arrival in Washington. It all begins to make sense to her now: John's several trips to the States, the improvement in his mood. He'd been planning
the move without telling her.

An hour goes by, maybe two, she doesn't remember. She's on auto-
pilot, feeding and bathing herself and me. Tucking me into bed. Waiting
and wondering what is to happen next. Her thoughts are filled with José
Antonio, his easy wit and generosity and *cariñoso.*

It's with resignation that she answers the phone.

"I've just come from your lover's house." John is shouting. She can't remember the last time he shouted. "What's his name, José? Never expected
you'd go for the younger type. What do you have, eight, nine years on
him?"

"You went to his house?" she asks, shocked.

"There are pictures of you and Alysia everywhere. How the hell do
you think that makes me feel?"

My mother can't respond, rubbing her temples instead, and pacing as
far as the phone cord will allow. The cord is like John, she thinks, restricting
her movements, keeping her posted and confined. She's ashamed but she's
also angry. Was she expected to suffer through a lonely marriage forever?

"How could you? All you do is work, you leave me alone. What did you
expect?"

But he's not listening. "Pictures of my daughter and my wife with this
man. How the fuck am I supposed to handle that?"

"John—"

"Is she even mine?"

My mother doesn't answer, and the question hangs heavy in the air.
Finally, he speaks.

"Jesus Christ, you don't know, do you?" He slams the phone down.

•   •   •

A FEW MINUTES later, he calls again.

"We're returning to Washington," seethes John. He is only sightly more calm.

"When? Tell me when we're going to Washington."

"We're scheduled out on the four P.M. plane."

"Four P.M. when?"

"Tomorrow. God, I can't believe you did this—"

"What do you want me to say?"

"The obvious. That you'll have your things sorted by morning."

"Please come home, John. Can't we talk about this?"

But he's not listening. "I want you to tell him that your relationship is over, and I want you to come back with me. You know," he says darkly, "you can't stay in a Communist country. You can't live on pesos. I *know* you."

She sighs. "Where are you?"

"I've checked into the Nacional. I . . ." His voice has changed tone and is quieter. "I need you, I've always needed you. You know I'm no good without you. Please come home with me tomorrow."

My mother softens. She knows too well her husband's emotional handicaps. She partly blames herself for their distance, for not attending better to his needs. She also knows that her mores would never allow her to leave her husband, no matter how strongly José Antonio has wrested her heart. Even if she wanted to, she reasoned, how could she live under an enemy regime?

JOSÉ ANTONIO ARRIVED within minutes of her call. He'd never been inside a diplomat's home, and he bristled at the luxuriousness of my mother's surroundings. When José Antonio's chest puffed, when he stiffened at her embrace, she knew her clever husband had anticipated José Antonio's reaction to their wealth. It was John's profession to know his enemy, and he understood all too well how American prestige could demoralize a foe.

John had to have believed José Antonio would come to my mother that night, she reasoned, knowing she'd never leave her sleeping daughter alone. John had to trust that if José Antonio pled a case for love in the intimidation of their home, then the defense would surely score a defeat.

But my mother felt she could live drunk on the love of José Antonio and the warmth that glowed from his family. A family she wished could also be hers.

My mother wrote that their conversation lasted until dawn. How they were by turns angry and sad and passionate. She wrote that she agonized over staying in Havana with the man who excited her mind, ignited her body, and gave her the greatest *regala.* Her child.

José Antonio told her that in his country, people were poor, but they were happy. He told her that a daughter should know her real father. That material possessions were second to the love of a good family.

But it was my mother's Southern sense of propriety that won out, just as June, her sister and my aunt, had suspected. My mother believed herself unable to change the motion of her life, or to impose upon the strictures of marriage a new thinking. Hadn't she promised until death? José Antonio countered: Staying in Havana, he pled, would be following her life's true path.

My mother said she would be strong for both of them, and tearfully refused to give in, citing the unrealistic dreams that sprouted in the heat of passionate love.

They were together for the last time on the rooftop, under the stars, my mother imprinting their patterns in her mind. The distant lighthouse, the same one that signaled the beginning of her affair with José Antonio two years before, directed its beam through treacherous waters and crossed the terrain of their bodies. As the sun rose, the reach of the lighthouse faded, and with it the beacon she'd come to depend upon.

As they held each other, she heard him swear he would come and find her. That he was determined to know his daughter.

He promised me, too, leaning over my small body in the bed where I slept.

"*M'ija,*" he said, tears in his eyes. "Go with your mother now. We'll be together again soon. Your father promises to find a way."

57

Camila's house is abuzz with family and neighbors as I burst through the door, my address in hand, my breath having run out on me. Tito is barking in the excitement, and I scoop him up.

"Well, if it isn't Matías Pérez!"

Two centuries ago, a man named Matías Pérez tethered sheets and silks to a basket and set off from the Malecón pumping hot air into his makeshift balloon. A crowd assembled and watched, in astonishment, as his strange contraption elevated. No traces of Matías Pérez or his hot-air balloon have ever been found. Some swear he will one day soar from the sky and recount the tales of his devilish ride.

But today it's Camila who's swooped in from the clouds. Beaming in gold jewelry and a new baby-pink Valentino suit, my *amiga loca* tells of her adventure amid the chatter and din.

She floated on the clouds all right. She floated on a plane chartered by her Syrian sweetie Farouk, who whisked her off to Damascus. Farouk's father had been in need of triple-bypass surgery and, as a friend of the Cuban government, Farouk arranged for the talented Camila to perform the operation on his father, a high-ranking Syrian. For security reasons, Camila explains, she hadn't been allowed to tell anyone of her whereabouts.

"*Oye*, it was a private plane," gossips Camila, drawing *coños* and *mentiras* from the crowd. "We stopped for fuel in Paris." Everyone's eyes are shining now. "I saw the Eiffel Tower!"

"Are you going to marry him?" asks someone.

"Will you move to Damascus?" asks another.

Camila shakes her head in horror. "Heavens no. I'd never live there. Women have no rights." She leans in. "I was the only woman surgeon in the entire hospital!"

The neighbors find this incredible. Later, Camila pulls me aside. "It was the worst trip ever," she says. "I didn't want to worry my family but . . . Except for the surgery, *mi vida*, it was a disaster."

"What happened?" I ask, stepping farther into the back of the house.

"Farouk was totally different from the way he is here. Telling me how to dress, what to eat. Horrible. I hated it."

"He dumped you, didn't he."

"Like a rotten mango." She shakes her head and sighs, and I give her a big bear-hug. It may be the first time on record Camila has suffered a romantic rejection. Later on, over Hemingway daiquiris, I commiserate with her about her loss, and we share the joy of my procured address.

Camila wipes her nose. "Alysia, at first when I met you I befriended you out of charity. But now . . . You are so important to me. I know you can't promise me, but could you at least pretend you'll never leave?"

I've less than two months before I'm permitted to return to Washington, and the idea of staying here is about as appealing as the doughy, half-baked peso pizza sold on nearly every street. But I don't tell her so.

CALLE M, NUMBER 3051.

I keep the cardboard as a talisman, for luck, but the address Victor gave me several days before is burned in my memory.

I don't have the guts to go there. If it's not my father's house, I'm back where I began nearly one year ago, living like a local, without benefits but with every stitch of their heartaches.

I want to keep this moment alive, this moment before everything changes. If it's not the house, if it's another dead end, then I've little choice but to return home defeated. If it's the right house, then the scenarios are too numerous to settle. My father could be irritated. He could be disbelieving. He could be dead.

Camila comes to Calle M with a bowl of chicken and black beans, and plops it down on my lap. She orders me to eat; I beg her to whisper. She shakes her head and arranges herself in the bushes. We're across from

No. 3051, in the darkness. I've been watching the comings and goings for several days now. I'm driving her crazy.

"How long are you going to do this?" she asks. I shrug.

The island is buzzing over the rumor of an American attack: storing food, boiling water, calling family. The madness affords me solitude, to sit undetected in the foliage across the street. I watch the house, a sprawling two-story colonial with faded yellowy paint, in Vedado—once the forbidden hinterlands of Havana—and just six blocks from the hospital where I was born.

Thus far, the residents I've detected include a grandmother, several baseball fiends under age twelve, and five or six adults, including one attractive man my age with a sizzling boyfriend.

"You know, I'm so happy I went abroad," says Camila, scratching Tito behind the ears. "It's the one thing I'd always wanted to do. Now I know I'd never live *anywhere* but *mi patria*."

"My mother didn't want to leave, either," I say, peering intently at the house.

"*Mentira!* She wrote that in her books?"

I nod, shooshing her with a finger to my lips.

"She seems like a very sad woman to me," says Camila, choosing her words. "She didn't listen to herself very carefully."

"Morty gave me a thousand bucks," I whisper, changing the subject. "I can pay you back now."

"Did he whip out his, what does he call it, his 'nambycane'?"

I nearly howl at the visual, but cover my mouth. "No, thank God. He swears you're his only *mamacita*." Camila laughs, but I quiet her as another boy leaves the bustling No. 3051.

Suddenly serious, she asks: "*Mi vida*, what are you going to do if you do find your father? Will you return to the U.S.?"

"Do I have a choice?"

Camila answers with a raised eyebrow and a shrug. Her mouth settles tightly, suggesting she's biting her tongue. She pulls Tito into her lap and tries to get comfortable next to me, and the two of us sit for what seems like hours, watching and waiting.

A mango tree grows like a merry weed on the side of the house. Kids from the neighborhood steal the green fruit and whack them with sticks to the outfield. Duct tape X's serve as bases. It's a happy, chattering, clamoring brood, and I hope to God they're mine.

"You have to just go," says Camila, pleading with me. "I can't stand watching you watch them. You're building your expectations too high." I know she's right, but I can't do it. Every older man who walks in the door makes my heart stop cold.

58

White slips of paper flutter on the main doors of Havana's houses. People look to the sky, waiting for bombs.

Camila tells me the white paper means the military is welcome in that house, its owners having agreed to feed and shelter soldiers during an attack. An attack. It's all they talk about now, in these days after May Day, after a speech raising the ire of the island.

There's no way to confirm if it's just hype, if the U.S., a country with a powerful Cuban constituency, would attack an ancestral land. When I say I don't think so, that the fear is fed by propaganda, a way to make people forget crackdowns and dissidents, no one seems to listen.

Despite my Cuban blood, the U.S. passport I carry makes me untrustworthy now. They say they love the people in the U.S., that it's the government they loathe, but I feel misplaced nonetheless. No matter how local I feel, earning my way like many Cuban women, I'm still an *extranjera*, a foreigner. My paperwork says I may leave in a few short weeks. And that makes all the difference.

I'm awakened late at night by Rafael. I'm thrilled to see him, it's been two weeks now, but he's cold and curt. He leaves his 1956 Chevy on idle and stands at my door. I reach for the heirloom gold cross that hangs around his neck and caress it between my fingers. I must have phoned him twenty times.

"You've forgiven me?" I ask, feeling ashamed.

"*Oye*, I've heard you found your father's address," he says, taking back his chain. "Camila told me."

"I'm so sorry," I say quietly, unable to meet his eyes. "I should have told you about my *jineteando*."

"It's incredible. That you won't go meet your family."

"Modesta says the Russians roughed you up."

"After everything you've been through to find them."

"*Perdóname*," I say. Then I stand on my toes and impulsively wrap my arms around him and, finally, he reciprocates, and the way his body slowly relaxes into mine suggests I may have been forgiven.

"*Mami*, why don't you come home with me tonight," he says, his voice low and soft. "Tomorrow I'll take you in the Chevy to your *casa*, to see if it's your family. You shouldn't go alone." I think of the entrance, of my father's face when he sees his *jinetera* daughter with a *jinetero* boy pull up in a *jineterismo* Chevy.

Well, I figure, José Antonio has got to know the truth. And I realize then it's what I'm hiding. There's a fear my father won't respect me for what I did to find him, won't understand what I gave up on the off-chance I'd track him down so many years later.

Last year, when I began searching for my father in Havana, I ran into Dr. Ruth, the sex guru, in the bar of the Hotel Floridita, during a jazz jam. She said hello, but there wasn't much to hear, with all the music. Dr. Ruth was surrounded by sexy young men and women drinking mojitos. They had no clue who she was. Yet I'm certain, from the pale tourists on their arms, she knew who they were.

I didn't ask her what she thought of what she saw. But I think she would have understood that there's nothing new about sex as the *devise du pays* for luxuries; that after the war French girls fucked American GIs for stockings and canned fruit; that some girls in New York won't date a man unless he charters a Gulfstream G5.

She might have said that sex isn't just currency. That it's also communication; it reflects the hopes of who we are, or what we yearn to become. In Cuba, *jineterismo* isn't just for stockings. It's about throwing a penny down the well, and wishing. A middling tourist, defeated at home, is anew in Cuba, virile and potent, with a pocketful of cash. A peasant girl, with a little love, transforms into the sophisticated charge of a heady man. Dr. Ruth would say there's nothing new about that.

It's because of my new complex relationship with sex that I can't sleep with the one man I have feelings for: Rafael. He understands, he says, and we just hold each other all night and, in the morning, I keep my promise to him. The one where I agree to shunt my fears and knock on the door of the house at Calle M. To see if, indeed, it holds a history that belongs to me.

So I pull up in the Chevy and the kids squeal when I catch the mango—fly ball!—and I step onto the porch. The door is open, and voices beckon me inside, into the house filled with liveliness. With Rafael's hand on my back, Tito at my feet, and my heart in my mouth, I blurt out my story to the first friendly face I see, and I repeat it again, upon request, and then there's more astonishment and rapid-fire Spanish and hoots and laughter. Then come the hugs and I realize something is happening, though I'm not sure what, and I keep answering questions, yes I was born here, yes my mother was a Yankee, yes she was the blonde with a quick laugh, and it all starts to make sense, to them at least, to my uncles and aunts and cousins, and when I hear myself ask about my father, there is silence.

"He's gone," says the oldest woman, finally speaking.

It figures, I think, putting my hands to my face. I can't cry, because the room is jumbling around me with embraces and smiles, and now the neighbors are coming in, and it's hot, the curse of latitude.

Rafael tugs at my hair. "Listen," he says.

"My son is gone, *mi niña*," says the old woman, gathering me in her arms. This must be my grandmother, I think, feeling her loose flesh cover mine.

"But he'll call on Sunday. He always calls on Sunday from Miami."

59

On the plane to Washington, my mother whispers good-bye to Cuba and José Antonio forever. With me asleep in her lap, she reasons that her romantic urges had to come secondary to the welfare of her child, and she tries to leave it at that. She remembers gently squeezing John's hand. With rare tears welling, John tells her he can't live without her, and embraces my mother tightly as they nose through turbulence.

Shortly after we arrive in Washington, a dozen Cubans break into the Peruvian embassy in Havana and demand asylum. Rather than turn over the offenders to the Cuban government, the Peruvians relent and issue exit visas.

Within hours—Radio Bemba alight with the news—nearly eleven thousand Cubans join their forerunners at the Peruvian embassy. In a chaos few can forget, asylum-seekers climb gates and walls, ram the entryway, and camp atop the embassy, all demanding their ticket out.

My mother hangs on the story, disbelieving the irony of wishing to return to a country the *cubanos* are desperate to leave.

Twenty-seven miles west of Havana, in the Port of Mariel, a natural bay and former British naval station, officials quietly clear cargo ships from loading docks. Shortly thereafter, the port is announced open to all who wish to leave from it.

Boats arrive immediately from Floridian shores, and captains and crew rescue their relatives and friends. Those without *norteamericano* contacts scramble to construct makeshift flotations. These rickety contraptions are heaved to sturdier craft. A flotilla is formed. Together the weak and the strong, the fiberglass and the scrap wood, tie their lines together and make the notoriously deadly crossing.

John briefs the administration in Washington. Over the ensuing months, he watches as nearly 120,000 Cubans ply the Florida Straits. But John is unsettled. Handling the exodus from the U.S. Interests Section in Havana—instead of from his new base in Washington—would have made his career. He silently blames my mother, or so she perceives, and the foundation of her decision begins to crumble.

Perhaps she had made a mistake in not following the longings of her heart.

What my mother would never know is that José Antonio, in keeping his promise to his daughter, would take his few possessions, leave behind his mother, sisters, brothers, nieces, and nephews, and a respectable career, and jump on a Coast Guard ship bound for La Yuma.

60

When I was small, my father would play with me at this pastel, rambling house on Calle M. Everyone knew me then. Photographs of us are still here, but are too delicate to touch without them crumbling.

When my mother and stepfather packed up to return home, José Antonio reported to his family he couldn't argue with his lover's decision. He thought it was best his daughter go to the United States, so she wouldn't have to live like a Cuban.

What I learn from my grandmother, in the snippets she'll disclose, is how José Antonio left for the U.S. shortly after our departure. He believed *la familia* to be the most important thing in the world. He wanted to know his daughter. And once he was in the U.S., sending money to his family back home became his other priority.

How long had he been looking for me, I wonder? Had he turned up on our doorstep in Washington? Had my mother shunned him? Could he have known of our long foreign assignments, an aching in his heart awaiting our return? At night, I sift through my mother's diaries, trying to put the pieces together. But in them, I find nothing to graft.

My grandmother, my *abuela*, refuses to answer most questions directly. As do my uncles, aunts, and numerous cousins. Their dancing eyes hint of sorrow when I talk about my mother and José Antonio, or the twenty-three years of longing they've felt in his absence. No one will tell me why José Antonio has never returned to his homeland to visit his loving kin.

He's on his way to see us now. To see me.

He said I've gone far enough, and booked a charter flight to Havana. His voice was gentle, and he said he couldn't wait, that he'd been dreaming of meeting me again. I've plenty of questions.

Just hearing him speak with relief and happiness at hearing my voice is more thrilling than I'd ever imagined. He's alive! He knows about his daughter! And he's coming back home.

I am Alysia Vilar, *née* Briggs, and I've found my father at last.

Filled with a new confidence, I storm out of the Calle M house to confront Walrus, who is standing under the mango tree, playing outfield to the children's game.

"Well," I say indignantly. "I'm not going to be here much longer."

"Don't be so certain," Walrus says, chucking a mango to first base.

"Don't you hear me? You can stop following me around," I say, trying to play tough, although our size difference makes my scorn more than comical.

"*Mi niña,* you've been quite entertaining," says Walrus. Holding a battered mitt, he doesn't need to watch as a mango whizzes near his head and lands with a smack in his waiting palm. "But I promised José Antonio I'd keep an eye on you until he arrives."

"My father?" I ask, my eyes narrowing. "You *know* my father?"

"*Disculpe,* but I'm sworn to secrecy."

At first, I'm perplexed that my father may have known all along that I've been in Cuba. Then I'm angry that Walrus had likely been aware of my family's whereabouts all along. When I question Walrus, he again refuses to clarify.

"*Mi vida,* I have not told your father everything. What we say on the telephone is listened to by many. There are ears everywhere." I look carefully at him, and he lowers his voice further. "I knew he was doing everything in his power to get back home. I did not want to worry him with . . . with the details of your misfortunes." Walrus tosses the mango overhand and turns back to me. "I will leave it up to you to be the first one to tell José Antonio about most of what's happened with you."

For a few minutes, I hang my head in shame, wondering what he will think. But I realize it's fruitless. I'm not afraid anymore of his judgment or anyone's. I'm a kin of this land and we all do what we must. *A lo cubano.*

Things will change, I think, watching the breeze jostle the military notices that are tacked to doors. Cubans are waiting for Washington's bombs. I'm waiting for a charter flight to arrive. Looking up at the empty sky, I'm hoping for the best.

61

*C*hinese pistols are cocked. Young men and women run drills in the streets. Public weapons stashes are unlocked, checked, and relocked. Underground tunnels built to withstand a U.S. attack are cleaned and readied. Cuban flags glued to rough wooden posts wave proudly in shop windows and homes. A sense of urgency seizes even the desultory.

If Yankee soldiers are going to show up, they'll be in for a surprise.

In the streets, a rendition of Picasso's antifascist mural *Guernica* is unveiled defiantly in front of the Spanish embassy—where my mother first met José Antonio all those years before—and protests loom over Madrid's agreement to join in the bombing of Iraq.

My Cuban family ignores the signs of brewing trouble. For here on Calle M the news has been longer in the making, and tonight there's to be a fiesta in honor of a daughter's return to Cuba. Cousins drag a wooden cart down the street, one carrying the pink shell of a butchered pig, head attached, gutted and skinned and wrapped in palm leaves for roasting.

At Calle M, there's been no sparing of expense, under the orders of my *abuela*. The same *abuela* who taught me dance moves twenty-three years ago, and on the same chipped and faded Spanish-tile floors. I'd recognized their patterns immediately, on some level, a morsel rousted from the memory of childhood.

I help in the kitchen as the women prepare rice and beans—known as *cristians y moros,* Christians and Moors. We mash and salt and fry green plantains into *mariquitas.* There's shrimp in red sauce, baked beets, and a salad of cucumbers and tomatoes tossed in vinegar and salt. Boiled yucca is smothered in a garlicky *mojo* sauce. Cuban bread, so light it transmutes into air on the tongue, is toasted and drizzled with butter and garlic and parsley.

Outside, the men turn the pig on a spit, and down the Belgian-inspired Cristal beers, one dollar a can. As they sit on wood stools and rock on stoops, I watch the new men in my life, and the women who cook for them. In all, I have three uncles, two aunts, and fourteen cousins of both sexes, and of various sexual persuasions. Most of my family is *blanca*, but the most beautiful are my *mulato* cousins, their skin adding a heavenly shade to the family tree.

My father's sister is telling me that my father is a *mango*, a sweetheart, and how she, too, can't wait to wrap her arms around him.

"He never got over you," she says wistfully. "You can't imagine how happy we all are to have everyone here, in Cuba, where we all belong. *Gracias a dios.*"

The phone is for me. My *abuela* doesn't look me in the eye when she hands me the receiver. It's José Antonio, and his trip has been postponed, and there's a hint of anxiety in his voice, but he offers no reason. Just promises to arrive shortly. Although I'm able to leave in six short weeks, he again insists on meeting me in Havana.

Camila bursts through the front door bearing gifts of her mother's caramelized flan and coconut cakes and flummery. She takes me aside in the fresh coolness of sunset.

"Something's strange," I say, relaying my conversation with Walrus. "And why could it be so difficult for José Antonio to get here? Why does he insist on meeting here, and not back home? It's just weird . . . I mean, he's gone twenty-three years without even coming to Cuba to see his family. They've missed him *so* much."

Camila looks concerned, and tucks flyaway hair neatly behind my ears. "If you expect nothing, you won't be disappointed. But it worries me how you've built this up so much in your mind."

"*Eso es.*" But it's all I can do not to get my hopes up.

"Whatever happens to your father, you can't forget that you already have what you came to Cuba for."

"Them," I say, nodding my head toward the house.

"A wonderful family, *mi vida,* you are superlucky."

"Alysia!" Daya struts around a corner, giggling and holding hands with a boy whose eyes are so green they radiate from a block away. She's hooched up in a red stretchy miniskirt and rhinestone-encrusted heels. It's a rebellious, anti-Richard ensemble, and Camila and I offer a guttural howl.

"If the termites haven't fallen on the piano!" laughs Camila, shaking her head.

Daya introduces the teenage *cubano,* Diego, and then pulls me aside: "I broke it off with Richard."

"*Mentira!*"

"I told my mother, no more *yumas.* I quit. I'm through. *Nada mas.*"

"*Mi amor,* what happened?"

"My dance teacher happened. I told her about my first letter, the one the police gave me in Morón. She said if I didn't stop with the *yumas* I'd lose my place in the troupe. I would *die* if I lost my place in the troupe." She mimics a knife across her throat. Then she flips her hair and winks at Diego. "He's my new boyfriend, isn't he *guapo*?"

I nod vehemently. "And your mother?"

"*Ay,* she's angry." Daya shrugs and flicks her fingers with a snap of the wrist, a common posture that means "*dios mío*" or "*en candela*" or "you wouldn't believe." "But she'll get over it."

"That's wonderful," I say proudly. "*Felicidades.*"

She lowers her voice. "*Coño,* if this boy learns about Viagra, I'm dumping him!" Daya grabs her crotch and grimaces. Diego looks at us and sports the wince of a male who's accidentally wandered into the scary hinterlands of *chica* talk. A blush burns his cheeks.

At this, Daya and I laugh.

ALL THROUGH THE night there's music and dancing and then stories about José Antonio and a blonde toddler who left with her *norteamericana* mother. And how, twenty-three years later, she sat in the bushes across from the house, too scared to walk in and say hello. There is speculation at how many times we may have passed each other in crowded streets, and I tell them of the eerie preciseness of the Santería priest's geography.

My family is loud and funny and loves their rum. Growing up an only child, with no cousins on either side, I'm overwhelmed by the multitude of names I'm expected to remember, or how we all relate in our complex web.

My cousin Manuel and his boyfriend Paulo rectify the situation by grabbing exotic fruits from the kitchen and arranging them on the floor. A banana is an uncle. A melon is an aunt. Mangoes and *guayabas* and *fruta bomba* correspond to the personalities and physicalities of my many cousins, and no one can stop protesting their assigned vegetation.

As the imagery of my extended family begins to form in my mind, they bombard me with questions as well. Where did I grow up? Why so many countries? Wasn't my mother in love with José Antonio? What does John think of me looking for José Antonio? And then the one everyone hangs on: Once I meet my father, am I going to return to the U.S.?

At this, I catch Rafael's expectant stare. He's been at my side all night, and I've found myself studying his profile, his relaxation as he moves through crowds, the way people's eyes linger on him. Not letting it go to his head. With ease, he makes fast friends with those he doesn't know, crafting with them the fraternal bonds of those whose daily life is the same kind of weird hardships, the same shortages, and the *inventando* that spurs a motivation and rewards cleverness.

Shortly after midnight, a blackout shuts down city lights. The backyard at Calle M is aglow with candles, and neighbors without them make their way over to the raucous fiesta. Everyone is dancing *casino* to *Charanga Forever,* even my *abuela,* who grabs my hands and shows no chagrin at my waxen hips.

"*Mi niña,* I taught you well," she says, happily taking credit for my skills.

Camila tosses me a snide glance and raises her glass. "*Candela.*"

Everyone smiles. Tito barks. But Rafael's face tightens. In the rhythm of a new romance, the natural time for first sex is upon us. But later, at his house, the candles flickering in his bedroom, the music setting an easy tempo, I suffer stage fright before my jeans fully unzip. It'll be enough to have to leave my father and return to my country, I don't want to also be missing Rafael. It would be too much to bear.

62

The cells distributed throughout our bodies contain the evidence of memory. If our hippocampus—the area of our brains that recalls memory—is injured, the cells in our bodies provide a backup, albeit a hazy one. It's a phenomenon that psychiatrists and scientists hold in awe.

Cells are also believed to hold the memory of their own particular history. Collectively, the cells in an injured knee will forever recall the pain. A torn ligament remembers its past. And I also believe that cells retain the memory of senses, the feel of long-ago touch and the sound waves produced by the voice of loved ones.

The cells in my body from childhood, despite long having flaked off and regenerated, are being put to the task today. Because today is the day José Antonio arrives at José Martí International on a charter flight from Miami.

My grandmother had offered to come to the airport, for moral support. But like every similar invitation from friends and family, I've declined. I believe I can recognize my father. Knowing my cells' memory shall prove a guide.

Terminal 2 is where most charter flights land, and where I show up several hours before the flight is scheduled to arrive. "Terminal" comes from the Greek, and means boundary, or the place that connects one life to another. The word is derived from an ending, and I know this Havana terminal will deliver an end to a life without my father, and the beginning of one with him. Or so I hope. Will he know how far I'd gone to find him? How many humiliations I'd suffered along my journey? Will he know from my face, today a year older and slightly lined, that I'd become a modern-day version of the Greek's renowned hetairai?

Three hours in the theater of the terminal are spent pondering my upcoming fate. I watch families part. The wealthy leaving for abroad, the poor returning to their daily *inventando*. Will a similar farewell play out with José Antonio and me in a few short weeks, when my papers are cleared and I'm allowed to return to my other homeland?

In the heat, perspiration forms on my face. The humidity wrinkles the suit Camila had lent me—quite possibly the most conservative outfit ever to hang in a *cubana*'s closet, and one procured on her trip to the Middle East. ("I'd last one minute where fashion says to wear a blanket on your head," Camila had said.)

Smoothing down the imperfections, I feel a hand on my shoulder, and my skin goes cold. When I look up, I realize no one is there. Gratitude warms my freezing skin. I knew she wouldn't let me do this alone.

I feel him somewhere, too, and I stand up, as if on my mother's directive. My eyes scan the crowd and then I see him walking through the gate. He drops his heavy bags. Looks straight at me.

It's a long, long moment, and it is spent in the irises of each other's eyes. José Antonio. My father.

I run to him.

PROTESTS BEGAN AT dawn. A million people were rousted from work and sleep, from cities and villages, and now bang their fists in the air. Spain and Italy are being denounced today as fascist, a direct retaliation for their vote in the European Union, one that would punish Cuba economically for imprisoning its dissidents and killing the hijackers a mere three days after a summary trial.

Crowds stall traffic. The taxi driver throws up his hands. My father appeals to him to drop us in the Jewish quarter of the old city. We drag his bags to the Hotel Raquel, a restored Art Nouveau building on Calle Amargura, near the St. Francis of Assisi Square. In the cool lobby restaurant, the Garden of Eden, we find a paradisiacal respite from the heat and anger just a few blocks away.

"I want an egg," says José Antonio in a low voice, as if it were a forbidden fruit. "I dream of the eggs in my country. I've been dreaming about them for twenty years."

I can't look at him, I'm so nervous. I stare down at my menu, unseeing. José Antonio takes my hand.

"I've been dreaming about finding my daughter for longer."

My father is the physical antithesis of my stepfather, John. He's medium-built, with broad shoulders and a quick, sincere smile that spreads across his face like honey on toast. His dark hair is framed by graying edges, and I'm pleased he doesn't follow the Cuban male custom of erasing grays with flat, black dye. He's stocky and strong and with an unfettered energy that belies his fifty-three years. But it's José Antonio's eyes that bring the most happiness. They can't seem to look away from me.

Here we are, ordering breakfast. The two of us. Like a normal father and daughter dining together at a Caribbean hotel.

"There are about twelve hundred Jewish Cubans still living here," he says, chattering nervously. "The government allows them to buy beef for pesos." My father is referring to the widespread shortage of beef, available only at expensive dollar stores, and the draconian laws preventing anyone from slaughtering cows or buying black-market steak. "The temple is around the corner. I remember it from when I was young. Most of the Jewish folks left just after the revolution. They'd built successful businesses, and weren't interested in living without that opportunity."

We're talking about religion and politics, because even controversial issues are less sensitive than a conversation about our pasts, and the future they may decide. I've dreamed about this moment for so long, but never anticipated my mouth would be dry and no questions could tumble from my lips. I think of nothing to say. My vision is reduced to one focused line, and my knees begin to hum.

"Where do we begin, Alysia?" asks my father quietly.

"You start first," I reply. "At the beginning, the Spanish embassy, am I right?"

A smile crosses his face. "There was flamenco. I couldn't keep my eyes off her." And so starts the first thread in a long unraveling.

When breakfast plates are cleared, we sit until lunch, picking over salad and soup, and when lunch is over we move to the terrace with *café con leche.* Later, we wander the former Jewish quarter, on Calle Acosta, which once housed kosher bakeries and butcheries. Later, still talking, we have dinner and Hemingway daiquiris. It's a free-for-all, a putting together of the last pieces of a jigsaw puzzle of our entwined histories. It's the making of connections in times and places. The story begins to form, its shape appears, and a clarity is realized.

There were questions from him about my mother, and the contents of her diaries. There was the news of her death, and the way the tears came down his face, and the long and soulful silence that followed. There was the story of John. Finally, a silence.

"Walrus?" I ask.

"Who?" says José Antonio.

"El Gordo, who has been following me."

"*Ay*, Salvador," he says, laughing. "Salvador's an old friend." His laughter cools, and he drinks from his glass of water. "There are no secrets here, as you must have gathered. When you signed up for the university, you were on a special list, and it was flagged in the computers. Someone in the Interior phoned me, a good friend. I asked Salvador to keep an eye on you. Guess he did a good job, he was once a G-2 man."

"An eye on me?"

"To make sure you didn't leave Cuba before I had a chance to find you. If you were going to leave early, I had instructed him to approach you and tell you about me."

José Antonio fiddles with his water glass, concentrating on the beads of condensation dripping down it.

"Had I any idea your money was stolen . . . It just never occurred to me you would have been in financial trouble." He looks up at me now. "If Salvador had told me, I would have been here the next day, I hope you believe that."

His eyes are full of deep remorse and it's then I understand he knows about my nighttime wanderings.

"We don't have to talk about everything," I say, finally speaking.

"Let me just say one thing about this: your coming to find me, and doing everything that entailed, has touched me in a way I can't describe. I must do all the work now, Alysia. Being your father for the rest of my life is a pleasure I can't wait to experience in full."

"If Walrus—okay, *Salvador*—knew why I was here, why didn't he just take me to Calle M?"

"He didn't know why you were in Havana. No one did. You were signed up as a student, remember? I didn't know what you knew, or what your mother told you, or why you were here. I suspected. I hoped. I prayed you were looking for me . . . But you never went to Calle M. I assumed if you were here to find me, your mother would have told you all you needed to know. Of course now that I know of her death . . ." His voice trails off, but I'm more confused and I need a moment to sort my feelings.

José Antonio coughs. "What I haven't told you"—he coughs again and takes a sip from the glass— "is that I cannot leave Cuba now; I won't be allowed back in the U.S. That's why it's taken me so long to be here. Had I been able to leave when you first arrived in Havana, I'd have been on the first plane. You must know this, *mi niña*."

His words hang in the air, and the waiters, who've long left us alone, look over because I stand up abruptly, spilling my coffee.

"Sit down, please," says my father, standing up as well. "I'll explain." But I'm upset and afraid, and when we are seated again, he begins slowly. "When I left through Mariel, I was processed in Miami at Immigration. We camped at the Orange Bowl, the football stadium, like many others. Immigration asked if I had worked for the Ministry of the Interior and, of course, because I had, as a translator, I said yes. What this means is that although my job was mundane, and I knew no state secrets—I translated from Spanish to Russian and German." He sighs heavily. "I'm considered suspect simply because I was employed through the Interior. So I was allowed to stay in the U.S., but it meant I was monitored, and told that if I returned to Cuba even for a short visit I wouldn't be allowed back in the U.S. There are many Cuban operatives living in America. But I'm not one of them."

It's still to much to process, and so I take a deep breath. Slowly, I say this: "Why all the delays in coming here?"

"The reason"—his voice is crackling now—"I took so long to get here is that I applied for paperwork to overturn that decision, but I was rejected. I did what I must: I've sold my home and shut down my affairs. I'm afraid my coming here is forever, Alysia."

"Why didn't you tell me?" I ask. "My visa here ends in a few weeks, I could have met you in the U.S.—"

But he cuts me off. "I'm sorry, Alysia. My only goal in living in America was to be with you while you grew up. But your father, John, made that impossible. Now that I've found you—*mira*, in fifteen, twenty years I'll be an old man. My father died in his sixties, as did his father before him. I want to be here with my family now. I don't want to die without ever seeing them again. I don't want to grow old with strangers. No matter how comfortable life can be in America."

"But it's so hard to live here," I say, incredulous. "Why would you *choose* to wait in lines and suffer blackouts and never have toilet paper . . ." I drop my head on the table. I can't believe what I'm hearing. It's way too much.

He takes my hand, and with the other gently lifts my head. "I have moderate savings and a pension that starts in a few years. I can make do." I can't look at him, and tears are starting to roll down my face and splatter on my borrowed clothes.

"Alysia," he says, his voice soft. "I've changed my whole life to look for you. I went on a boat across the Florida Straits. I left my family for twenty-three years. I made a life in Miami, missing my Havana every day. It was all to find you. *Pero*, now I've found you. *Gracias a dios.*"

"It's so hard to live here," I repeat.

"My wife, she's a lovely woman, a *cubana*, she will be joining me in a few months. It is her wish, too, to return here and be with her family. We are prepared for the sacrifices." But he says this without looking me in the eye.

Then he takes my other hand. "Alysia, *m'ija*, blackouts and toilet paper are inconsequential, at least in the big picture. I love my country and I can't—I *won't*—wait until it's perfect to live here. My body may not make it that long. I have the same feeling about this system as I'm sure you've come to have. It's imperfect and sometimes very damaging. But I won't *not* have another egg in my country. I won't *not* live near the house of my mother. I won't *not* wake up every day to feast on the beauty of *mi patria*. I won't die with hatred and regret. I've put those feelings aside and will make the sacrifices I need to make to be here with my family. I hope—*dios mío* do I hope—that it includes you, *mi niña*."

We don't speak for a long while. There's nothing in me that doesn't understand what my father is saying, but I'm not certain I can live in Cuba, and I'm not certain I can live without him. Not after having finally found him.

He studies my expressions. After a moment, I ask a question I don't actually want answered, and it comes out in a resigned whisper. "What did you mean about John?"

My father takes a long breath and calls to the waiter for more water. He takes a long drink and a deep breath. He leans over the table. "John raised you, I know this," he says. "So I don't want to speak badly of him. But the truth is this. The truth, Alysia, is that when I settled in Miami, I eventually found your mother in Washington. It took me a long time before I had a job and could afford to find you two. But you all were in and out of the country so often . . . I had to wait until you'd return to your apartment—"

"At the Watergate?" I ask, imagining our long-term Washington residence and the place where my things have always had a permanent home. "You went to our place?"

He nods. "I flew to D.C., hoping to speak with your mother. To discuss a way, at least, for me to see you. But John intercepted, and ordered me to leave. When I came back to Miami, two of his men came to my door saying I had to keep away from your mother and you. And if I didn't . . ." He shakes his head sadly. "Well, John would make a big deal about my Interior records, embellish them, and see that I got deported. I was stuck."

"Completely stuck."

"I couldn't ask your mother to let me see you, and I didn't want to be forced back to Cuba, where it would be nearly impossible to find you, *ya tu sabes.* So I made a career as a translator, married a wonderful woman. Went on and hoped your mother would soon tell you the truth. I guess I naïvely believed John would tell your mother I was looking for you, and where I lived . . . I don't know. I was just dreaming. My wife and I, we never had children—she couldn't. So, Alysia, you are even more special to me."

I'm stunned, and find myself disbelieving that John would leave me to rot in Havana, broke and homeless, knowing I was looking for a man living on American soil all along. I can't believe it, and I find my face flush with anger. John couldn't have been so cruel. I need to believe this.

We leave in a taxi and ride in silence. There's a lot to process.

José Antonio is to have an emotional, long-overdue reunion now with his mother and family. I've insisted on giving them privacy. He and I make arrangements to see each other in a few days. When I get out of the car at Camila's house, he hugs me with a ferocity I never felt with anyone, much less John.

"You know, you can come back and forth between the U.S. and Havana. But the U.S. will only allow one brief visit every three years. It won't be the same at all as if you'd just live here with us." He backs out of the hug and pleads. "We've lost so many years already, my beautiful daughter, I can't stand the thought of spending our future apart as well."

Sadly, I watch the taxi zoom off. Rather than being a blissful denouement, meeting my father has churned up more confusion about my family and my past. Not to mention my future.

63

On the hour anyone will answer their phone—at four A.M., too comatose from sleep to screen calls, too stunned to let it slide into voice mail—I phone my other father, the one who raised me.

John's voice is thick and groggy, and I hold back a torrent of accusations.

"Alysia," I say, in answer to his question.

"Wait a minute, let me splash some cold water." A woman's voice in the background surprises me, though it's been years since my mother's death. I can't help but be happy for John, hoping he has found someone to soften his edges.

"I'm glad you phoned," John says. "I'd thought of sending one of the staff down there to bring you home. We have some financials to sort out. Are you still in that rotting city? How are you faring?" It takes all the calmness I possess to not burst into an angry tirade. How does he think I'm faring—broke and trapped in a country where it's impossible to work?

Instead I say this. "Yes, I'm still in Havana."

John sighs. The water stops running. "I hope you're ready to come home and start a career now. I think there's been enough gallivanting."

"I've found José Antonio."

"He's gone back to Cuba, has he?"

I sigh. "Do you miss me, Dad?"

"You know, there's no real proof. That he's your biological father. Your grandmother is convinced of it, but I'm not so sure."

"When I come home, can we have a real relationship? You know, maybe have breakfast once in a while? Spend holidays together?"

"We can get you a nice post in foreign service, forget all about this."

He doesn't even get it, I think. He doesn't understand what he's put me through in refusing to help me out of Cuba, when all the power to do so has been easily within his reach. And how cruel, I think, not to tell me José Antonio had been in the U.S. all the while.

"Alysia—" he says tentatively.

"Do you miss me?" I repeat quietly.

He says nothing.

Sighing, I start to say good-bye.

Then he interrupts. "Wait, Alysia?"

"Yes," I say.

Another long silence. "Um . . . Never mind."

"Good-bye, John," I say, my voice cracking. Then I whisper it one last time. "Good-bye."

Gently, I click down the receiver. Looking around, I find myself in the lobby of the Hotel Nacional, an empty phone card in my hand. Standing at the same pay phone I used twelve months ago to call for John's help. This time, the *jineteras* gliding through the lobby don't faze me. I touch my face and tug at my tight clothes. The girl who stood here one year ago is gone forever.

64

Rafael greets me from behind the wheel and I slide onto the bench seat. Tito licks my face and I squeal over his affections. Shyly, I kiss Rafael's cheek. In the back sits a tourist couple from Canada, and we exchange greetings. They've hired Rafael to chauffeur them to Three Kings of El Morro, the prominent castle and fortress atop a cliff overlooking Havana Bay.

Walking through its hallowed grounds, Rafael scoops me up and sets me on *la cortina,* the curtain wall blunting a steep drop into the harbor. Soldiers in red uniforms pump gunpowder into a cannon pointed at the sea. Each night's cannonade is at nine P.M., the ritual hour Havana's city walls were locked and barricaded three centuries before.

Paranoia is running high over a putative U.S. attack. But the only heavy artillery raining on Havana now is the cannon's friendly fire.

"You have to trust me," Rafael says, instructing me to stand tall on *la cortina.* "Everyone jumps when the cannon goes off. But I'll grab you so you don't fall backwards into the bay."

The Canadians are safely on the ground, their fanny packs unclipped and held tightly to their chests, and the fire's glow flickers on their bodies. I lean over and whisper in Rafael's ear.

"My father is staying in Cuba for good," I say. "My visa runs out in a few weeks."

"So renew for another year," Rafael says simply. But my face twists at the suggestion. He sighs.

I stand up straight and feel the night's rippling breeze through my hair.

Below the precipice churn dark waters. Fishermen on inner tubes float through the darkened bay with string and hooks.

Rafael sends me a grin, but I'm frightened, and so he grabs my other hand. The fuse is slow and languorous, and when it goes boom, I jump, but Rafael keeps his promise and catches me, and I slide down his body. It's a good move, and I tell him so, though wondering if it's been perfected on the countless women before me.

We drop the Canadians off at a disco, and Rafael uses the money earned shuttling them around to treat me to dinner in Chinatown. It nearly feels like a real date back home. Rafael wants to know how things went with José Antonio and what my plans are—what *our* plans are. I love how he hangs on my every word and lets me speak without interruption. I recite a *Reader's Digest* version of yesterday's conversation with José Antonio.

"*Mira,* Alysia, it's a big decision," Rafael says, feigning indifference. "Don't you want to spend time with your father after all that's happened to find him? If you stay, he'll take care of you, *verdad*?"

"He's offered. But I'm not sure I'll last very long being taken care of by anyone. Besides, he's not a rich man."

Rafael toys with the shrimp on his plate. That I'm to leave Cuba soon hangs in the air and kills a merriment we normally share.

"I feel something very strong for you, *mi vida,*" Rafael says. He folds his arms on the table and looks away, as if transfixed by a point on the distant horizon. "All my Cuban girlfriends in the past have understood that my business with tourists is my business. If I'm gone a night or two or a week, I have to have that freedom. *Dios mío,* I don't *want* to go out hustling. But I'm the head of my family. I have my mother and brothers to look after."

On reflex, I reach out and touch Rafael's cheek with the back of my fingers, feeling the smoothness of his skin against mine. A rare sensation gnaws at me, one I can't quite place. Then I recognize the emotion: jealousy. I'm imagining the foreign girls who pine for him, and the *cubanas* such as Modesta who can't get over him. I'm jealous, awfully jealous. All my life I swore to myself I'd avoid the emotion, that it's not sensible or ladylike, and certainly not in the Briggs family lexicon. But the creeping presence of jealousy, this *celosía*, signals a deepening of my *cubanidad*. The environment is stronger than me, and is altering my beliefs.

Rafael waits expectantly for a reply. For the first time, I consider the possibilities. Could I actually live in Cuba? Would I manage to thrive among the *jinete*, as surely my occupation would remain? And as a *jinetera*, could I be the girlfriend of a *jinetero* and all that it entails?

Truth is, my mother didn't want to leave José Antonio Vilar of Calle M, and I don't, either. My mother regretted leaving her Cuban love, and I don't want to regret leaving mine. Could my mother in her afterlife be nudging me to live my life differently? To damn convention and rational thought and go with the basic instincts we're provided to see us through?

"Some days," Rafael says, "I have to spend six hours to find one light-bulb, *m'entiendes*? Tomorrow, I have to go to the *barrio* and buy three or four ounces of cocaine for some tourists in Havana Vieja, and then I need to use my profit to repair the roof on our home. Next week, a group of Italians I know are coming back to town and will want teenage *jineteras*. Do you see? *No es fácil.* You, all you've done is put a flower behind your ear and pretend to be *cubana* for a year. You've scammed some handsome tourists, you've gotten some presents. But the real *vida*, Alysia, the way things really work here is forever *luchando*. I want you to stay. *Dios mío*, I want you to stay. But I don't know if you can deal with Cuba, not when it's *permanente*."

"Maybe you're right," I say, also pushing my plate aside. I think not just about my father, but also about my aging *abuela*, spry and funny in her housedresses and clip-on earrings, and her daily José Martí recitations and French-language endeavors. How long will she be alive so that I may know her? What about Camila and Daya and the people whom I've come to love in their support of a Yankee stranger? If I leave Cuba, I'm leaving more than frustratingly long lines and a life of *jineterismo*.

I'm leaving behind my own dream.

I've seen my mother's body attack itself in her sorrow, in her not fol-lowing her heart and staying with José Antonio. I saw John, in my early childhood, become the man he dreamed of being and, when he lost my mother, bury himself in the refuge of what was familiar, in the politically showcased family that placed little premium on love.

If I stay, I think, I'll continue missing the fragments that made up my comfortable life. I miss my platinum American Express card, which sits unused in my wallet, and also my bank accounts, as these have once been relied upon to provide a well-being and safety that comes from having access to money. I miss the doorman at the Watergate, a room of my own, and the feel of fresh, clean towels tumbled dry in a machine—unlike the stiff, sun-baked cotton that passes for bath gear here. I miss my indulgences, the face creams and department store cosmetics and shampoos, and the certainty that the lights will be on to apply them. I miss America and twenty-four-hour pharmacies. I miss sashimi and TiVo and world news. But these, of course, are small things.

To stay in Cuba would be to suffer considerable losses. There is John, who, despite our fallout, retains a place in my heart. And there is Susie, and my other friends. How many of their weddings and new jobs and babies will I not be there to celebrate? And what of my own?

John always told me that, when making a decision, it's best to write down the pros and cons in two columns, and measure them up, side by side. But that isn't helping me here. For every minus, there's a corresponding plus, and for every bounty reaped there's a deficit. As I parse down the good and the bad, I realize I'm angry. What kind of world is this? We're a mere ninety miles away from the U.S., and though it's a lonely path across mean seas, I'm irritated that forty-five years have gone by and no bridge has been built to close the chasm. The divide is temporal and spatial, and the distance so great I feel like I might as well be on the moon.

"When you do go back," says Rafael sadly, "don't ask me to exchange addresses. I can't do that. Not with you."

I sigh. The only thing I am certain about right now is that I'm ready to go home with Rafael tonight and feel what it's like to slip between his sheets. I need a vacation from the inside of my brain, and to attend to the other parts of my body that are ignited. This urge for him is overwhelming and I convey it none too subtly. But when we arrive at my home, Rafael's lips barely scrape my cheek, and he drops me at the road, refusing to come in. Standing at my doorstep in a cloud of pollution, his Chevy zooming away, I feel rejected and even more confused.

A few hours later, he phones.

"If you were a tourist," Rafael says, "there'd be no way I'd have turned you down tonight. I wouldn't care about you, I'd just be scamming. *Escúchame,* but I can't sleep with you—you're going to leave. I do *not* have a passport. I can *not* come after you. I am trapped in Cuba. What kind of man wants to know he cannot pursue the woman he loves?"

65

Tears are flowing outside the house at Calle M. It's still dark, and my plane leaves in a few hours and I'm trying to keep it together while I say good-bye to Camila and Daya and the aunts and uncles and cousins whose distinctions I barely recall.

That my entire extended family has arrived to see me off so early in the morning is overwhelming.

Whispering in Daya's ear, I hand her a sack with the jar of peanut butter and strict instructions to give Limón the gag gift if ever he's released, although whatever humor it once held seems to have deflated now. Daya's thumb is in her mouth, and she kicks at a few pebbles with a dancer's pointed toe. My grandmother pushes up the thick glasses on her nose and starts to cry. She can't believe her granddaughter is yet again leaving *pa' la Yuma.*

"Tell Rafael . . ." I whisper in Camila's ear. "Tell him I understand why he didn't say good-bye."

Camila nods and throws her arms around me. "Alysia . . . *Ya tu sabes.*"

Any second I'll start sobbing, and so I hand Tito to my grandmother and climb inside the taxi. My father settles next to me and I'm grateful he's saving his farewell for my departure at José Martí International. I need to say good-bye in stages.

We're quiet on the drive, and I don't feel the usual heady rush of excitement that comes from the anticipation of travel. That, too, seems to have disappeared in Cuba.

"*M'ija,* I wish you had met my wife," says my father, finally speaking.

"Aida . . . I'd love to."

"You'll come back as soon as you can?" His voice is cracking and I, too, am unspeakably sad. It's only been a few weeks since I met my real father, and I'm hardly ready to leave him. I sneak glances at his profile and try to impress his features to a canvas in my mind, like silver crystals to film.

Two years ago, I can't help but remember, I was studying my Aunt June's profile as our taxi took us down this same road.

I double-check for my passport, and it falls open to the stamps I've acquired in my travels. I finger the red-ink outline of the Pearl of the Antilles as imprinted 364 days ago, and the visa that expires tonight.

José Antonio, too, studies my passport, and I wonder if he's thinking of how it transported me and my mother away from him for all those years. Then a palm smacks his forehead.

"Your map," he says, fumbling in his shirt pocket. "I almost forgot. Camila unpinned it from her wall. She wanted to make sure you kept it."

Unfolded, the map takes up the taxi's backseat. My father holds up the western end of Havana and I the eastern end and the sandy *playas*. My red, girlish stars were drawn over vital places as they became known to me, and I show my father the trail that led to the treasure of finding him. The hospital where I was born (and where I convalesced from the temperament of the Russian, but I don't tell my father everything); the house with the thieving doctors; the depressed landlady; Camila's happy home; and, lastly, the sacred pastel *casa* on Calle M. A smaller star rests on Rafael's beachside apartment, and my finger lingers over his street.

My mind settles on a memory of my dance lessons with Camila, and how she told me there's a flow to everything, and if you think too much and feel too little, you miss the important signals. This map has always been in front of me, all along, since the beginning of my search, and at times I've stared at it hard, wishing it could magically plot the road to my father. Pinned to the wall above my modest desk, this map had been shining like a beacon during my year in Cuba—even in the darkest days. But I'd chosen to ignore its fundamental importance; to not see the real message it has been conveying all along.

Until this moment.

"*Oye*, driver," I say, suddenly flustered and bright-eyed. "Make a right here."

"*M'ija*," says my father, gently correcting. "Your plane leaves from Terminal 2. Terminal 2 is to the left."

The map crinkles as I lurch forward in my seat, repeating my demand.

"I know the terminal is to the left," I say. "But I'm reading the map, and it says to turn to the right."

66

José Antonio and I walk through the Havana botanical gardens. When the sun reaches its peak, we take cover in the shade of a Japanese pavilion. From there, we admire the arched bridges and carved bonsai trees. In the pond below us, golden-orange koi nip at floating insects.

I'm laughing at one of my father's jokes when a stunning woman in her late forties approaches. Her hair is black and curly, and she's dressed in white, with an aquamarine brooch on her chest.

Aida kisses our cheeks and hugs us both tightly.

"Look at you, jabbering away like two West Indian parakeets," she says, situating herself on my father's lap.

Many things about Aida remind me of Aunt June, including her lively wit and abiding kindness. When Aida arrived at the airport a few months after I met my father, I knew then I'd made the right choice to stay. Something about her and my father together cemented the idea for me. That I was home, and I belonged.

"We're having Camila and *abuela* over for dinner," says José Antonio's wife, leaning back into the summer sun.

"What, no Rafael?" asks José Antonio. Then sternly: "Have you replaced him without asking your father?"

Aida playfully scrunches José Antonio's cheeks. "You keep out of her love life," she warns.

"He'll be there," I say, rolling my eyes. "He wouldn't miss Aida's cooking for a new set of Firestones."

At my new home is my map of Havana. Sometimes I look it over, to remind me of the journey. To see the stars I'd drawn over the places I knew, like my family's home in Miramar, and the places I hoped to find. Lately, my fingers have traced the journey from Havana along the ocean-front road that leads to Mariel, and the port where my father began his circuitous journey to find me.

My father speaks often about the Mariel boatlift. His Coast Guard cutter was tied to rafts, and rafts were tied to each other, and the seaworthy and the makeshift held strong together through the canyons of waves that make up the Florida Straits in hurricane season. They were bound together by the ropes of determination and hope and might, and plied collectively the uncertain seas before them, strung to one another's fate, their common aim the shores of Florida. And, they hoped, a life of fulfilled promise.

My map has been covered in new markers, and this time I've portrayed the flotillas we've created on dry land. On my map I may now chart the Cuban families—bound together by blood, or geography, or the fortune of friendship—that make up neighborly fleets. Ties that connect rafts of people together through rough waters of the unknown, through the journey that is life in modern Cuba. Patiently allowing the interminable winds of change to dictate their direction.

Above all, they are together, we are together, shoring up our strength for whatever may be ahead. Peace? Prosperity? Who knows? Perhaps someday a tear-drenched reunion with our families to the north and south, east and west, like the broken heart of a locket, the pieces coming together again, and creating a final harmony.

I am on such a raft. I am a necessary line in the flotilla, and my weight, my pull, my physicality is an equilibrium. I salve wounds; I salve mine and my father's, and I am there for those whom I love. And they are there for me.

Each day I grow more convinced this was the destiny my mother turned her back on; a destiny that was hers, perhaps, and certainly, un-equivocally, mine.

Part of my duty now is to keep tuned my own moral compass, one that provides space for my life as a *jinetera,* as well as for holding on to an integrity that allows me to retain my pride.

In Cuba, where anything goes for the sake of the holy dollar, I've learned to create my own boundaries.

I've watched a proud shop clerk steal from the change owed a tourist. Ten cents here. Twenty cents there. When held accountable, he burns with indignation, and it's the part directed at his soul he most wrestles with.

I've seen a noble family of doctors and engineers let rooms to sex tourists for $20 a night. The kids and grandkids huddle in the basement, listening to the hurricane of a fifty-year-old white Spanish guy pound a nineteen-year-old black Cuban girl in rooms the generations grew up in, gave birth in, honeymooned in, died in. And it continues, the next day scraping up condoms and wrappers and shrugging it off. Laughing—and admirably so—but for how long?

How long, these lamentations?

I don't know. I don't understand the vicious stalemate between my American land and my Cuban one. And while the nations wrestle, while they teeter-totter on my hyphen, on the fulcrum of my Cuban-American identity, I can only pray for a quick resolution, so that my people who've been scattered around the world may again claim their homeland, and together we may heal.

My father muses that in a Japanese garden it's nearly impossible to know where nature ends and art begins. As we walk slowly through the grounds, José Antonio takes the hands of the women he loves, and we admire the delicate structure of each plant and tree and flower, and its place in the landscape. It's then I feel my mother's presence, and her warmth on my bare shoulder. This touch is less powerful, less sad, and I feel instinctively she's saying good-bye.

Leaving me in good hands.

Acknowledgments

Alison Callahan believed in this book before a syllable of it was written. Once those were arranged, her philosophic pen cast a magical spell over my story, and all improvements are in her name, and any mistakes mine alone. *Gracias* also to René Alegria, who had a vision not only for this novel but for Rayo and for an America whose bookshelves hum with Latino stories.

Stéphanie Abou has all the attributes a girl could dream of in a great friend: loyalty, perseverance, humor, genius—and a fabulous fashion sense. Lucky for me, she's also my agent, and for her prodding and pulling and cheerleading I give this Parisian import a big hooray.

For honeyed encouragement and smarty-pants facts, applause goes to: Karen Croft, Anne Kostick, Marc Serges, Christine Debusschere, Whitney Woodward, Peter Watrous, David Sesser, Jackie Weiss, Joel "Bishop" O'Brien, Jeanette Perez, and the staff at HarperCollins. Kenneth P. Norwick and Jay Berg wowed with their legal vetting. For the space and love to write, I'm obliged to Oscar and Mike and Nancy in New York, and to María and Cristóbal and Azie in Spain.

Late night Havana gossip sessions were an indulgence on par with *café con leche* and *pastelitos*. Lena, Christine, Esther, and Beth kept me saturated with the latest whisperings and watched my back all those crazy 3 A.M.'s in Cuba.

Thanks to my family—my heroes!—for immeasurable support and for having the courage to follow their path. The arrival has been so sweet.

Besitos to my rock, Pablo Vilar, for being there. Always.

Finally, the heaviest debt is owed to my *amigos íntimos* in Cuba, none of whom would benefit from having their names printed here. I arrived in Havana with a *corazón roto* and a cleft stick; they gave me a compass and a map.